WORK TRIP

WORK TRIP

CHLOE FORD

HEAD OF ZEUS

An Aria Book

First published in the UK in 2025 by Head of Zeus,
part of Bloomsbury Publishing Plc

Copyright © Chloe Ford, 2025

The moral right of Chloe Ford to be identified
as the author of this work has been asserted in accordance with
the Copyright, Designs and Patents Act of 1988.

All rights reserved. No part of this publication may be: i) reproduced or transmitted in any form, electronic or mechanical, including photocopying, recording or by means of any information storage or retrieval system without prior permission in writing from the publishers; or ii) used or reproduced in any way for the training, development or operation of artificial intelligence (AI) technologies, including generative AI technologies. The rights holders expressly reserve this publication from the text and data mining exception as per Article 4(3) of the Digital Single Market Directive (EU) 2019/790

This is a work of fiction. All characters, organizations, and events portrayed in this novel are either products of the author's imagination or are used ficticiously.

9 7 5 3 1 2 4 6 8

A catalogue record for this book is available from the British Library.

ISBN (PB): 9781035913213
ISBN (eBook): 9781035913190; ISBN (ePDF): 9781035913176

Cover design: Gemma Gorton

Typeset by Siliconchips Services Ltd UK

Printed and bound in Great Britain by
CPI Group (UK) Ltd, Croydon CR0 4YY

Bloomsbury Publishing Plc
50 Bedford Square, London, WC1B 3DP, UK
Bloomsbury Publishing Ireland Limited,
29 Earlsfort Terrace, Dublin 2, D02 AY28, Ireland

HEAD OF ZEUS
5–8 Hardwick Street
London EC1R 4RG

To find out more about our authors and books
visit www.headofzeus.com

For product safety related questions contact productsafety@bloomsbury.com

To my husband (who will probably never read this) and my son (who I hope never will).

Author's Note

As a self-proclaimed country girl who would pick being deserted in the Scottish Highlands over the London Underground during rush hour, let me tell you, this was a fun one to write as my characters are quite literally of the opposite opinion. It was interesting to see this world through their eyes and wonder at how magnificent, but also terrifying, it actually is to be so remote with limited supplies and zero connection to the wider world.

Before I started writing, I did attempt to plot the route Fliss and James would take, but over the course of drafting and edits my author license has taken control. While some of the names of towns and places are real, the general route they end up on has been manufactured for extra swooning and fun-filled plotivities. So, although I want you to adore this version of Scotland, please do not try to figure out the route as it does not exist (and you might drown lol).

Happy reading!
Chloe x

One

He's done it again.

I can hardly believe it. No, scrap that. I can absolutely believe it. He does it all the time, actually. The words in his email roll through me, soaking into my blood system until my limbs are rattling. I breathe in for three then slowly exhale away the stress for ten. Amongst the background noise of work chatter, gossiping and coffee machines hissing, I find peace in this modern glass building. I will not let him destroy that peace.

"How do you say, '*You're a total dipshit, I hope you and your idea fall into a pit of misery and despair*,' without it sounding unprofessional?" I ask my assistant, Gemma, who looks up from her desk, her hazel eyes blinking over her screen.

"I think it's 'I appreciate your interest in this matter. However, the situation is in hand'?" Then in a lower voice, she whispers, "What's he done now?"

I massage my eyebrows as I stare furiously at my laptop. Gemma is used to these altercations now. She's a seasoned employee here. "He's trying to say he can make more money using our cosy lounge area for our VIP customers by putting another hospitality marquee there instead."

I delete my last comment: *Are you actually kidding? Or are you maybe a bit stupid?*, and try for something less sassy whilst also retaining that tone of – *you're a sneaky weasel and I'm going to get you back*. Professionally, of course.

"Is it direct to Michael?" Gemma asks, a flit of concern in her expression.

I peek across the modern office and notice our CEO, who is the key decision-maker around here, talking to someone in the main kitchen.

Well, at least he isn't reading his emails yet.

I nod at Gemma, angry-typing as I respond. I write, *Thank you* so much *for your idea. I can see you put a lot of thought into this. However, as you already know, we are far too close to the event to incorporate these changes.*

"Yes, it's direct to Michael," I say. "And I've only seen it because Fiona copied me into a reply. He's a sneaky…" There are too many rude words to choose from so I trail off, undecided.

Fiona, our Head of Finance, tends to take my side on things, but I'm pretty sure she enjoys fuelling the drama. She's always the first to hit the karaoke at work events. And since she mostly organises them, there is nearly always a karaoke. Often Abba themed. Her red hair, once fairly natural looking, has been getting brighter by the month. She mentioned she was battling greys, now in her early fifties, and she's often trotting off to the hair salon down the road. I imagine her colluding with the stylist, picking a colour closer to atomic red each time she goes.

"Rajesh has already shown his support of the new idea," I add with a pained sigh. Rajesh being the Head of Operations. He's almost impossible to get to respond to an email, so I assume the enemy had to practically lean over his shoulder to get his written endorsement.

I take a deep breath, trying to push down the tight pang of panic building across my abdomen. I've done well to secure Head of Marketing by my thirtieth birthday. Even if I must say so myself. But it's taken sheer determination, long hours, magically forgetting I haven't used even half of my annual leave and networking with the Board of Directors on what some might describe as arse-licking levels. I have dignity, it's just not as much as other people. I'm driven and I know where I want to go.

I joined The Starr Agency six years ago and progressed my way up the ranks by showing dedication to the cause. We work with local parks in the city, throwing pop-up musical festivals. The company has been growing fast because we offer a range of options to suit those on a lower budget and corporate clients who want to spoil their customers with a suave dinner in a specially designed pop-up restaurant.

It's been growing in popularity, to the extent we are now being invited to major sporting events to run mini festivals within their larger events.

It's great for business. It's bad for my social and mental wellbeing.

But it's worth it. Michael Starr, our esteemed leader and creator of the company, has been hinting about making me a director. Only last week, in my monthly appraisal, he said, "You're now portraying all the behaviours we'd expect to see in someone even more senior than yourself." And the other day, his email to the heads of departments very clearly set out his plan to promote internally since his very strange (incredibly handsy) and elderly uncle stood down from the board. When I've finally shown my worth, I can start reeling in the money in a big way, and all the sweat and tears I've committed to this point will be worth it.

Only problem is, there's a hurdle.

A greasy-salesman-shaped hurdle.

James Boatman.

And he's a real pain in my arse.

I growl as another email comes through. Gemma sits taller, rolling her chair back to stand and make her way to the kitchen. She knows how I like my coffee and I'm guessing she's sensing an incoming implosion. The machine rumbles to life, hissing the liquid into my mug. Our little kitchen is mostly a cupboard with a sink beside our cubicle. I got it installed so I didn't have to waste time going to and from the main kitchen all day.

"Michael's just replied suggesting we discuss James' idea further in this morning's meeting. *But what is there to discuss? Seriously?* We're three weeks out from the event and we've sold seventy per cent of the VIP tickets. We'll easily sell the rest. What do we do for those who've purchased it already? Downgrade them? That'll go well." I suck in a big gulp of air for mental strength before pressing my fingers to my eyelids. "Why is everyone trying to make me cry? Why can't Gloatman just back off this one time!?"

James' surname is Boatman, but since he makes a point in the end-of-month company "show and tell" to make a huge song and dance about every single bloody sale he makes, it was my genius idea to call him Gloatman.

Ok, so it's not particularly clever.

It was annoying when he found out what I was calling

him, and instead of being incredibly offended, wrote it at the top of his sales board as if he was proud of it.

I don't know what he calls me, but I'm sure he does call me something.

Oh god, there's a prickling behind my eyes. I shake out my limbs. I will not allow myself to cry. Part of being a successful businesswoman is being able to offset the tears in a moment of weakness and let them flood out at a point when nobody can see.

Which, admittedly, is becoming increasingly frequent.

"Drink this," Gemma says, placing a milky coffee down in front of me. It'll have three sugars in it. The rich aroma wafts into my nostrils in a sensational way.

My battle drink. My sweet kick of fury. My caffeine booster.

I nod, murmuring a thanks to my loyal colleague as she returns to her desk. I roll my shoulders, slap my palms together a few times and sip in between aggressive typing. Then I hit print on our ticket sale statistics for last week.

Once I'm ready, I leave our corner of the skyrise office opposite Liverpool Street station and head towards the other side where Michael's conference suite resides. I try very hard not to bristle when I spot James already sitting in the chair closest to Michael's, leaning back casually as if he hasn't purposefully beaten me by arriving seven minutes early. He has his usual classic salesman appearance. Matt-black hair gelled immaculately. Gleaming shoes. A fine, expensive-looking three-piece suit with a teal tie that brings out the blue in his eyes. I'll give him something, he has a nice nose. It's long, with a little bump in the middle. James's appearance oozes with an irritating confidence that I've always thought gives off Matthew McConaughey vibes.

"Gloatman," I say.

He smiles, but it's not a friendly smile, more calculating. I imagine he's saying my nickname in his head. The fact that I don't know what that is only irritates me to the extent that I want to turn this building upside down in order to retrieve it.

But no… deep breaths. *Deep breaths*.

Finally, his smile fades as he turns his chair back towards the table where he has a notepad. He fiddles with it in his lap, using his long fingers to spin his pen. "Felicity."

"It's Fliss."

"I know," he replies without looking at me.

Then say, FLISS!

My christened name is Felicity and nobody except for my parents (and Gloatman) have called me it in about twenty years. Granted, it was an error on my part. James started at Starr a few months before me, and on my first day, as I was being shown around and introduced to everyone, my nerves got the better of me. I said my name was Felicity. And he's never forgotten it, even though I sign off my emails as Fliss.

I take my seat opposite his. This way I'm close to Michael if not exactly closest thanks to the oval shape of his office. I'm a stark contrast to James, in his dark tweed suit, with my flowery patterned dress that flares from the waist down to my knees. My dark brown hair, which I attempt to straighten every morning into a semi-acceptable state, is naturally thick, pulled neatly backwards by my fuchsia Alice band. My nails are currently painted a pastel blue, my kitten heels are from Irregular Choice and are exactly that, covered in sequins.

James always looks as if he's about to step onto an episode of *The Apprentice*. Whereas I look more like I'm going to a summer wedding.

"Did you see my email?" he asks, raising an eyebrow in a telling way.

I look up, fixing him with a narrowed stare. He knows I've seen it. "Did you get a chance to read my reply?"

He makes a face, a sort of arrogant smirk, which suggests he did. Damn it. I should've added a read receipt. "Unfortunately, I haven't had the pleasure. I'm sure it was incredibly insightful."

Bastard!

Before I can load a useful response on my tongue, the rest of the team starts filing in. There are five main departments at The Starr Agency: Events, Sales, Marketing, Operations, Finance and HR. HR is literally Mel in her own little office where people go to be fired or hired.

They take their seats, sipping on their drinks whilst I watch my nemesis across from me. We smile overly politely. The room is too hot, or at least I am, so I remove my cardigan and hang it on my chair. James has gone back to making notes on his pad. What's he writing? Does he have a plan for this meeting? He often comes prepared with his irritating ability to woo people.

Except me, that is.

I see right through his appealing front door, past the lavish exterior, the dark blue eyes and toned arms – tight against his sleeves, and see the arse that he really is. He knows the consequences for me and my team if we don't hit our targets for ticket sales. We don't earn as many bonuses as the sales team. In fact, we earn only one a year and our success is hinged on this event he is trying to ruin for us.

"Good morning, Dream Team," Michael sings in his jubilant way as he enters the room, walking round to take his seat at the head of the table.

Admittedly, Michael's a strange one. Some would call him quirky. I value his input and calm leadership here. But he does have this tendency to sway between marketing and sales like one of those old-school gameshows with the spinning wheels. He could land anywhere. It makes me both tense and agitated, whilst also maintaining a sense of hope that I have a fifty per cent chance of taking the enemy down.

He's pretty reliable in some ways. He always wears a white shirt, no tie – a few buttons undone at the top and a pair of standard grey work trousers. Even when this office is verging on chilly, he'll only wear the shirt. And yet, he's also the most unpredictable decision-maker I've ever met. It makes him hard to work for. Never really knowing what he's going to do next.

I try not to grind my teeth when he touches James' shoulder as he passes. "How were your weekends?"

We all look around waiting for someone to speak first. It's one of those frustrating moments because none of us actually care how each other's weekends were. However, it is an unwritten rule that we should at least pretend to.

"I went fishing with my cousin," Rajesh offers. I inwardly sigh. Rajesh is in his late forties but looks older. He's lovely, but frustrating to communicate with when his stress levels peak at ten, yet mine can launch well over a thousand in a matter of minutes. It's hard to get him to understand the sheer depth of importance of some tasks. For example, branded signage being positioned in the correct places for maximum visibility. Or sponsored merchandise being worn by our event staff. I suspect he thinks we're all a bit mad.

"Marvellous," Michael grins, his teeth glinting.

Michael, the man behind this whole enterprise, comes from money, I think... Actually, I only assume. We don't know very much about him at all. With his silvery-dark hair and spookily pale eyes, he's a mystery to me in many ways. He never seems to be tired. I regularly receive emails from him in the middle of the night and I'm still yet to see him eat.

Obviously, there are rumours. I don't involve myself in them. But I know people around the office joke that he's a vampire. Or a ghoul. Someone once suggested he was a cannibal.

I silence my mind in case he can read it. At that exact moment, he turns his head to smile at me in his eccentric way, full mouthed, stretched cheeks, as if he heard me thinking. I open my mouth to say something, but James beats me to it.

"How was *your* weekend, Michael?"

Slimy git.

"Exactly as you'd expect it to be, James. Kind of you to ask," he replies. Ever the mystery.

James gives Michael a polite nod before turning to me with a slightly less enthusiastic grin. "What about you, Felicity? Get lots done?"

I laugh in polite corporate. He knows I did. The reason he knows is because we were the only two sad fools to be logged in on Saturday afternoon, replying to Michael's many emails. "It was sublime, thank you, James. And how was yours? Did you manage to get away from your laptop for a few hours?" I round this off with a pity face.

"Hilarious," he mutters, his grin faltering. "Yes, thank you, Felicity."

There's a moment of strained silence. I physically feel it in my chest but force myself not to fill it with some unhelpful nonsense. No. We need to get to the heart of the matter. I, however, will not be the one to cause the friction in our first meeting on a Monday morning.

James purses his lips before finding his stellar grin again, leaning towards Michael in his typical flirtatious way. "What did you think of my idea then, boss?"

Let's bloody go…

I say, "If you had gotten to my email before this meeting, James, you would have seen that it is *far* too late to be incorporating changes…"

"As I said a moment ago, Felicity, unfortunately the sales team were very busy this morning, so I was unable to make time for your reply. However, if you had fully read the email thread, you would've noticed my idea has already been endorsed by the ops team."

He means Rajesh. He means he walked up to Rajesh and told him to write a response.

My smile is corporate cyanide as I lace my fingers together on the table. "That's really great. I'm so glad you took the initiative to get this project signed off by Rajesh. And I did see that part of the thread. Thank you for highlighting it to me again. The trouble is, you have forgotten that you need both Marketing and Finance to sign this off too."

Michael looks between us, as James blinks at me. I notice the quiver in his cheeks and along his rigid jawline. He knows he's got to play his best cards to win this because I'm not going to budge.

He talks quickly, clearly. "As Marketing will remember…" I'm *Marketing* now – hilarious. I'm not a person, I am an entire department. "… we've almost sold out of hospitality places for the final event of the summer. We could easily close out another marquee. The profit would absolutely annihilate anything VIP tickets can achieve. Although I admire and support all the work Marketing have done to bring this about, Marketing should be realistic about the way business works."

The way business works? What a patronising…

My smile is making my jaw ache, but I must win this battle now. Time for some swift blows. "Of course, Marketing is very aware of how business works. Thank you for your concern in this matter." I cringe as I say, "It would help, however, if Sales were more aware of the work that goes into the last efforts of organising the events, as it mostly comes down to the dedication of the other departments to achieve this. For example, where would you put the kitchens?" I ask, tilting my head in a patronising way to mirror James' tone. "What about the menus? Sales have less than three weeks to finalise it. And the sales team aren't always as reliable as we would like—"

James laughs with volume to interrupt me. "Don't go for my team," he says, his pitch raising slightly, his teeth gritted. Ooh, he's protective of his aggressive slime bags. I'm yet to meet a salesperson in his team who has any kind of office-kitchen etiquette. At work events they're always the loudest, rudest and most inappropriate. Annoyingly, Michael tends to turn a blind eye.

We, being my lovely marketing crew, are usually trying to have a pleasant evening of laughter and food whilst they're mashing it up with *shots, shots, shots* and glugging beer back like it's going out of style.

"Sales needs to consider the fact that there's absolutely no guarantee you can sell the tables in that timeframe," I reiterate. "And even if you can, what about the sixty people who've already paid for the VIP tickets? Marketing sold another twelve last week alone. We're at seventy per cent capacity. Marketing can easily get this to the one hundred per cent."

Gosh, even I'm talking about myself as if I'm an entire department now.

"The sales team deserve the chance to exceed their bonuses, and this would allow them that," James says directly to Michael, not even bothering to include me now. He gets straight to the heart of the matter. Money. That's all he cares about anyway.

"Erm... excuse me? When making business decisions, please consider all the departments it will affect," I say. In other words, stop being a selfish prick.

"Thank you for pointing this out, Felicity," James says. "Unfortunately, when you look at the bigger picture success of the company, you'll know the bonuses your department achieve are incredibly minimal compared to Sales so—"

I scoff. "Marketing *deserve* their bonuses too."

He makes a face. "Sorry, I wasn't aware the middle of my sentence was interrupting the start of yours."

Ugh. Shots fired. I have no response to this. I glare across at Gloatman. In fairness, I did interrupt, but he's done it to me too.

After a moment, he continues, "And besides, you're only marketing. You don't mind working on your salaries. My team require bonuses for motivation."

"Isn't selling their job? Like marketing is ours?" I ask through the last shreds of my cheek muscles.

James gives me one of those oh-you-poor-thing expressions, wrinkling his nose. "You don't understand how this works."

I laugh, frustration lacing the sound. "Although I appreciate your concern about my understanding, sales are in constant need of financial incentive. Their motivation levels are lacking, and it may be time for their leader to look inwardly at this challenge. They've already hit their bonuses. Why do they need to *exceed* them?"

James turns back to Michael again as if I haven't even made an iota of a point. I notice I'm clenching and unclenching my fist on the table. The line between professional behaviour and physical violence is sometimes scarily thin.

"The profit target has been met. Sales can exceed it. Let us do this. It will look so, *so* good to the board. You know it too. Rajesh has already endorsed my idea. The kitchens can be extended. The furniture can be hired. It's all ready to go."

"No, no, no..." I say, leaning in towards our leader too. "What about our clientele? We can't just let them down. I thought your vision, Michael, was to bring joy to local communities. If we continue to remove affordable options in lieu of expensive corporate stuff how does that impact our long-term goals?"

"Our long-term goals don't mean shit unless we're driving a steady profit," James retorts.

"Which we are..."

"No thanks to Marketing. You'll find the real profit is achieved through Sales."

"Which is consistently supported by Marketing," I grin, but my teeth are set together.

"Entirely against the point. That is the purpose of your department."

"As is Sales to… erm… What is their role again?" I make a show of tapping my chin. "Oh yes, that's it. *To. Sell.*"

Gloatman is giving me his full attention now, nervous energy seeping from his pores. Maybe it's the way he's gripping his pen. I have a feeling he's already committed to his idea. I have a feeling he's already sold some of the tables. I have a feeling he's not going to let this one slide.

Well, hard luck for him. Neither am I! We stare each other down as if the other might crack.

"I see this is quite the debate," Michael intercedes. "I support both your points of view here. You make very strong arguments. As you know, I like to be led by my team, and if Fiona is in support of Fliss, then it means we are split down the middle."

We all turn to Fiona for her wide-eyed nod of confirmation. She's an angel. Always has my back. I'm convinced I hear James curse in response.

Michael is no longer smiling but watching us with a worried expression. At some point during the discussion, he's rolled his shirt sleeves up, and I notice his arms are completely hairless.

Vampire…

"I think the whole team needs a break," he says calmly. "A nice corporate away day to boost morale and rejuvenate."

Oh, absolutely not. We're three weeks out from an event.

There's so much to do. He's done this before, dragging us to some random event in Paris for a "learning experience", and it was a nightmare. I ended up working through a whole night to get everything done.

"No. No, it's fine—" I say, as James says, "I would advise against—"

Michael holds up a hand. "I think we *all* need a break." He smiles again in his unnerving way. "You are my team. I can't have you disagreeing like this. I will make a decision about James' idea after our... away day." He nods to himself as if he's having his own internal discussion about this. "Yes. I think some team building will be good for all of us. An adventure. Somewhere different... Yes. Somewhere but nowhere."

"We really need a quick decision," James pipes up.

He's silenced with a calm but stern expression. "No decisions should be made in such a rushed way my fearless leaders. You require time to choose wisely."

James opens his mouth to object again, but Michael goes on. "Don't worry. I think we should go away imminently. Clear your calendars for the rest of the week. No exceptions. I'll let you know the details by end of play today. Team dismissed."

Two

There's a whiteboard by our flat's front door with a list of problems on it. Our landlady is supposed to come around to fix them but we have only met her once when she moved us in five years ago. The biggest, most critical issue is the hole in the floorboard in the hallway, large enough to drop a shoe down. That has been on the list for three years. There's a sorry-looking corn plant covering it, with a red bauble dangling from the top leaf. Our rendition of a Christmas tree. But it is now May, and nobody has bothered to move it. The mould in Jen's room is home to three slugs. The window in the loo doesn't shut, and we have a worrying crack across the ceiling in the living area.

Our three-bed flat is home to five fully grown adults because there are two couples living here. I'm pretty sure it's illegal, but they share some of the overall rent, so I work very hard to pretend not to notice.

The kitchen is one and a half metres wide. There is only one tray in the oven. The sink is rusty. The fruit bowl is full of random things nobody will claim as their own: an out-of-date condom, a random key, a dead fly and a half-used pack of Kleenex. No fruit.

Living here is actually not conducive to a healthy lifestyle. But it's in a nice street so, I guess, you give, and you take.

I've procured a dehumidifier in my room that also acts as a clothes horse. It's badly ventilated in here without the windows open but it's too cold in winter to open them. As I shrug out of my dress and into my cosy pyjamas, I realise it has already gone nine in the evening. There's an ongoing battle between myself and James as to who will leave the office last. Michael stays late and I would hate for him to think I'm not invested in my job.

I am.

But the issue is, so is Gloatman.

Luckily, he got a call that had him sighing, running a hand through his perfectly shaped hair as he strode out of the office, giving me one last miserable glance. Thankfully, it meant, despite our battle in the meeting earlier today, I had triumphed. But on top of this I actually had a lot of work to get done, or reassign within my team, thanks to this last-minute work trip that Michael has flung on us.

His email came through at four fifty-five, just as my team were giving each other anxious glances about when it might be suitable for them to leave without looking uncommitted to the cause. I don't expect them to hold the same standards as me, but it would be nice if one of them showed an ounce of willingness from time to time. I'm pretty certain they think I'm a workaholic.

Over the past couple of years, getting back to my room has been the worst part of my day, and I struggle to pinpoint why. I can cope with my messy, damp-infested flat. If anything, it's character building. It's the way my heart starts juddering at an uncomfortable rhythm as I lie back. It's the way, despite adding a softer mattress and the weighted blanket to my bed, my limbs seem to go rigid as I try to relax. It's the way my breathing becomes laboured even though I'm just lying here doing nothing at all.

My brain spins, going over the day, the commute, the meetings, the challenges. I scrutinise every part of it until I'm on the verge of throwing up. I should've said something else to Michael. I should've held my tongue with James. I let him get to me. It's not long before I sense my cheeks are damp. The room is dark, somehow both stuffy yet cold, and I take a shuddering, calming breath as I realise how very tired I am.

"I love my job. I love my job. I love my job," I preach quietly into my pillow.

Maybe I do need a break? I'm not sure the break I need is the one Michael has organised. No. I think I need to do a *Mamma Mia!*, find an island in Greece and a long-lost auntie who has a half-ruined farmhouse I can do up. Hopefully I'll bump into three gorgeous men over one summer and have some exciting, wild affairs under the sun.

Instead, we were sent our boarding passes for Inverness. Inverness! And our return flight isn't until Saturday. He didn't even ask us if we had plans at the weekend. The man just assumes we're free.

I am. But that's against the point.

I love my job. I can do this.

I sort of wish one of my housemates were around so I could chew their ears off about this whole thing, but alas they're all out working their second jobs. For a moment, I'm thankful I earn at least enough to avoid that. I honestly think a second job would kill me. Especially as sleep claws over me now, my eyes heavy, weary.

Before I drift off, I set my alarm for 3 a.m. An overwhelmed cry falls from my lips.

I love my job.

Heathrow is quiet at this time in the morning. There's a lull in activity for a few hours each night, and Michael appears to have booked our flight at an unsociable time. I sit in sleepy silence at the gate, waiting for my flight to be called, and when it comes to boarding, Gloatman and the rest of the team are still nowhere to be found. Apparently, Michael would be finding his own way there, and Mel in HR decided it would be more conducive to a healthy work environment if she stayed. An appropriate decision, considering Gloatman's team can be total arse wipes to my team.

For a moment, I sense a pocket of adrenaline bursting inside of me. Where are they? Why am I on my own?

I open my phone and dial for Fiona. There's no answer. I frown at the boarding queue getting smaller by the second. I haven't got long to decide. I think about calling James briefly to see if he's on his way, before realising that I hope he isn't coming anyway, and this may be the best thing that's happened to me in a while.

This does feel suspiciously weird though. I look behind me at the way I came into the terminal. I could turn around now, travel home and slither back into my bed for a kip, all before 7 a.m. That's not how you get promoted though. *Must remember to show willingness.*

The queue is getting shorter, and they've already called for final boarders. This is it. I need to make a decision. Oh, flip. I bite my bottom lip, considering. What's the worst that can happen? If it turns out Michael cancelled the trip last minute and forgot to tell me then I'll just turn around and come home. I'm a grown woman. I shouldn't be afraid to get on a flight on my own. And yet, uneasiness is bubbling under my skin.

I sigh, stepping towards the cabin crew waiting to scan my pass, then board the plane.

Once seated, I pretend to enjoy the flight, despite the worry of what's to come from my unpredictable manager making me fidgety, whilst peeking out of the window as the light, fresh blue of morning leaks into the night sky. There's a slight orange tint, the promise of summer just around the corner. It's such a short flight, I don't even get offered a hot drink. Luckily, I bought a bottle of water at the terminal that I sip on slowly, popping my ears as we descend.

Scotland from this height looks like a lot of water and barren land.

I peek at my phone on flight mode and realise I haven't called Mum back yet. She rang whilst I was still in the office yesterday evening, and I didn't want to let that vulnerable side of me leak into my fierce façade. Mum has a way of making me fragile. My dad, on the other hand, has a way of making me a little cross and bossy. Their divorce, when I was fifteen, felt very personal to me.

They made me sit at the head of the table as Mum took my hands into hers. She was a bit teary; I remember that. Dad looked more resigned, tired. Mum said, "We're getting a divorce."

Dad said, "It's been a long time coming."

To which Mum made a gasping sound, as if he'd personally slighted her. "We never really loved each other at all, to be honest. We only stayed together because I got pregnant with you."

My dad rubbed his face, shaking his head in exasperation. "What your mother means is that we love you very much and it meant the world to us to raise you together but that we haven't ever been truly happy. Not really."

Of course, at first, I'd been devastated. There was this ever-present need to feel all the warmth and cosiness of my life prior to their breakup. Baking gingerbread with Dad on Christmas Eve whilst Mum watched from the dining table, sipping on eggnog as festive tunes rattled on in the background. Opening presents on my birthday, watched dotingly by my two favourite people in the whole world. The summer barbeques with Mum's exquisite array of salads and Dad's charred black burgers we'd have to scrape before we could eat. It was all gone, and nothing I tried with them individually could ever match what we had had.

And besides, they'd explained none of it had ever been real anyway.

For some reason, even now, we all play this fun game where we don't talk about any of it. I think it was, *and is*, better that way. I still juggle Christmases between them, and so far, it runs relatively smoothly. Bringing up those discussions would more than likely cause a rift. There's a lot of life admin to consider with separated parents, but the worst part, with Mum single, is how her emotional baggage falls on me.

That's why I decided to ignore her call earlier on. I can't

be talking her down off a ledge over a bad date whilst I'm at work.

I sigh inwardly. That's not fair.

She's a highly empathic woman; something I try to smother in myself. And I think she has this ability to spark deep and traumatising fear into any man she meets. She's a crier. And she's been known to do this on first dates.

This may have happened to me one time. But in my defence, there was a puppy.

As we come in to land, I promise myself I will call Mum as soon as I'm in the privacy of my own room. *I really hope I have my own room.* The air in Inverness is cooler than it is in London. There's a fresh nippiness about it. It's as if they're in early spring and not the start of summer. I'm glad I chose tights this morning, knitted black ones that go perfectly with my little red ankle boots, red cardigan and black skater dress with a high-cut neckline.

I've always enjoyed mixing it up with colours. Dressing blandly draws attention to my otherwise plain self. There's nothing particularly exciting about me underneath my clothes and makeup. I'm average in many ways: height, waist circumference and ordinary green eyes. They're not even bluey-green or hazel. Just green. I wouldn't call myself pretty and yet I wouldn't call myself unappealing either. I'm right there in plain Jane world. So, I add some colour, to make myself memorable.

I wrap my cardigan tighter around my shoulders as an icy breeze whips off the sea and across the taxi pick-up area. There's a saltiness in the air. The stench of seaside lingers here. Rather than the lovely aroma of beaches and ice cream, there's the waft of rotting seaweed and dampness.

On the planning email Michael sent last night, he advised that he had arranged a car at Inverness to collect us, which now turns out to just be me. What am I supposed to do with that little information? The details of where and when this car would be here are missing from his instructions.

I glance around for a sign of some sort. Something, or anything, that will make me feel just a little less flustered and frantic.

Surely my colleagues must be here by now? Did they take another flight?

I pause with a huff. *This is ridiculous.* I open my phone and try for Fiona again. It's 7 a.m. now so she must be awake. But, again, no answer.

Gah. I so do not want to have to call James for clarification. He probably knows all the details. What if Michael has cancelled, and now, I'm the only prat who flew to Scotland? He'll be so smug. I give the small airport one last scan to check for their familiar faces but, alas, they're still nowhere to be found.

I dial for Gloatman, a defeated feeling weighing heavy on my shoulders. His phone doesn't even ring. Straight to voicemail. Well, damn.

I decide to walk a little further towards the taxi rank. To my surprise, I spot a driver holding a sign for The Starr Agency. I let out a small gasp of happiness that at least something seems to be going to plan, but then, once I reach him, I realise I know nothing about this strange person I'm about to get into a car with.

"Felicity Rainer?" he asks, his bushy eyebrows rising.

"Yeah, that's me," I confirm. "Just quickly though: do you know where we're going? Are we waiting for anyone else to join us? Do you have proof Michael booked you?"

The man looks at me curiously, but to my relief, he doesn't seem offended by my questioning. "Sorry, lass, I was booked by the company. I don't have any proof other than that. You can call 'em though, if you like? Sally in the office might know more. All I know is I am picking you up and taking you to Davey Castle. It's about a forty-minute drive from here."

I contemplate calling this Sally, but then again, his black SUV does have branding on it and all the relevant registration plates so he must be legitimate. And in addition to that he seems friendly and kind. He's only an inch taller than me. I think about who would win in a physical confrontation. He's quite old. I reckon I could take him.

Fine. Since I'm out of options, I let him load my small suitcase into the back of his taxi. He then speeds out onto a faster single carriageway towards this mysterious castle destination.

I check the time. It's only just gone 7 a.m. My stomach is rumbling, and I have this sudden urge to lie down for a moment. Must be the stress of the morning getting to me. Something tells me, however, that Michael won't have sleeping in mind.

The scenery is vast and bare here. It's both rocky and green, with lakes and long stretches of sea clawing its way through the landscape. We follow a road along an estuary that dips and burrows its way beside the sea, through grey hills and past small, sparsely populated villages, until the landscape becomes thicker with sharp, thorny bushes that seem to have grown harsh in the bitter weather and trees that grow tall but thin.

The car takes a right turn onto a driveway, surrounded by a magnificently green golf course with manicured lawns. Well, that's how it appears anyway. I know nothing about golf, of course. I'm sure it's the sort of dull activity you'd find Gloatman doing to network with his clients.

I roll my head from side to side to loosen my neck. I really hope whatever this retreat turns out to be, James doesn't make it. He'd just be trying to find a way to win Michael over to his idea. At least if he doesn't show, I can act as if that argument never happened. I can prove to Michael I am a calm, creative, gentle employee who favours image over money. I see the bigger picture. The longevity of the business.

The car follows the drive until it arches around in front of a grand castle. The front is all grey and menacing with its turrets and gargoyles, but the windows glow a light orange in a friendly, welcoming way. There's the faint smell of brewing coffee and cooked breakfast that makes my mouth water.

Just looking at this place has the stress melting away from my body.

I take a deep breath of the fresh Scottish air once I'm out, holding my bag with a smile. Maybe this won't be so bad after all. Maybe this *is* what I need. Maybe this week will help me get rid of the anxiety that lingers inside of me, never wanting to shift.

"Felicity," a deep voice comes from behind me.

I jump, spinning, as my calm composure evaporates like

water thrown over a volcano. "*You!* But you missed the flight."

James is dressed in another tweed suit jacket, beige chinos and a white shirt, a few buttons undone at the top, a whisper of dark hair on show. Although it's still a smart look, it's more casual than usual. Wait... Is that the same outfit he had on yesterday? Just without the tie?

He shrugs, unbothered. His face is one of bored confidence, as he says, "I shared the jet with Michael."

I try not to let it irk me that James got one-on-one time with Michael. I bet he used the time to chew his ear off.

Another thought occurs to me. Is he considering James for the director role too? No, he can't possibly be. James is an idiot. He's only interested in money. He doesn't see the bigger picture at all. Directors need to be able to see the bigger picture... Don't they?

I feel a sudden urge to stamp my foot. I was already tired. Now I'm irritable too. And still hungry.

"Yes, it was the perfect opportunity to discuss business ideas and my potential promotion," he says, giving me a knowing look, his eyebrows lifting. Well, damn. Why hadn't I even considered James would be in the running for director too?

But, of course he would. He's always trying to find ways to slither into Michael's schedule. And his ideas! His stupid bloody ideas! They've been more frequent recently. I should've seen this coming.

Michael never said there were two of us in the running... This changes everything.

There's a tingling in one side of my brain and if I don't turn away from James soon, he'll catch an eye twitch.

"Where's Michael and the others anyway?" I demand, peering around the car park, trying not to make eye contact with Gloatman.

But as if saying his name somehow conjured the man, Michael appears to our left. I have to physically catch myself from gasping and stepping backwards.

He softly places his hand on my shoulder and does his magnificent, if slightly creepy, pearly white smile. "My team!"

I give James a look. Wasn't he with Michael all morning? Surely this isn't a surprise to either of them.

"Follow me," Michael says, whooshing past us both towards a beat-up minivan.

Three

I'd be more concerned if James seemed to know what was going on, but since he's frowning too, I assume he's also in the dark. A thankful sign. Not much chatter can have occurred between the two on their way here. Michael, for once, has dressed differently from how he is in the office, in his black jeans and tight-fitting turtleneck.

Michael spins to face us. He claps excitedly, a little bounce in his knees. "We're going on a secret adventure." He nods towards the dented white minivan. "I'm borrowing this from the hotel. On you hop."

"Where are the others?" I ask. "And why aren't we staying here? This castle looks lovely."

Michael's excitable expression doesn't shift. "No others. Just you two. Don't worry about the castle. I have better plans. Let's go!" And with that he practically skips round to the back of the van, motioning for us to follow with our bags.

James peers down at me. He's at least a foot taller than I am, at my measly five foot three, but he's relatively lean. Not one of those hulking great big rugby types. I imagine he takes great pride in his image. I've heard he does a lot of running alongside weight training. Some of my marketing team go all bashful whenever he's nearby. It irritates me no end. And anyway, he's not exactly boyfriend material. After all, there are rumours he sometimes sleeps with customers to get their business.

It wouldn't surprise me.

"Do you know what's going on?" he asks in a low voice.

"I thought *you* would, considering *you* shared a jet with Michael this morning," I hiss back. I'm not hiding my annoyance anymore. I'm going to get to the bottom of it at some point. It's not fair he had one-on-one time, and I was forced to travel alone without even being offered a refreshment.

James holds my stare for a moment as if trying to decide whether I'm being honest or whether to jeer back at me. Instead, he rubs his face, groaning as he strides forwards, handing his large rucksack to Michael, who places it carefully in the boot. Once we're all in, we're off again.

Michael drives carefully, calmly. But I can't enjoy the scenery or the gentle driving as I'm too busy racking my brain for clues. Where the hell is he taking us? I'm a fun person when I want to be. I think… But I don't like surprises. They play with my emotions. Tease me. And a teased Fliss is a tearful one. God, do I hate and distrust her. Especially around James.

He doesn't EVER get to see me cry!

The main road we follow initially is long and winding, taking us through small villages and rugged countryside.

After a good hour, I chew on my bottom lip as we turn left onto a narrower road that could be mistaken for a farm track. It's gravelly and full of potholes, and the weeds are clawing over it as if they're trying to claim it back to nature. Beyond the sheep wire fencing lining the road, is an incredible backdrop of mountainous Scotland that goes on forever. Below the clear morning sky, lakes, rocky inclines and patches of forest dot the landscape. My jaw drops in awe, my eyes taking it all in.

This is the same island that my crappy apartment is on. How can that be possible?

When I peek to see if anyone has caught me gawking, I catch James frowning at me suspiciously. I give him a *what?* face. He looks away, huffing as he leans further back into his chair, rubbing his chin. He's possibly more disgruntled by this whole thing than I am.

Good. Probably means I'm winning.

After another hour of venturing into the deep wilderness, I check my phone to see that, firstly I have no signal (*shit, I have no signal*) and secondly, we've been driving for over two hours.

I'm not sure why neither of us have mustered the courage to question Michael about all this yet. Maybe I should? But I don't… I would hate for him to think I'm complaining. And at least the scenery is nice. Besides, if James thinks I'm ok with all this, then hopefully it will psych him out and he'll be the first one to buckle and ask.

Or even better, complain.

Another twenty minutes roll past. I keep checking my phone. I haven't had signal for a while now. It appears phone companies don't know this place exists. I mean I guess I didn't a few hours ago.

I'm just about to cave, ask Michael how much longer to go, when the van makes an alarming sputtering sound. My heart lurches as it practically hops along the road. I grab the seat and pray for my life. Luckily Michael handles it well, pulling off to the side in a well-placed layby right by an expansive lake.

"Oh, what was that!?" Michael exclaims, frowning briefly before turning his head to look at us with a wide smile. "Not to worry. I'm sure it's nothing. James, be a good lad and come check with me."

Of course, Gloatman leaps at the opportunity to help him, pulling the door back and bouncing onto the verge. Inside, I tap my foot against the seat in front, waiting for a report. They mutter outside for a moment before I peer out to see James running his fingers through his hair in that agitated way I often see him doing at the end of bad months when it comes to reporting his sales figures.

This is not good.

Michael pokes his head back through the doors. "It's bad news I'm afraid. We've blown a tyre."

"Shit," I say. "What the hell do we do now?"

I get up from my seat, hopping down from the minivan, and walk round to where James is uselessly blinking at the blown tyre. I stop beside him, looking to Michael. "Well, do you have breakdown cover? Can you call the hotel? Surely, they'll sort the insurance."

He sighs. "Probably, but no signal." He waves his phone at me.

"Tell me you have signal?" I say to my enemy.

James props his hands on his hips, giving me a disbelieving glance. "Ah, yes. Despite the fact nobody else has it... Don't worry, Felicity, I have a super phone."

"Don't be a dick."

I cross my arms, staring at the wheel like it might

magically fix itself. For a moment there's a stunned silence whilst we all rack our brains for ideas.

"Does anyone know how to change a tyre?" James asks. More silence.

"Is there even a spare one?" he adds.

Michael looks around the van, underneath, behind the back doors, and returns with one of his dazzling smiles. This smile makes my blood fizz. I can't help my face from contorting into an angry stare. How did this man think it was a good idea to drive us out into the middle arse-end of nowhere without a spare tyre? I bite my lip again and fold my arms around my middle a bit tighter to prevent a full-scale meltdown.

We're stuck. We're stuck here in... *God knows where!* And we're down one too many tyres with no signal and no hope.

Oh shit – are we going to die!? We might bloody die!

"Stop freaking out," James mutters without even looking at me.

I realise my breathing has indeed increased to an audible level. I puff out a long stream of air in the hope it might settle my lungs. I like the countryside. I'm a big fan of sheep and grass and trees, but I also like to be within walking distance of civilisation. We must be miles away from anything here.

"I'm not freaking out, *actually*. But *what the fuck* do we do now?" I whisper-hiss back.

"Someone will have to follow the road up to the nearest village," Michael says. "I'd better stay in case help arrives early."

Sheer horror crosses James' face. His mouth opens slightly, his eyes widening as if he's just been confronted by

WORK TRIP

a ghost. "I'll go on my own!" he yells about three octaves louder than necessary.

For a moment, a sense of relief flows through me like when you climb into a warm bath. Well, that's wonderful. I don't fancy walking in my little boots that far anyway. It'll wear them down and they're already second hand. But then the gritty competitiveness teases into my blood system and *hell no* am I letting this man steal this victory.

"I'll go with you!" I announce, matching his volume.

"Great!" Michael says with a clap just as James says, "You can go on your own then."

"What!?" I step backwards. He'd let me go on my own? Out here? I might get lost. Or murdered. Or kidnapped. Of course, he wants me to go alone. Bastard.

"I think it would be wiser to go together. You're a great team!" Michael adds jubilantly. We both give him *are you kidding!?* expressions but his smile doesn't slip.

"Give me strength," James mutters under his breath, before shrugging out of his jacket, despite the chilly breeze rolling off the nearby lake. "Come on then, Felicity. Let's get this over and done with."

Four

When I was sixteen, I went on a walking holiday with Dad and his then fiancée, Sasha. She was pretty but she was a bitch, and despite the walking part of the trip away being *her* idea, she found an excuse at every opportunity to complain about it.

Despite this, I felt this deep need to show Dad how much I liked her. I'd made his life miserable enough up till then. If she made him happy, then I was happy.

So, I gritted my teeth, held my head high and forged on ahead despite her constant whinging.

Sometimes I do worry witnessing my parents' failed relationship somehow set my own romantic life up for failure. They've hardly been good role models. It forces me to be extra focussed on my job because, what if that's all I really have to show for myself? For my life? I'd better make it good.

And that's why I am not going to let James, who is striding ahead of me on his long powerful legs, bother me. I'm pattering down the road behind him, my heels clinking on the tarmac, doing two strides for each one of his.

"Will you slow down?" I complain.

"You're the one who insisted on coming. You can keep up."

I groan audibly. "You know you can be a real arse sometimes. Actually no, you always are. You're always an arse. A great big, dick of an arse."

"That doesn't make sense."

"You don't make sense."

He laughs, bitter. "Burn."

A thought occurs to me now we're totally alone, the minivan no longer in sight. "What did Michael say on the jet?"

"None of your business."

"Just tell me."

"I don't want to."

I scoff. "Fine, whatever. Just surprised you supposedly spent the morning with him but seemingly have zero knowledge of what the hell is going on right now. Why are we in Scotland anyway? Why here? Why pull us away from our busy working days without any access to our emails at all for… for this! What is this!?"

"I know as much as you, Felicity."

James keeps walking ahead as if he can somehow outstride me. He could. Absolutely. In fact, if he started running now, I'm sure he'd disappear in moments. I wouldn't stand a chance. Even if I had appropriate footwear, he'd escape me like a greyhound racing a guinea pig. Which is intriguing, because why isn't he?

He's only walking fast enough to make it slightly difficult for me. I reckon he could go faster if he wanted to.

James' phone bleeps. He tugs it out of his pocket so fast

you'd think it was burning a hole through his chinos. "Shit. Low battery."

"How do you already have low battery?"

"There wasn't a charger on the jet."

"But you didn't leave home with it charged?"

"I didn't go home last night."

I laugh, roll my eyes. Not a surprise. I wonder who it was this time. Honestly the man has no shame. "Shock."

He pauses then turns around, tilting his head with a frown. "What does that mean?"

I shrug, marching past him. "I've heard the rumours."

His eyebrows shoot up. "Oh, you have?"

"Everyone has," I say, listening to his steps behind me.

"Go on then, if you've heard them, where do you think I was last night?"

I'm just about to answer with something that, I'm sure, is very witty when we hear a rumbling sound in the form of an engine. We both step forwards to get a better look. After another moment, an ancient blue tractor rolls around the trees in the direction of the van.

We give each other a relieved look then start waving like crazy. It takes longer than I thought it would to reach us, so there's a lull in our waving, but the man driving has seen us and slows to a stop, opening the cabin door.

"*Madainn mhath*," the man says.

James runs his hands through his hair in exasperation. "Do you speak English?"

"Aye," he replies.

"Oh, thank god. We've blown a tyre in the minivan down the road." James points back the way we've just walked. "It's parked up on the side by the lake. Can you help us?"

The man grunts. He's got muddy, green, full-body overalls on. I know he's a farmer but there's a small part of my brain that thinks maybe this man might murder us. As long as he goes for James first then I have a chance to get away.

"Go on up to the town."

"How far is that?" James asks, a bit less friendly now, disgruntled this man is not a sucker to his charms. We immune folk do know how to wind him up.

"'bout another ten minutes' walk. Must be on me way," the man says, slamming the door shut.

"Well, he wasn't very friendly," James says.

"Do you expect everyone to be charmed by your perfect hair, Gloatman?"

He takes a deep breath. "No, Felicity. If you must know, I expect people to be generally kind. I distrust petty people," he says, before adding, "Like you."

"I'm not petty!"

"Next time you're near a dictionary, search for the word, because you'll be amazed to find your picture in there."

"That's so not true," I say. "You're the one always making my life difficult with your stupid ideas and schemes."

"The ideas and schemes that promise to make the company more money?"

"But threaten to ruin the image—"

"The image?" James scoffs. "God, you and the fucking image. What does that even mean?" He does that thing he does where he places his hands on his hips and juts one long leg out like some kind of Austen hero. Obviously, he's far less refined. And comes without the absurd sideburns.

I'm aghast at his question. "I knew you weren't paying attention in any of my presentations! We have a brand,

James! A brand my team and I have worked bloody hard to create. It doesn't just boil down to the corporate hospitality sales. You know they only make up thirty-five per cent of our overall revenue, right? And even less in profit when you take off the topline.

"We're trying to create a long-term brand that people rely upon. You know, like Nike or Burberry or freaking McDonalds! We want people to know what to expect. But if you keep on ruining our consumers' nights by trying to downgrade them a few weeks before, because you want to make more money in hospitality, then it's going to damage our brand. Do you understand that?"

James ponders this for a moment. "I hadn't actually thought about it that way, but hospitality is growing, and fast. Thanks to the hard work of *my* team, we now have a thriving client base who regularly and consistently buy tables off us. They have an image in their minds too. I think it could get so much bigger on my side."

He looks away as if he's suddenly transferred to his dream world where everyone and their dog can afford the packages he sells. Well, they can't. "You still don't get how important this is to me… I mean to the business."

"But mostly to you."

"Urgh, let's just get this done with, please, and agree to no further chatter. You're making my head hurt." And he actually is. A throbbing sensation is growing right behind my eyes. I want to lie down in a dark room. I do not want to be walking down a chilly road in quite possibly one of the farthest parts of Scotland with the worst person I know. This is my idea of hell.

"Smartest thing you've said today," James replies before

stepping ahead of me and lifting the pace just enough to make my feet scream in pain again.

"This is a town?" James asks, squeezing the back of his neck with both hands.

I try not to get distracted by the way his shirt goes taut against his core muscles and force my eyes ahead.

The town is a small church, a few grey stone houses and what looks like a tiny school building. It's surrounded by a magnificent estuary, with boats anchored, dotted around or tied up on one of the rickety docks. Gentle grey waves lap against them making them sway or dip. I have the urge to pin my nose. Clearly, the smell of rotting seaweed I experienced in the airport originated from this village. The gusts are so strong I can lean my whole body into them and stay upright.

A bearded man looks up suspiciously from his small blue fishing boat about fifty metres away. He's probably not used to seeing new people around here. And if he does, they're probably not wearing smart office clothes.

"Go talk to him," I say to James, nodding in that direction.

He frowns. "Why me?"

"You're the salesman. Isn't talking to strangers like your key skill?"

I think he's about to fight me on this, argue against it, but I guess I've already worn him down because he just rubs his face in his hands and walks slowly over to where the man is trying to avoid eye contact with us. I follow behind, leaving enough distance between us to show that I am the submissive one when it comes to this conversation, my arms folded to protect myself from the wind.

"Morning," James says, with a friendly wave. He really is confident with this sort of thing. I'll give him that.

The man looks up and around as if James might be talking to someone else. I look too. There's literally not another soul in the vicinity. Who does he bloody think we're talking to?

"We've broken down a few miles back that way," James points, not bothering to wait for the man to respond. "Can you help us out? Do you know where we can find a phone?"

"There's one in the church," the man says, going back to unknotting the fish netting on his deck.

That appears to be enough for James, who, without looking at me, storms in the direction of the steepled building in the middle of the town. I totter along behind him.

As we step into the church a calmness comes over us. The wind isn't invading the thick stone walls at all. Inside there's a peaceful serenity. Again, nobody to be seen. It's pretty bog standard as far as churches go with the pews, the wooden carved crosses and the organ taking up a whole corner. Right in front of the dark porch there's a desk, a chair and a phone complete with wires and number pad.

"Blast from the past," I say.

James ignores me, inspecting the ancient device. There's a list of contacts beside it, plus a Yellow Pages. We sift through it until we find a local breakdown recovery service. Turns out there aren't many breakdowns around these parts and the man says he's off right away.

After that, James shoos me out to make a personal call. With only a minor grumble, I step back out into the fresh air to see the fisherman is now out in the water, slowly feeding the netting back into the estuary. There's the sound of school kids playing, but other than that it's eerie how quiet this place is, except for the wind whistling through the gaps between the houses lining the harbour.

"Let's go," James says, marching on in front of me.

"Everything ok?"

"Do you really care or are you just asking?"

"Back to silence?" I suggest, not enjoying his arrogant tone.

The walk back takes us longer. Turns out we'd been going slightly downhill the whole way to the village. But now we're heading uphill, my heels are rubbing themselves raw at the back of my boots. It's making my eyes water, but taking them off is not a solution. The ground is damp with sea mist and my knitted tights will soak it right up like a sponge.

As the lake where the minivan broke down comes into view, James' step falters. I nearly crash into the back of him, giving him a little shove with both hands.

He moves to the side enough for me to see the conundrum.

"Where's it gone!?" I demand. "Where's the van!?"

James is speechless. He stands completely still for a few more seconds before ramping up to a flat-out sprint in the direction of the layby. My heart races in my chest as I *tap, tap, tap* behind him. He's way ahead of me, stopping once again beside what appears to be two large hiking backpacks. He lifts and reads something, then he lets out this low-pitched, agonised wail that echoes off the surrounding water and rocky hills.

I slow as I reach him, coming to a stop just as he walks away down towards the water's edge. He collapses to his knees, holding his head in his hands. Awfully dramatic, considering Michael will probably be back soon.

My eyes fall to the piece of paper James has dropped beside the bags. A fifty-pound note has been folded and pinned to the top. I lift it up and walk down to sit on a boulder a few metres from where he is having a mental breakdown.

I read out loud. "Well done on finding a recovery driver so quickly. Most impressive! Now here's for the real fun. I was going to drop you off in the fishing village and brief you, but I feel this has worked out for the better." I realise this was written by Michael, so begin using my best imitation of his voice. "Recently, James, you told me a story about backpackers who get the cheapest flight to Europe with only fifty euros cash in hand and must find their way home. It sounded most riveting."

James moans into his hands at this part and I can't help giving him a look. *Oh, Gloatman, you and your stupid stories and ideas.*

I continue reading. "I thought you could try that in Scotland. It should take you less time than in the whole of Europe. Think of it as team building…" My voice wavers. James pulls his hair out of shape as he looks across the water. I want to tell him to calm down but now my hands are rattling as I read the last part.

"Find your way back to the hotel by Saturday morning so you don't miss your flights! It is imperative that you take the most scenic route you can, to ensure you are maximising your team-building opportunities. I want to hear all about your journey. I've packed you two bags so you have all the essentials you should need. In order to proceed to the next step in your career you must overcome the need to compete and find a way to cooperate. I would like to hear how you worked together as a team. See if this week will shine a light on your management skillset. Don't let me down! And good luck!"

Five

James spends a few more minutes trying to pull his hair out before getting up and walking away from me further down the edge of the lake, kicking stones into the water with his black work shoes. His hair has already started to lose its shape as the fierce winds drag clouds in, bringing with them a thin sea mist that mars the scenery into a grey nothingness. Every now and again, he looks back towards where I'm sat on the boulder with a pained expression.

I've tucked my dress underneath me as if I'm out for a leisurely picnic. What you can't see, though, are the blisters on my feet from this morning's walk. I take my phone out and see I've got just over sixty per cent battery left. I'm not sure why I'm calm right now but I've heard that the human mind is conditioned to act in accordance with those around us. So, as we both can't freak out right now, I think I'm compensating for James with a rational mindset.

Maybe my turn will be later.

I switch my phone off, tucking it back into my dress pocket.

As James finally makes his way towards me, I look away, not enjoying the expression he's got plastered across his face. He's really hating the thought of spending time with me. I also hate the thought of spending time with him. But he's horrified by the prospect. Am I really that bad?

"I've got hardly any battery left. We could call 999 on your phone," he suggests. "It should connect with a satellite or something like that."

"Calm down. It's hardly an emergency. And besides I've turned my phone off to preserve battery."

James blinks. "But we're abandoned, *Fel-ici-ty*. Don't you see?" He spins in a circle, hands out to demonstrate our tragic situation. As if to prove his point the cloud thins, and light raindrops spatter down onto my nose. "We need rescuing."

"We don't need rescuing. Michael left us a very clear note with instructions. And besides, this is a test, isn't it? Don't you want to pass, since you're supposedly in the running for promotion too?"

James sputters. "Oh god, you're actually insane. You think I'm going to hike across Scotland dressed like this? Not a chance."

"Why not? It'll be an adventure…" I'm really grasping at straws here. I don't really want to do this either, but Michael has set us a challenge and he's going to be very disappointed in me if I don't at least give it a go. "Aren't you trying to impress him too? He said we should cooperate. Find ways to put our competitive natures aside."

James watches me curiously for a moment, his eyes searching for something. The note maybe? It's tucked into my dress pocket for safekeeping.

"I'm going to sue the bastard," James says, nodding to himself. I watch as the smart quiff at the front of his head flops down onto his forehead from the weight of the, now fatter, raindrops drenching us. "Oh bloody hell!" he sobs.

"Don't be such a baby. It's just a bit of rain."

"Ok. Ok. I'll go this way. You go that way. The first one to reach someone can call for rescue. If you stick to the main road, then I'll find you."

I laugh. "Oh, I get it. You're scared."

"I am not. He's abandoned you, Felicity! He's abandoned you with a man you despise in a place with zero phone signal and no help whatsoever. We have nothing. What if one of us has a heart attack? What then?"

"Then we have my phone. I'll save the battery for real emergencies. Come on, don't be so dramatic. Let's find shelter; I'm getting drenched through."

The rain isn't even that hard but it's somehow soaking into my clothing with efficiency. My cotton cardi is plastered to my shoulders, my hair is sticking to my forehead and my tights feel as if they've been glued onto my legs. I climb up from the boulder, peering around at our surroundings. Well, there are certainly no buildings in sight. A few trees poke out between the layers of low-lying cloud, huddled together at the top of a hill some way in the distance.

"Look over there," I say positively, pointing in their direction. James gives me a frown to show he's listening. "Let's get the bags and walk up there. It's higher up, so we can use it as a viewpoint. And the trees will make a shelter. We can plan our next steps from there."

James continues to glare me down, so, I take off on my own, expecting him to follow but deciding I'll have to go alone if he insists on being a mopey git. Michael wants a character assessment of me, well, he'll get one. No challenge is too big. I'll take on the Scottish Highlands like a falcon.

Ok, so I'm maybe more of a pigeon. But I'll fly, nonetheless.

I grab the smaller hiking bag, assuming the bigger one is for James, and hoist it onto my shoulder, tucking the note into a side pocket along with the money.

"Come on, Gloatman," I call. "We might have snacks in our bags. No point opening them here as everything will get wet."

"Shouldn't we stick to the roads? In case a car comes?"

"Have you seen any in the past few hours?" I ask, pointedly, turning to face him but walking backwards in the direction I'm headed. "All I've seen is a tractor."

James pinches the bridge of his nose, watching me leave with a stormy expression. "Look at what you're wearing. How the hell do you foresee yourself hiking in those boots and that dress?"

"I'll be fine... Sometimes I walk to work instead of getting the bus in these things, and they're *fine*," I say, ignoring the pain pulsing in my feet.

"Not across the bloody Scottish Highlands," he mutters. "I'm sure people have died from doing stupid shit like this."

I don't respond to this. But have they?

It'll be ok.

We won't die.

We have fifty pounds and a mobile phone for emergencies if needed.

I give him one last prod. I raise my eyebrows in his direction, a telling quirk in my lips. "I dare you," I say.

James watches me, his lips pressed together in a firm line. I experience a sudden rush of heat wash through me as our gazes lock. Finally, he throws his head back, closing his eyes against the rain, which has now trained his hair into a long, floppy mess. I never knew it could look so shaggy. Then, as if he's conjured up the energy to deal with me, or has realised he'll have to take part in order to out-character-assess me, he follows on behind, grabbing the other bag as he goes.

The trees are further away than I thought they were, especially when we discover there are patches of swamp, multiple slippery, rocky surfaces and long stretches of rough terrain to cross on the way there, whilst also wading through thick patches of thigh-high bracken. There's a lake we have to walk around – not fancying the swim, despite already being damp through.

Every now and again I hear a huff behind me, followed by some choice words about our esteemed leader.

Michael's not perfect but he isn't evil. He didn't do this to punish us. I mean, there's clearly a passion tax that drives a lot of the events industry, and I'd be a fool if I said I wasn't victim to it. I'm not totally money driven. But I would like to one day have my own flat. One without mould. Or a hole in the floor. And a wardrobe instead of a dehumidifier acting as a clothes horse. That would be nice. And yet, in the meantime I do love working in the events industry. It's more interesting than working for, say, an aluminium company. I'm aware, however, that they do pay significantly more for marketing people. Probably because it's so boring.

"He doesn't pay me enough for this shit. And to abandon me with…" James pauses.

"Go on, say it," I dare him without looking back, trying and failing to cross a patch of swamp with only a few naturally placed stepping stones to help me. There's not really a footpath. At least, I'm not sure anything round here is forged by human feet. Anything path-resembling was formed by roaming wildlife. I lose my balance and my boot lands in the mud, coating the beautiful red suede in an unrecoverable way.

"*Noooo*, fuck," I hiss. Yanking myself out to the drier piece of land, I try to stamp it out a bit but there's no hope. And despite trying really, really hard to hold it together in front of Gloatman, I can now feel the prick of tears threatening to ruin me.

I swore I would never cry in front of him.

James opens his mouth just in time to distract me from it. "I have nothing to say you don't already know."

I roll my eyes. I knew he hated me, of course I did. But part of me was hoping it wasn't quite so bad. That maybe it was more of a respected rivalry. "Let me guess. I know you think I'm the definition of petty. You probably think I'm a busybody. That I dress too brightly for work meetings? I once heard through a colleague that you criticised my makeup choices." I sometimes go big on colour with lips and eyeshadow too. "Hmm... What else—"

"I never did that," he interrupts.

"What?"

"I never said anything personal. How does what you wear matter to me? Whoever said that was either projecting or lying."

"Projecting!?" I gasp. "So other people think that about me?"

"Oh hell, you need to stop caring what other people think so much. Just let it go."

That's easy to say, I'm sure, if you haven't grown up in a battlefield where all you can think about is what other people are thinking and how you can adapt your behaviour to prevent them from being upset or cross or stressed. I doubt, very much, that James has zero concerns about what other people think. It's human nature. "You're telling me you never care what other people think about you?"

He stops beside me, staring at my mud-sodden boot. I could *weep*. I sniff, as my nose starts to sting. Everything stings.

They're only boots, Fliss. Let them go!

James shrugs. "I don't."

I frown at his face, expecting him to expand on the why part of his statement, but he says no more, striding ahead, leading us towards the trees. And by luck, he seems to be better at picking out a decent path, taking extra consideration to avoid muddy, swampy patches.

We're both puffing when we reach the top of the incline where the tall trees have once been planted in a circled-out plot of land. It's too perfect to be naturally formed. We venture in, James using his hands to separate spider webs draped between the trunks. I shudder as we take a seat on the twiggy ground, looking out across the valley we've just covered. The clouds are thick across the sky still, bundled together like big damp pillows leaking down on us.

The rain has dried up and left behind the sea mist. It's inescapable, even sheltered below the thick branches of leaves above us. It's sort of like sitting in one of those steam rooms at a spa. Except it's cold. And there are no fluffy slippers and dressing gowns patiently waiting for us to grab on the way out.

James sighs audibly, shaking out his wet hair like a damp dog. Drops of water splash on my face. I growl at him, shoving his shoulder.

"Let's check these bags out then, shall we?" he suggests, ignoring me. "He better have packed spare phones or something in here."

There's noticeably more contained in his bag than mine, which is baggy at the top, whilst his is packed full. We unzip them, quietly taking out a few items. James has a small tent in his that pretty much pops out fully made, with a bag of pegs and folded poles. I fiddle around in my bag too. I find some walking trainers (*thank you, Michael*), a pair of hiking trousers, spare vests, knickers (which I discreetly hide from James' view and pray sweetly that this was in fact packed by Michael's secretary, Millie) and a thermal jumper. I suspect Millie guessed I'm a size twelve pants, size ten top, because we're similar sizes.

"It's sort of annoying me that he put so much thought into this," James says.

"Why?"

"Because it means he was planning it for a while. And I don't think he was alone. At least he's packed toothbrushes and toothpaste," he adds. "And empty bottles."

"I guess we fill them with natural water."

"As opposed to fake water?" he asks, raising his eyebrows.

"You know what I mean."

It surprises me when he actually laughs. I smile too. "You've been looking like the Joker for the last hour by the way. It's been entertaining to watch your face melt." And there it goes.

My smile snaps into a glare. "Nice hair, Gloatman.

Did you drag it backwards through the half-submerged hedgerows back there?"

Now his smile fades too. "Great, no hair gel."

Thankfully, it's my turn to laugh. "Have you found any snacks yet?"

James fiddles around some more. He discovers a pack of baby wipes and some deodorant in his bag. In mine I find a can of dry shampoo, but unfortunately Millie or Michael neglected to pack a hairbrush.

I've been so busy dealing with the shenanigans of the day I've totally neglected to acknowledge my rumbling stomach and now it won't go unheard. James gives me a startled look when it grumbles again. "Was that your stomach or thunder?"

"Stomach. Keep looking for snacks... I'm terrified of considering the alternative."

"You mean hunting?"

"Not hunting. Nope. Won't do it. I'm more of a gatherer than a hunter."

James blows out a breath. "Of course, you are. Here," he says, passing me a protein bar. "They're in the bottom compartment. Do you have one?"

I lift my bag, unzipping it from the side, and as I do, six boxes of tampons fall onto my lap. "What the hell?"

"Jeez, how many boxes do you need?"

"I didn't pack this, James," I say. And for goodness' sake. Why am I blushing? I'm a thirty-year-old woman and here I am blushing over a man seeing my tampons. They're not even *my* tampons! "I don't even need these right now."

"And even if you did," he says, "one-hundred and eighty of them for a few nights away is a bit extreme."

"How do you know that? Do you secretly have a girlfriend you hide from the office?"

James shakes his head, unwrapping and biting into his protein bar. He chews on it whilst saying, "Sisters, three of them."

"You have three sisters? How did I not know that?"

"Why would you? You never asked."

I suppose he has a point. I do tend to avoid conversations with him as they nearly always end in an argument over something work related.

He takes another bite, staring out into the scenery as a large bird glides by. Must be some kind of hawk or falcon or something. I sort of wish I had binoculars and a bird book so I could identify it. "What about you?" he asks.

"Huh? Me?"

"Siblings?"

"Oh no, just me. Only child, my parents are divorced." I cringe. Not sure why that's relevant.

James nods as if he understands. "My dad left before my youngest sister was born."

"Sorry," I say, shuffling as the twiggy surface below me is starting to grow uncomfortable.

He shrugs as if it's of no importance. "Sophie's in labour. The eldest of my three sisters. She's a year younger than me. That's who I called earlier. Well, not her. Her husband. But he's not answering and I'm sort of shitting myself right now."

"Oh god, that's... Did Michael know that?"

James bites the side of his cheek, pulling it into his mouth, leaving a hollow. "Not in detail, I guess. He doesn't really ask about our personal lives, does he? But that's why I shared the jet. I was late for the flight because I was at the hospital with Mum. Was hoping that meant I was off the hook. But nope." He takes a long sigh. "I'm going to fucking sue him, Felicity."

I frown. This is the most I've ever heard James talk about himself. It's annoying because I'd prefer to keep him at arms' length, but also, I feel bad for him and slightly resentful of Michael for dragging him out here – even if he wasn't fully aware of his situation. And yet, I can't bring myself to say anything bad about him, or even agree.

What's wrong with me?

James finds another zip inside the main compartment of his rucksack. He pulls out a beige bag, fastened at the top and frowns as he opens it. Without putting too much thought into it he sticks his hand in and out come a handful of condoms and a bottle of lube. My mouth drops open as James panics, stuffing them back into the bag and to the side of his lap.

"Was that…!?"

"Mmmhmm."

"Oh my god! *Oh my god!* What does he think…?"

"I don't want to think about it," James mutters and I'm sort of relieved when I notice colour flooding into his cheeks too. Only problem is, I can't tell if he's embarrassed or outraged.

"Where's your tent?" he asks, changing the subject, a notch forming between his brows as he peers across at my now-empty bag I'm busily stuffing tampons back into.

"I'm not sure…" That's when it hits. I grab at the sleeping bag, still fastened into its packet. "This is all I've got. Does he think I'm going to sleep under the stars?"

James shakes his head, a sympathetic— *actually no*, a patronising expression crossing his face. "Do the math, Felicity. One tent. Twenty-something condoms."

"Is he... Is he pimping us out to each other?"

He looks back at the scenery ahead of us, broken up between patches of cloud. I've been in tall buildings in London before where you feel like you're higher than the weather. A white blanket blocking out the world below. It's somehow slightly nerve-racking seeing it here though. I didn't think we were even that high above sea level. Or maybe it's just low-lying cloud.

"So, let me get this straight," I say, clenching my eyes closed as I exhale slowly. "We've been abandoned in the Scottish Highlands with one tent, two sleeping bags, some empty bottles and a few protein bars, twenty-something condoms and a bottle of lube?"

"And one hundred and eighty tampons," James adds helpfully.

Six

"I don't know what he's thinking…" James mutters. He moves his bag again, shifting it away as he pulls out an Ordnance Survey map and begins to unravel it. There's a clinking, rattling sound in his bag as it lands with a thud.

"What was that?" I ask.

He frowns, as he finds another zip in the main compartment, opening it to find a bottle of clear liquid. "Vodka…" he muses. Then he laughs. "Christ, what sort of shit does he think we're going to get up to?"

"This isn't funny… He's given us empty bottles for water but a full bottle of vodka?"

James passes it across to me as I'm busy using my sleeve to wipe away some of the smudged makeup from my face. I use my spare hand to take the bottle. It is indeed straight vodka. An expensive bottle too. "He could've at least given us some lemonade to mix it with."

James laughs again but holds his face in his hands like he might also cry. "Oh, bloody hell. What the fuck are we going to do?"

"Get drunk?" I suggest.

"We need to get back. *I* need to get back. My sister… I can't be here, Felicity."

"Ok…" I nod, acknowledging his predicament.

James' phone pings again. He grabs it out, groaning whilst cradling his chin in his hand as the final vibration signifies the end of his battery supplies. "Shit."

A moment of weakness leaks into my heart at the sight of his sorry expression. Who knew the man had feelings? I really try to stop my mouth from opening. I try so hard but… "I have power. You could use mine if you wanted to?" I suggest. Gosh, why am I being so kind to this man all of a sudden? "Not that you deserve it really."

He doesn't respond to my quip. Instead, he stands up and walks away from where I'm sat with all our things, as the skies clear enough for the sun to peek through. A ray of light pushes down and settles on his head, glittering on his damp, dark hair. He stops. And although I can't see his face, I can tell by his shoulders and the way he thrusts his hands into his chino pockets that he's taking some deep sighs. I should stop looking at him. If he turns around, he'll catch me staring and his ego is big enough to assume I'm perving.

I take in my surroundings and my original idea to get to higher ground to decide where to go next is flawed. There's nothing up here to pinpoint exactly where we are. I take out the map, but it's all colours and shapes to me right now. I'm hungry and tired, and my brain is pulsing thinking about all the things I should be doing but am not doing. We're three weeks out from an event. I trust my team to cover a lot of the work. The issue is, they shouldn't have to.

And now I have a new set of challenges. But I must not let them detract from my overall objectives. I suppose I should add another one, which up until a few hours ago I took for granted.

Objective one: Work up to director position at Starr.

Objective two: Earn the only bonus I expect to earn this year, which means not letting James sneak his idea through Michael.

Objective three (new): Stay alive. First two objectives rely heavily on the success of this one.

"I did my Duke of Edinburgh," I shout across the space between us. This is probably useless to mention since it was fifteen years ago, and I tagged along with a very knowledgeable bunch of scout leaders who looked after me most of the way. I also remember the walking draining me, and taking a few days to recover.

James laughs, not bothering to look back at me. "Of course you did."

"Hey… What's wrong with that?"

"Posh girl," he says. I don't know where James gets this impression, but he's convinced I'm some sort of nepo-baby. I am not.

"What? Didn't they do it at your school?" I ask, remembering most of my friends from other schools at least had the option to do it. I hardly went to Eton. It wasn't private or anything. Arguably though, my parents played the postcode lottery well. And could afford to do that.

"It cost money," he says. "And we didn't have a lot of that around."

I chew on my bottom lip as I look down to fiddle with my sorry-looking boots. I don't want to pry further. I don't remember the Duke of Edinburgh costing very much and so he must've been in a very tight predicament if he couldn't afford to do it. But also, he could be manipulating me somehow. I wouldn't put it past him.

"Are you wearing a watch?" I shout. "Do you have the time?"

I've stopped wearing mine recently and now rely on my mobile phone but that's turned off.

"It's just gone three," he shouts back.

"Should we find somewhere to set the tent up?" I ask. The tight pang of anxiety resurfaces in my stomach. I can't believe I have to share a tent with this man. It's actually not ok.

"Stop freaking out," James mutters, as he walks back towards me.

I gawp. How can he tell from a distance? And he's one to talk. "Says the man who was pulling his hair out down by the lake earlier."

"That's because I've been abandoned with a lunatic."

"I'm a lunatic? You're a total psychopath."

"You're having one of your epic meltdowns. You know, I can almost hear it happen when I send emails sometimes. It's like the mood shifts from *Great British Bake-Off* tent to the Death Star in a flash. The air thickens. And it's not just me who notices."

"Shut up," I say. But... "Who else notices?" I realise he's purposefully baiting me, and I am absolutely falling for it. It's not true, of course. And, well, maybe he shouldn't send emails to make me go all Darth Vader. "Whatever... We just... *I don't know*."

Objective three... Focus on objective three, Fliss.

"We need to find somewhere to camp. We need to find water. Do we just fill our bottles up? Do we have those tablets that disinfect it? Or are we going to risk getting poisoned?"

"I'm pretty sure we're safe drinking Highland water," James says, looking down at me in that stupid hands-on-hip pose again. It's a pose I usually appreciate in a man, but on him, it's patronising. He's looking at me like I'm a child.

"Do you know how to put this tent up?" I ask, climbing to my feet, patting my soggy dress down. "I need to get out of these clothes." I glare at James waiting for a smart comment, but he just tilts his head as if to suggest he'd never. "And soon…"

"Well, I guess we might as well stay here tonight then, yeah? Don't know about you but I'm knackered, frankly. We can look at that map properly and work out how to get to the nearest town. Don't see much point in heading back to that other one. Do you?"

"They did have a phone."

"But we only have fifty pounds. That's not going to get us a taxi out of here."

I nod. "Besides, I've already decided I'm doing this challenge. We spend a night here then tomorrow we hike."

James drops his head as if this plan fills him with dread. "Tomorrow, we hike. God help me."

I'm not sure when it happened but as the sun began to lower over the horizon and a navy-blue sky rose above us, the wind seemed to drop. The clouds have cleared. There's a promise of a gorgeous starry night sky. The ripple of water from a nearby waterfall I found earlier and used to fill our bottles, trickles in the background. And as the beauty of Scotland's summer evening curls around us, so do the midges.

"It's like a fucking apocalypse," James complains as he tries once again to wedge the tent pole in. He spits as he tastes a few.

"Do you mean the Exodus?"

"The what?"

"Are you referring to the locusts?"

"They're midges, Felic-*puh*!" James spits more of the buggers out, batting his hands around his face. He shakes his head before ducking down again to fight the pole into the tent.

I give up the discussion, concluding I'm right and he's wrong. I'm standing uselessly beside the tent waiting for him to erect it so I can finally get dressed. "I think you're doing, *puh*, it wrong-g," I say through spits.

James tenses all over, throws the pole he's wrestling with down on the floor and gives me a glare. "Do you want to do it then?"

"Fine," I say, shouldering past him. He straightens and steps back to let me past.

"No, it doesn't – *pah* – Christ, these midges are making me mad! It doesn't go like that." I can see the faint outline of his shadow pointing at my progress.

"Look, let's just peg it in and hope for the best," I say. He goes quiet and I realise too late I've used the word "peg" around a child. When I turn around, he's looking up to the sky, hands on hips again, doing that irritating foot-tapping thing. He's biting his lip, so I know he's trying not to laugh. "It's literally a peg though."

He laughs. "Come on, Felici-*puh*... Get that peg in."

"Grow up," I say, turning to place the peg in the ground, then standing to squish it in with my foot. Once it's in, and the tent is manageable, for one night at least, I grab my bag and dive in to change out of these knitted tights I may very well have to peel off at this stage.

James, however, seems to have the same idea and is already sat inside with his legs crossed.

"Get out!" I demand. "I need to get dressed."

"You can't seriously expect me to stand out there whilst those midges eat me alive?"

"They don't eat flesh… Do they?"

He gives me a funny look. "What, midges? God, I don't know."

"Out," I say, nodding behind me as I crawl in too.

"I'll turn my back," he suggests.

"Oh my god! Get the hell out! *Now!*"

James huffs. "Fuck's sake," he mutters as he climbs back out of the tiny space. And, shit, it is a tiny space. Definitely a two sleeper. It narrows in height so you must have to sleep with your head at the top, toes pointing down. Once I've done the zip up behind me, I can hear James telling me he's not going to wait long so to "hurry the fuck up". So, despite claustrophobia creeping in, I peel my clothes off, unclipping my bra too, and pull on some clean, dry items that Michael packed for me. Interestingly, despite his (or Millie's) keen attention to detail, he did not pack me a spare bra. I suppose I should be grateful he doesn't know my bra size. My bra is wet too but if I hang it somewhere (*where to hang it without James seeing?*) I can maybe dry it overnight ready for us to get started in the morning.

"You have ten seco-*puh*-onds!" James yells.

"Alright, alright…"

Practically throwing the rest of my stuff on, I start to

climb out just as James grabs the zip. He dives back into the tent as if he's outrunning wolves. He lands with a thump on his sleeping bag.

At least we have two of those. Ever the optimist.

I slide my feet into my trainers and, whilst whipping my hands in front of my face, look around for a suitable place to hang my bra. Thankfully, there's a low branch on a nearby tree, which I lay it over, mentally reminding myself to get up first tomorrow and remove it before James sees.

Cannot let the worst man in the world discover my bra size. It would be like feeding candy to an arsehole.

Once I've clambered back into the tent, I see James has managed to change super-quickly too and is now studying the map. "Do you even know where we are?"

"Nope."

"What about here?"

I squint. The light is waning quickly, especially in the tent. Without a fire or any sort of torch, we're kind of screwed. "Maybe we should do this tomorrow."

James exhales slowly. "What do we do now then? Talk?"

"Definitely not… We should, erm…"

We sit in silence for a moment. I've tucked my legs into myself in order to avoid touching him. It's not a sustainable position. He's taking up most of the space. I'm going to say it's a 70/30 ratio. A shiver racks through me. My hands and feet are freezing. As if James notices, he raises his eyes to mine. "You should get into your sleeping bag and start warming it up. You've probably got a chill from walking in the rain. Don't need you going hypothermic, do we?"

"I'm fine," I say. But I climb into the bag anyway, awkwardly shuffling around, then end up sitting there like a slug, with my legs pointing down the tent, only my face visible with the hood up.

James pretends to be busy with his bag but we both know there's nothing left in there.

"Tell me about your sisters," I say after about ten minutes, meeting my silence quota for the week. I find silence suffocating. I always have. It's probably partly to do with my people-pleasing tendencies. Silence means I'm not doing anything to ease the tension. And the tension pulls at my weak self until I cave and talk nonsense.

James climbs into his sleeping bag too, lying down beside me, and I think this might be the weirdest moment of my life so far.

"Josie, Hannah and Sophie. Josie's the baby. She'll be twenty this year. Hannah's getting married in two months. She's twenty-eight. And then Sophie, well, she's possibly a mum now… She's thirty."

"I'm sorry you can't be there for her."

James shrugs. "I'm sure I wouldn't be much help at this stage. It's not as if I'd be in the room. It's weird though, not being there. We've always been close. There's only ten months between us in age." He's quiet for a beat. "I should be meeting my nephew."

"You will," I say.

"Yes, but I'll have missed the birth, missed the first week of his life. I shouldn't've come. I should've stuck to my guns."

"You were going to bail?"

I turn my head to get a proper read on his face in the dying light. He's staring blankly at the roof of the tent. "I told Michael I couldn't come. I'd missed our flight anyway.

Sophie called my mum to say she was in labour. That's who I called at the church in the fishing village earlier. Dean, her husband, didn't answer, but I suppose it was an unknown number. So, I don't know how she's getting on."

"Well, I guess now we know why Michael insisted on you coming?"

James' eyes lock with mine, the dark blue almost black in the dark. Something about the intensity sends a shockwave through me, forcing me to look away. "Please don't tell me you're apologising for him? You know he's an arse-raving lunatic, don't you?"

"You said I was a lunatic earlier. Maybe you're the problem."

James laughs with frustration. "You are! You're making excuses for him in your head. I can hear your brain ticking."

"Whatever... I want to like him."

"Why? Because you can't keep providing free labour for someone you hate?"

"I get paid..."

"Not enough for the hours you do. What's your salary? Let me guess. You're Head of Marketing but your negotiation skills are lacking."

"Excuse me!" I scoff, insulted. "Anyway, it's against HR policy to talk about salaries."

"Forty," he says.

"*Forty grand?*"

"More?" he guesses.

I look back at him with a frown. "What do you earn?"

He faux gasps. "Are you breaking HR policy? *Felicity...*"

"Don't be annoying. Just tell me."

"You really want to know?"

I blink. Do I? I feel like the answer might hurt. I've always assumed he was on the same base pay as me. Of course, he earnt bonuses on top of that. One of the perks of being a salesperson. The shit part being all the customer interaction and pimping out of oneself that's required. It was the way he guessed forty grand… It's like he knows I earn less than him. But by how much?

"I'm on sixty grand basic, with potential to earn forty per cent on top of that."

I swallow, looking away into the darkness at the far corner of the tent. I'm not sure what to say, I didn't expect it to be that bad. I bite my bottom lip. I should end this conversation. Wherever it's headed, it's not going to help me. Besides, I don't particularly want him to know how much I'm on. It feels like a failing somehow.

James cringes at me. He's noticed my hesitation. "Go on then, your turn."

"I'm on less," I say quietly.

James doesn't say anything, instead he lets the silence linger on, which is somehow more annoying than having a smart comment or two.

I lie back down, staring up at the ceiling of the tent too.

"A lot less?" he finally asks.

I shrug. "More than half what you earn. But not by much."

He blows out a breath. "No wonder you're after the promotion."

I don't want to say more in fear of revealing myself. I feel somewhat betrayed by this news. How can it be that he earns that much more than me? What did I do wrong?

As if James can hear my thoughts out loud, he says,

"Could be that marketing generally earn less. It's business, but not the ugly part. People actually enjoy it. You can stay in your comfort zone. You don't have to put yourself out there. Sales is the battle. Marketing is the banquet."

I'm speechless – annoyed with myself for even asking the question before. Annoyed that James is right and I'm sticking up for someone who clearly doesn't have my back in return. Someone who has literally all but banished me to the swamp whilst he sits comfortably in his castle.

James must realise I'm not in the mood to talk anymore. There's a slight shiver running through my limbs, despite trying discreetly to warm myself up. My toes are now numb. I don't want to talk in case there's a quiver in my voice – I don't want James to know I'm struggling. He unzips the tent, leaning up to peer out.

"Hey, Felicity... Take a look at this."

I roll to the side so I can peer up out of the tent too. He holds the flap open for me. There, in the sky, is the most beautiful thing I've ever witnessed in my entire life. My eyes water as I stare up at a vista of stars scattered like sugar in the dark sky. We settle for the night with them twinkling down on us, mesmerised.

At some point I must've fallen asleep because a voice wakes me. There's a gentle hand on my shoulder. I startle, sparking awake. "What is it?! Wh-h-ere are we?" I say, a rattle in my voice, my teeth chattering.

That's when I realise how cold I am. The tent is freezing. I can't feel my feet at all. My limbs are vibrating.

"You woke me up with your shivering," the quiet voice

says, almost huskily, as if it might wake someone up. It's so gentle it's like a kind of lullaby. "You're freezing, you loon. You need to warm up, fast."

I hear a zipping sound in the dark. It's not clear what it is until I feel hot, firm skin collide with my arms. I'm too cold to think about anything. The heat is exquisite. I roll over, attaching myself to it as more zipping occurs. Limbs are rearranged. My face finds somewhere cosy, safe, as arms wrap around my body.

"It's ok," the voice says as I drift back off to sleep.

Seven

My face nestles further into the warmth. I'm swaddled like a baby, wrapped tight inside my sleeping bag. Usually, I would find this claustrophobic, but somehow the heat emanating off my pillow is settling me, melting my mood into a lazy puddle.

That is, until my mind slowly awakens. I move my leg and collide with a knee. A long, firm thigh that *definitely does not* belong to me is entwined with mine. I tense all over, my heart racing, heat pouring through me like my body is harbouring a volcanic eruption. I scramble, my legs and arms pushing against the boiling body beside me.

"Let me out!" I squeal.

"Jesus," the voice grunts as my knee collides with his unfortunates. "Argh!"

I somehow manage to spin around, unzipping the impossibly tight sleeping bag, and rolling to the other side of the tent.

I suck in a breath. *Bugger.* It's so cold outside of my cocoon. "Ugh, shitting shit."

"*What* are you *doing*?" James growls, zipping himself back up. "You're unhinged, I swear."

I grab at my discarded fleece, dragging it over my head.

There's absolutely no way this can end well. He's going to remember this moment of weakness and hold it against me forever.

How did I end up in his sleeping bag?

Last night starts to come back to me. I remember the voice. The warmth embracing me... Oh god! A rush of embarrassment pours through me. I want the ground to open up and swallow me whole. I need to escape.

James has turned over and is quietly breathing again as if he's fallen back to sleep, so I slide my trainers on and escape the tent out into the freshest air I've ever experienced. It eclipses my senses. There's a crisp breeze racing through the valley, slicing at my cheeks. I stand tall, watching a huge bird swoop down towards a shallow river that curves around the hills. My hair is loose without an Alice band to hold it back. The wind lifts it, forcing me to tuck it behind my ears.

This is surreal. How am I waking up here? There's not another human being in sight. Except, that is, for the man in the tent who is never, ever, ever, going to let me live last night down. I slap my hands to my face to cover my eyes. How have I gone from despising the man to using his body as a personal radiator in a space of twelve hours?

I let my hands fall to my sides and shake my limbs out. I find our bags, tucked under the front awning of the little tent, and take out a protein bar. Another thought hits me like a brick being thrown from a tall building.

An involuntary sob leaves my lips as I realise there's no caffeine in our bags. No tea, no coffee, not even caffeine gels. I'm going to have to rely on water. I'm going to have to push through inevitable withdrawal symptoms.

"Stop freaking out," comes a ragged voice from within the tent.

I try. But another sob climbs my throat, forcing its way out of me. I walk away, towards the treeline again where I find my bra, chilled from being left out, damper somehow despite the dry night. I tuck it into my fleece pocket to warm before daring to put it on. I perch on the cold, hard ground at the top of a steep incline that's smattered with thorny bushes, their wildflowers awakening within, showing off their colours in this early summer sunshine. Hugging my knees, I focus on a patch of bluebells, swaying lightly in the breeze, to ground me. A squirrel scurries past, pausing to eye me up, then shoots back into the overgrowth.

I hear the tent opening again. A scrunched-eyed James clambers out, squinting across at me as he clumsily puts his trainers on. I look away, swiping at my eyes with my sleeve, sniffing. At least he's put a top on now. The memory of his bare chest pressing against me in the night makes me momentarily nauseous. Not because it wasn't nice, but because it was sort of, really, really nice.

He sits down beside me, unwrapping his protein bar too and taking a bite. "You were shivering and mumbling incoherently. I didn't know what else to do."

"Let me die?" I suggest, still refusing to look at him, rocking myself gently.

"I'm not going to let you die," he says, softly. I look back across at him as he rubs his tired face. His black hair is slightly lighter than usual in its dry, floppy mess. Tawny shades linger at the roots as if he's got natural highlights. I have a sudden urge to reach out and touch it. I guess I'm overreacting. Surely what he did was kind. I'm lucky he runs at a sweltering temperature compared to me. "It wouldn't be any fun to tell everyone at work how we cuddled in the same sleeping bag if you were dead."

And my mood dissipates. "You're such an arse!"

He laughs. "Whatever. I wasn't even going to make such a thing of it, but you latched on. You wedged your face right in. What was I supposed to do? Push you away?"

"Yes! *Yes*, James."

"You were just cold, it was methodical. What are you so worried about? And by the way, there's no way I can win in this situation because not only did you panic and knee me in the balls this morning, you also would've gone for me if I'd left you shivering."

I frown into the distance. "It's always about you, isn't it?" I quip. "Are you really going to tell everyone?"

James chews for a moment longer, takes a sip from his bottle. "No."

I release a breath which says more than I'd like it to.

"What's the plan today, then?" he asks. "Shall we look at this map again?" James suggests, nipping back to the tent to grab it, then spreading it out in front of us.

I peer at it with him for a few seconds without saying anything. It's all blurring in front of my eyes. It's all the same. Hills, and woodlands, and lakes… How the hell are we supposed to know where to start? "I need a coffee."

"Same," James grumbles. "I think we're here," he says, pointing to what looks like an incline, the lines closer together. He takes a deep breath as he tilts his head to the side. "What do you think that is?"

"That's a river…"

"Not that. I know what a river is, Felicity. I meant this, here."

"Oh, is that a castle?"

James frowns. "Or a hotel? Look, it has this drive all the way along here."

"There's no way that's a hotel."

"It might be."

"Maybe we should just follow the road back? It looks like a long walk…" I say, earning myself an exasperated look from James.

"I'm sorry. Is my route too far for you? The road will be further. At least this way we have a potential hotel. That way, we already know is a load of potholes and gravel. Do you remember my plan yesterday about walking separately in different directions to find help? Doing this was your idea. Did you not factor in long walks?"

I huff. This is ridiculous. It's such a risky, insane idea to send two of your most important staff off to the middle of nowhere with virtually no safety equipment and a £50 note. A thought occurs to me. The pang of anxiety that sits deep in my belly hasn't moved since early yesterday morning and it might be because… "Do you think Michael wants us dead?"

James laughs at my remark as if I'm joking.

"I'm serious. Do you think he's trying to kill us? I thought we were doing a pretty good job at Starr. I mean I get that we were at each other's throats a lot. That must've been awkward for the rest of the team. But in my defence, you're a real pain in my arse."

James opens his mouth to respond but I carry on before

he can. "But I think we're actually very good at our jobs though, right? And by the sounds of it, he's getting a real fucking bargain out of me. So, why kill us? Why do this?"

"I told you already. He's an arse-raving lunatic."

"No, he's not! He always has a plan… And his vision—"

"Stop!" James yells. "This is part of the reason I cannot stand to work with you. You're always on his side. I can't trust you at all. And neither do most of your team, by the way. And yes, I know this. You know how? *My team talk to me.* A few of them are actually dating people in *your* team. Did you know that?"

I gasp. "No? They wouldn't!"

"Wouldn't what? Date well-paid, charismatic people they work with?"

"*No…* Is that what you think you are? Charismatic? So humble. I mean my team wouldn't betray me like that. And we do talk, for your information. We talk *all* the time."

James huffs, shaking his head as he rises to his feet.

I snort, annoyed. He doesn't know how my team are with me. They're loyal and hardworking. They'd tell me if anyone from his team was flirting with them so I could report it… Wouldn't they? I glare at his back for a moment as he bends to take the tent apart.

He's just trying to get in my head. He's psyching me out.

Once we're finally packed up, and our rubbish has been tucked away neatly into our bags, we head off in the direction of the castle James is certain is a hotel, or something similar. There are no paths to follow once again, and it feels as if we're trudging through a jungle at points. The terrain is varied. It can go from hard and rocky with a slight layer of grass; to weeds; to boggy, wet ground that's exhausting to cross, all in a matter of metres. And now, after an hour of walking, we're heading towards forest. There are huge dragonflies hovering low to the ground, flying close to us, making us duck and dodge them as if they're not used to seeing people around these parts.

James is behind me today, barking directions every now and again. With my low energy reserves, and without my usual caffeine kick, I can't be bothered to fight him on the small things. If he wants to lead on directions today, then so be it. And anyway, if he royally screws it up, I can hold it against him.

And I will hold it against him.

Part of me is hoping and praying we can find somewhere with a phone or reception and call for help. I don't plan on wild camping again tonight. Especially with how it ended last night. James' body was not only toasty but firm and cosy. I hate to admit how comfortable I was with him entwined around me.

The conversation has waned completely since this morning's argument. So, I decide to bring it up again. "So you don't like Michael then?"

I hear James take a long breath behind me. "No."

"Have you ever liked him?"

"Not really."

I stare ahead of me. I never knew this. The way James hangs on his every word in meetings, the way he leans towards him in that flirtatious way, the way he always sucks up to him at events. It doesn't add up. "Well, you're a very good actor. Or maybe you're a master of manipulation."

"No... I'm a salesman. I've had to learn the skills to make people like me and make people believe I like them. Unless you're naturally extroverted or have had to fight for your meals on occasion, it's not something you'd understand."

I stop, spinning to face him with a notch between my eyebrows. James stops too, groaning and dropping his shoulders. "What now?" he says.

"You've had to fight for meals?"

He shrugs.

"I'm sorry to hear that."

He nods, peeking over my shoulder. "Please keep walking."

I roll my eyes at his attempt to push the conversation away. I walk on anyway but can't help myself from saying, "Still can't believe you don't like Michael."

"For crying out loud! Felicity! Why do *you* like him? He's ripping you off. You should be earning so much more. I hate you, I really do. You're a proper prim cow sometimes with all your rules and *don't-ruin-our-image* rubbish," he says. "But you are very good at your job and he should be doing a whole lot more to ensure you don't leave."

I swallow, unsure what to say. I honestly didn't think he felt that way. We have occasional meetings between ourselves and a few members of our respective teams to talk about marketing the hospitality offerings and he's always so quiet in them, letting others talk. I always assumed he didn't care or hated being in the same room as me.

"You like my hospitality marketing ideas, do you?"

"Of course, I do. We get great leads through them. Why do you think I don't?"

"You never say."

I can almost hear his eyes roll. "I forgot you need constant affirmation. Thank you, Felicity. I like some of your marketing ideas."

"Then why do you try to sabotage me and my department?"

"I don't. Only when I see a way to make myself more money."

I take a big step over a small stream, missing slightly, my heel landing on a slimy rock. My foot slips, and I'm about to right myself when a large hand finds the small of my back, pushing me carefully to the other side. "You alright?"

"I'm fine. I had it."

"Sure, you did," James says, removing his hand as he steps in front of me.

I frown at his back as he takes the lead again, his backpack bouncing as he strides ahead. "Is that all you care about? Money?"

"Yeah. What else is there to go to work for?"

I pull a face, using my hand to list off the reasons. "To inspire." James scoffs. "To motivate. To learn. To grow in yourself. To leave something behind in life."

"Trust me, nothing you do in your job is everlasting. Someone can replace you tomorrow."

I don't agree with that one. I've heard it said loads, but surely nobody could do what I do, day in, day out. Or at least they couldn't do it as well as I do. God, I sound smug. What I mean is, I'm passionate… But I suppose other people are too…

"Who's covering for you this week?" James asks.

"Well, I was planning on working in the evenings and

doing emails from my phone, so nobody was really expected to cover me."

He laughs. "Such a workaholic."

"So are you!" I argue. "You stay late so that *I* have to stay late. It's infuriating."

"I only do that because *you* do!"

"Then stop," I suggest.

"You stop."

"*I'll* stop if *you* stop!" I quip.

Suddenly we both laugh.

"What are you suggesting? We form some sort of an alliance?" I ask.

"A leaving-work-at-normal-time alliance?"

"I wouldn't trust you not to go back once I've left."

James snorts. "Likewise. And by the way, you are *way* more likely to do something extremely petty like that than I am."

"Ouch!"

"In fairness, since working at Starr, I've seen a lot less of my mates. I always try to make time for my family though. Do you think we really need to be at every weekend event these days? I feel like we could juggle the workload between us better," he says. "Just feels like our entire summers vanish and then I've missed out on holidays and seeing friends whilst the weather's nice."

"I like being at every event, I want to go," I say, unsure what he's getting at.

James frowns. "Really? Why?"

"Because I find it satisfying to see what all my hard work has achieved."

"You're so strange," he says with a gentle laugh. "Tell

you what. Let's make a deal. Neither of us stay at work past seven p.m. And on Fridays we leave at five." James holds his hand out for me to shake. Initially I glare at it.

I really don't know if touching him again will help the cause.

It's hard trying to impress people all the time but maybe staying late at work is something we can both let go of. It would be nice to get out more. Maybe I could really try hitting the dating scene again. Be more flexible. Open to openness. With more time anything feels possible. I let the breeze ruffle my hair as a sense of freedom blows over me.

I take James' hand and squeeze as he shakes mine. "Deal."

Eight

James checks his watch and announces we've been walking for around three hours. There's a growing ache in my shins, long and sharp, running up the bone. The part of my spine from my shoulders up to my neck aches from hauling the heavy bag around with me. We've crossed a few roads, but they were all abandoned, not a car in sight. I'll give it to Michael; he's really tossed us out at the far end of nowhere.

The terrain here is much sturdier. We've joined what looks like an actual, real human-formed rocky path crossing a green landscape, its sharp, thorny shrubbery thick and scattered about at random. Some of the bushes have pretty little red berries growing on them and I'm tempted to pick them as the protein bars are already boring me to death. But it's not worth getting poisoned. Especially all the way out here. I miss meals, and unlimited teas, coffees, biscuits, gravy, chips! It's only been a day.

Thankfully the sky is a bright grey where the sun is pushing through the layer of thin cloud, but there's no rain. Not yet at least. The temperature is fresh, and manageable during the day with my sweatshirt on.

We stop by a river that's approximately ten metres wide,

flowing fast through the valley, slashing and spraying as it hits the rocks embedded in the riverbed. I lean down at a calmer part to fill my water bottle.

"Is it time to panic yet?" James asks, holding up the clear bottle of vodka he's slid out of his bag.

I walk back to where he's perched on a soft bank of grass, taking a seat beside him. "I don't know… Do you think I should check if I've got signal?"

"Worth a try."

I open the back compartment sliding out my trusty pal. I turn it on and wait to see if any bars appear. After a few minutes it's clearly not going to happen. "Guess I should turn it off again."

James sighs, rubbing his face in his hands. "I wonder if I'm an uncle yet."

I don't really know what to say to that. "Let's toast to it?" I suggest.

"To me maybe being an uncle?"

I take the bottle, unscrew the lid then take a swig. I hate vodka. It instantly burns my tongue and throat, and I want to spit it back out. I make a brave face and swallow, trying my hardest not to wince and shudder as it goes down. "To you maybe being an uncle," I say, sounding quite exasperated.

I look up at James and catch the corner of his lips quirk as he takes the bottle from me, swigging some himself. The smile stays and he almost looks as if he enjoys the taste. "To me maybe being an uncle. Cheers, Sophie! Hope you're doing well," he says to the sky as if she's somewhere toasting him back.

"To Sophie," I say. Although I regret it when the bottle

is passed to me again and I feel obliged to take another sip. The liquid warms my stomach. It's probably a good idea for me to get drunk before nightfall if it might help me stay warm. Anything to avoid sharing a sleeping bag with my work nemesis.

Oh, I am *never* going to live that down.

"What about your other sisters and your parents? Will they be there?"

"Parent," James corrects.

I wince. "Ah, sorry. You did say."

He shrugs. "I doubt it. Hannah is busy with wedding stuff. And Josie is more interested in her studies at the moment."

"She's at uni?"

He nods, hugging his knees to his chest as the bottle swings from his hands. "Me and Soph made sure both Hannah and Josie could do that. We were close in age, us two, and it was around the time when Mum was trying to feed the five of us on a nurse's salary. She was working crazy hours. Our nan helped out a lot when we were kids, but she passed away when I was thirteen."

"I'm sorry," I say. "I've lost all my grandparents too. They all died at different times, with different illnesses. It feels like losing a piece of you, doesn't it? What I'm trying to say is, I understand how hard it is to lose family."

James nods. "Yeah. It was pretty hard on all of us. Especially Mum. Soph and I were sort of forced to leave school as soon as we could because of it. To support her, you know? I worked in a local corner shop, stacking shelves and whatnot. Soph was a dishwasher at the local pub until she was old enough to work behind the bar. I got bored easily so skipped around a few things. I've had a load of jobs. Learnt a ton. Found my calling as a car salesman."

I bark out a laugh. "*You* were a car salesman?" I don't know why I find this funny. I look at the shaggy-haired man beside me, with his relaxed, windbitten features. It's hard to imagine he even sold anything a few days ago. The other version of him though, the slick version in a suit: I can believe that.

He nods, smirking at my expression. "Sold second-hand cars. Made a shit ton in commission. Well, a shit ton for me at the time. I got the bug. I wasn't beyond putting my dignity aside, approaching people knowing they might well be rude to me. Or asking for a sale. Closing the deal. There's no dignity in being broke, so you grow a thick skin."

"And then you got into events?"

"Yeah. Worked at a few other places in between then found the job at The Starr Agency as Sales Manager and progressed from there."

I smile. I want to say that's actually quite impressive, and I find myself looking at his face for too long, his dark blue eyes connecting with mine in such a familiar way it sends an awakening shot of energy to my core. So, the words never come. And I'm glad because I'm still not sure where I stand with him.

"What about you?" he asks. "What's your story?"

I shrug. "Got a master's degree in marketing. Found a job in the city and never went home."

"Nah, I don't buy it. There's more to you than that. No one works as hard as you do for nothing. There's always more."

I blush at his comment. I feel seen. I don't like it. "Well,

I… I applied for the job, and I got it. I like working in events and…"

James snorts. "You don't even like what you do!"

My jaw drops. "Yes, I do!"

"Which part?"

"The creative part… The, erm… I like being in control of the whole marketing process. It's rewarding to see the hard work I've put in making someone's day. I like…" Well, fuck. What do I like? I frown across the river as I notice something dark brown worming its way through the current. An otter pops up at the other side, holding something in its front paw, then shoots away into the nearby grasses.

"You're addicted to it. Like I am," James states.

"Addicted to what though?"

"Success. The difference is mine is money. Greed, if you like. You're only addicted to the recognition. And Michael is very good at manipulating you with it."

I scoff. That's not right. That doesn't happen. And that's not the only reason I love my job. Sure, the recognition is nice. Michael always compliments our team on our design, press releases and radio advertising. I have a clever team underneath me who support all the challenges I face with fast-thinking, proactive and creative abilities. I can't say I don't enjoy that part of my work. Working with people.

"He doesn't manipulate me," I say quietly, partly because I'm busy juggling every memory I have of Michael and wondering if maybe I've missed something.

From the corner of my eye, James frowns, passing me the bottle again. This time I take a bigger swig.

"Didn't you want to go to university?" I ask, because it felt like the thing everyone was aiming for when I was at school. We went from this tight-knit friendship group to a loose-fitted version, scattered across the country, barely staying in touch.

"Never really thought about it. Wasn't an option."

"But you're smart," I say, despite myself. *Is he?*

"Not all smart people go to university, Felicity."

I roll my eyes at the use of my birth name. "Are you ever going to just call me Fliss? Everyone else does!" I huff.

"No, I prefer Felicity." He winks. I roll my eyes.

"What would you have studied had you gone?" I ask.

"Hmm, I guess I'd have studied sports science, or something to do with sport."

I give him a full body scan. He's certainly got a sporty physique. Although I've never actually seen him doing any sport. He's tall, lean and muscular, and wears a suit in the way you'd expect a professional sportsman to.

I close my eyes, looking away. For some reason, James talking about the human body has inspired a very naked image of him in my head. I will the image away but it's not leaving quickly. *Nope, must not think about him naked*. I haven't even seen him fully naked. How the hell has my brain jumped here?

By the time my eyes open again, I'm warm, and I can't tell if it's from the vodka or my dirty thoughts.

"What would you do? If you could do anything in the world?" he says, slightly changing the subject.

God, why are we talking about this! This is a scary question for me. I take a moment to consider it. I'm a very important, driven businesswoman, but there's always been a part of me who's imagined the home life I'd want. There's an image that finds me from time to time. I'll be sitting on my comfortable, expensive high-backed sofa in a Victorian-style front room, with pastel-coloured patterned wallpaper, and tall bay windows. I hold a book in my hand, occasionally peeking out at the green, leafy street I live on. He (whoever he ends up being) calls my name from the kitchen at the back of the house asking if I want a hot drink. Sometimes there's a dog, a small one with a long snout, cosied up by my feet. I imagine my cream-painted fireplace. The open shutters. The light breeze that tangles in the curtains. And that's my happy place.

The issue is that isn't my *real* happy place. It's not an attainable thing. And that brings with it this overwhelming sense of failure.

I'm thirty. The longest relationship I've ever had was ten months and he left me for a career move. I said at the time I couldn't go with him because of my own job, but the reality is he didn't even ask.

I should have a happy place in my current world. But I don't. So maybe I do numb it by making myself busy. Marrying myself to my work.

"Felicity?"

"Huh?" I start, realising I've been daydreaming.

"What would you do?"

I squint across at James, who's watching me closely, as if he's trying to record my reaction. I look down at my hands, fiddling with my laces, to escape his gaze. "I'm not sure, really. Think I want what most people want. A sense of commitment from someone else. A place to call my own." I shrug. "I'm happy with my job. I don't see me going anywhere else."

James sighs deeply, rubbing his chin in his hand. "You

probably shouldn't put all your hopes into becoming a director though."

His comment is like a punch to the gut. I'm instantly on the defence. "Why not? We're both here, aren't we? Doing this challenge Michael set us?"

He makes a face, looking away. We watch a large black crow hop along a grassy plane, pecking the ground. "I just don't think you're getting the respect from Michael that you think you are. I mean, look at where we are now," he adds, raising his hands as if to demonstrate his point.

My heart drops. I'm not sure what James is doing but it feels like some form of trickery. "Right," I say with a touch of venom, rising to my feet, shrugging my bag onto my aching shoulders and striding in the direction of this bloody castle again.

Nine

The path alongside the river rises and falls. When inclining sharply, it forces our heart rates to increase as we battle with the hill, dodging saplings, thorny bushes and fallen branches. James steps over them with ease. Sometimes I have to take off my bag, throw it to the other side, then straddle the thing to clear it. Occasionally, he stops to offer me a hand, but I hiss at it. I don't need his help. I never have before, and I don't need it now.

When the path is low there are spots, almost like little beaches, where we can pause to fill our bottles and take a break before climbing again. I notice the lids have a strange filter in them. Hopefully this is keeping us safe from any kind of sickness. I'm reaching a point where I may need to tuck into another protein bar, but the thought of it turns my stomach. They're all strawberry flavoured with a layer of yoghurt dried over the top. They're chewy to the point of making your jaw ache.

I once again think about dipping a salty chip into a pot of red sauce.

"What you groaning about?" James asks, taking a sip from his bottle.

"I'm hungry but I don't want to eat another protein bar."

"Me neither. Although I doubt you'd want to go hunting so I haven't suggested it."

I laugh, exasperated, resting my hands on my hips. "Even if I was ok with murdering a wild bunny – which I'm not, by the way – how would you go about hunting, Gloatman? Do you really know how?"

James rubs the back of his neck as he takes a big gulp of air, lifting his chest high enough that his black t-shirt rises, showing a little patch of belly-button hair and firm stomach. I bite the inside of my cheek, forcing myself to look away. I can't believe I had my hands and body plastered up against him last night.

"Never actually hunted anything before," he says. "But I reckon I could start a fire."

I frown. "Is that wise?"

"It'll be safe. And besides, have you seen any sign of civilisation yet? Looks like we're in for at least one more night in the wilderness."

I want to cry.

"Don't freak out," he warns, pointing at me. "What's the worst that can happen?"

"Are you seriously asking me that right now? I'm sure your risk-management levels are low, but mine aren't. If there's something for me to stress about, I've done it already. We could fall and injure ourselves. You might hit your head. I might hit *my* head. We could both fall and hit our heads! But worse than that, I'm going to have to shiver my arse off again for another night."

"No, you're not," James says, dropping his hands to his side on an exhale. "You can sleep with me again."

I freeze, my eyes wide like saucers. There's no way I just

witnessed him say that out loud as if it isn't the worst thing that I've ever done. Does he *want* me to sleep with him? Why doesn't *he* care more? Why isn't *he* traumatised?

"Don't do that…" James starts.

"Oh god!" I say, grabbing at my hair hanging loosely across my shoulders. "Is this the bit where I find out you've been in love with me this whole time, but it's taken you being forced into the wilderness with me for twenty-four hours to admit it?"

He blinks.

"Oh, shit! *You love me!*"

"Ha!" James' face morphs into this big fat clown grin. He leans forwards as he laughs, resting his hands on his knees. His laughter bubbles into full-on fits as he struggles to control himself. Finally, he rises again, wiping his eyes, making that stupid "ahhhh" sound. "That's the funniest… No, wait. That's the only funny thing you've ever said."

I pull a face, folding my arms across my chest. "No, then, I take?"

He restores his face to a calm expression. "No, Felicity. And I cannot stress this enough. You're annoying as fuck. Running up to this work trip, I had such little respect for you, I even contemplated abandoning you at the layby and taking off with the money. For the last six years you've repeatedly done anything you can to make my life harder at work."

"No, I haven't!" I object.

"You're a nightmare; you actively attempt to discredit all my ideas."

"Because they affect me! And my team!" I shout. My blood is boiling.

James scoffs. "You don't give me a chance. I was negotiating the loss of ticket revenue into the costs for my idea. I was going to make sure marketing got their piece of the pie!"

I stumble backwards, grabbing a branch for support. I'm not sure I believe him. I think about saying as much, but instead I decide to keep my mouth shut. It's not that I don't think he has the capacity for being good. It's that it's easier to continue to challenge him for the director role if I think he's a bit of a shit.

James shakes his head, turning towards the path again, but then stops, looking across the river. "We need to be on that side," he says, pointing. "Especially if we want this to be over with."

"Well, we can't cross it."

He points to the grassy slope on the other side of the fast-flowing water. "We could climb back up that side. And the current doesn't look as strong here."

"You're not seriously saying what I think you are. Because that would be insane."

"Oh, come on. You can swim, can't you?"

"Not in freezing-cold rushing water, I can't."

James rolls his eyes, pushing his hair back from his forehead – it's completely flat and floppy now. It would be cute, endearing, if it wasn't on an arrogant arse. "There you go again," he says. "Shooting me down."

"You're hardly an exotic bird, Gloatman. You can stomach a small dose of rejection. Might even do you good."

"And that means?"

"That you're way too confident and self-important."

He laughs, the sound rich with frustration. "I'm sorry.

Should I be more like you and require someone to be clapping for me at every step of the way?"

I scrunch my nose. "I don't need that."

"You absolutely do. And you don't like me because I refuse to pander to your childish insecurities."

Silence.

I realise at some point my jaw's gone slack and I'm standing here with a ridiculous face, so I shake it out and draw my folded arms even closer to my body, as if I can somehow protect myself from his words.

He's not right. Is he?

No. I don't require recognition. Is it nice to receive it? Yes, of course.

James taps his foot, as if waiting for something. If he thinks he's getting an apology he's got another thing coming. Probably in the shape of a knee to the groin.

I can't do this much longer. I certainly don't think I can do another night in a tent with James. Now that might be the last straw.

Looking across the water, I try to measure the speed of the current, the distance to cross, the depth. It seems shallow enough. Maybe it is a good idea. A mad one. But it could get us to the castle quicker.

An upper body shiver consumes me in an uncomfortable way. It feels wrong. It feels like I'm making a bad decision. But maybe that's just because it's Gloatman's idea. "Fine," I say, defeatedly. "I'll cross the damn river. But if I die, and I might, it will be your fault."

James nods slowly. "I'm not going to let you die, that would be fairly counterproductive to this mission, wouldn't you say?" He smirks. "But if for any reason you do die, I promise not to tell anyone about last night."

I groan, exasperated. "Yeah, right." I take my bag off my shoulders, have a sip from my bottle and consider how best to dress for this next step. I don't want to get my trainers soaked through. My only other footwear is my poor, unfortunate red boots. They might be salvageable now, but submerging them in the river will certainly destroy all hope. The next issue is my trousers. They're long, and I suspect there will be some swimming required.

"Strip down to your underwear," James says, as if he can read my train of thought.

I laugh. He's joking, obviously. I look at him. He's *joking*, right? I flash him a *what the fuck?* face. "You're kidding?"

But he's already got his trousers off and is efficiently rolling them up into his bag. He stands before me in just his boxer shorts looking quite proud of himself. I only take a quick glance to see if there's an outline. God, there actually is… and… it's… *Wow*.

Look away, Fliss. Look away!

And damn the heat rushing into my cheeks.

"It's the only way you're going to keep your stuff dry," he says. "We'll get our bags across on a float of some sort. That way we'll hopefully save them from getting drenched. Or at least the contents. The outer layer is waterproof anyway."

"But I'll freeze."

"And then you'll have dry clothing on the other side. You have spare underwear, right?"

"Yeah, but…"

"What?" James smirks at me in that patronising way

again, except there's a bit more softness to it this time. "Too shy?"

I blink, unsure how to respond. I've never prepared for this sort of argument. I'm not shy. Not fully clothed, anyway. However, I'm aware of my shorter-than-average legs and my slightly-wider-than-other-girls' hips. I have relatively large breasts that I don't know what to do with. And there's a small, but noticeable, roll on my tummy. It's not like I get time to do a ton of physical exercise outside of work.

James notices my hesitation and sighs. "Don't be weird. You've got a great body."

"Shut up, I don't." I sound too defensive. And wait, did he just *compliment* me?

Shaking his head, he slowly pulls his top off, pushing that into his bag too. There are a few moles dotted across his chest, abdomen and a noticeably large one on his hip. Maybe a birthmark. He has an *amazing* body. There's a light smattering of dark hair along his chest with a thin line that leads all the way down...

"Come on now, Felicity, you're making me blush," he says with a grin. "You going to just stand there and gawk or shall we crack on?"

How have I found myself in this nightmare again?

I sigh, turning my back on him as I slide out of my trainers and pull my trousers down. My skin is pasty white. I really need to get out in the sun more this summer. Factor fifty at hand, of course.

James rummages through his bag behind me. Probably trying hard to sound busy in order to put me at ease. Annoyingly, he is right about the clothes situation. I don't have a spare pair. I secretly curse Michael. What an arsehole! *Why didn't he pack me a spare pair of clothes?* Did he foresee this? I fold my trousers, packing them into my bag, cringing inwardly at the thought of being stood a matter of metres away from James in just my short black briefs, complete with mini side-ribbons.

Then I slowly lift my top too, pushing my hair out of the way. As I don't have a hairbrush, I know, even without a mirror, that my hair has expanded by about three times its usual fluffiness at this point. It's unmanageable. Best left alone. Hopefully a bird doesn't move in before we find a shower and hair straighteners. I don't see the point in using the dry shampoo without a brush. Surely it will just make matters worse. As I pop my top into my bag, a cool trail of wind whisks across my front. It's cold without even getting into the water. Luckily, there's an opening in the clouds and the sun sneaks through, warming the top of my head.

Unfortunately, I'm wearing a bra that I would deem on the smaller side, pushing my boobs up. It's not usually that noticeable when I've got a dress without a low cut or V-neck. I wore it because it suits the dress I had on. But out in the open like this, they're hard to avoid. And by the look on James' face as he swallows and blinks across the river, a slow blush creeping into his cheeks, he's *definitely* noticed them.

Crap, crap, crap!

I slide into my trainers again, seeing as that's what James has done, and hug myself as I wait for his next instructions. This is his idea after all. He looks at the bag and the small logs he's managed to grab from the nearby trees behind us. It's like he's doing a mental puzzle.

"There's no way you're going to make a raft for the bags," I say.

"Why do you doubt me so much?" he asks, mock offended.

He starts piling them into a rectangle shape, ripping the beige chinos he wore on his journey to Scotland and using the shreds to fasten the corners together. I wish he'd done this before I stripped down to my underwear. He keeps sneaking glances, and by the force of human nature, I can't help doing the same to him.

Admittedly, I've always known he was a bit hot. Truthfully, I assumed he was out of my league. Not that I'd ever have gone there – dated a colleague. He's not exactly boyfriend material anyway, what with all the rumours of his dating clients and stuff. I wonder if that's just a fun rumour or if it's true. Looking at the man before me, it's almost laughable. He looks more boyish than manly, with his hair ruffling in the breeze as he kneels down to make his raft.

Finally, once he's secured the bags and tied some more ripped-off strips together to form a loop to hold onto, he gives me a proud smile. Very boyish. Look how proud he is of his shitty raft. Let's hope it's up to the job.

"Right, you ready?" he asks.

"I guess so…"

James holds his arm out for me as if I'm going to hang onto him. I give him a funny look. "I don't need your help."

"You're tiny and buoyant," he says, giving me a once-over. "If you don't hang onto me, you are going to float off down the river like a rubber dingy."

"Hey!"

He laughs, shaking his head. "I'm sorry. It's a compliment,

honestly. And don't shout at me for noticing. I'm a man, I can't help it."

I sigh. "I usually put them away." But now I'm laughing too.

"I'm just saying."

As if his joking around has somehow made me more relaxed, I link my arm through his. The step down into the water instantly floods my trainers and I gasp from the icy chill of the water. I can feel the current wading into me even at the shallow part.

Oh hell, what's it going to be like further along?

The surface starts out crumbly, like a mixture of mud and pebbles. As we wade in further, there's a lot of large rocks covered in algae on the riverbed. They're slippery. I have to really think about where my next foot is going to land. James is focussed, trying to haul the bags over on his float. It appears to be heavier than he initially thought it would be. The current is pushing it downstream so forcefully he's having to practically haul it along.

As the river reaches our waist height, I take a shuddery breath as the water races around my stomach. James rearranges us so that he's protecting me from the majority of the current but he's also trying to maintain a hold on the bags.

It's all getting a little scary. I can feel my heart thumping in my chest. I'm panting. I can't tell if it's from panic, the effort or the cold.

"Keep going. That's it," James says, as softly as he can through gritted teeth. I can see he's struggling. I can hear it in his breathing. His whole body is tense, wading one step at a time.

Then I drop. Out of nowhere my head is completely submerged. I panic. The floor of the riverbed has vanished. The water has me. I slip through James' grip as my body is pulled downwards.

Ten

My head surfaces back above the water as I gasp for air. I'm gulping more water every time I take a breath. The raft with our bags on drifts alongside me. It's going too fast to be attached to James now. Unless he's been caught too.

Another current grabs me, whipping me sideways. I go under again.

My whole body lashes out, trying to find something, anything, to hold onto. I push downwards further to see if I can get a grip on the surface but it's too deep.

That's when my leg catches on something sharp. I cry out but I'm underwater. It sounds gurgled, otherworldly. I swallow more. My body goes rigid as it fights the intake. I think I'm choking.

Red droplets float beside me, dragged in the same direction.

Am I bleeding? I close my eyes as they start to sting.

The river bobs, flowing between two rocks and ebbs downwards again, like a violent mini waterfall. My face is thrust back above the surface as I take sharp, painful gasps of air.

"Fliss!" I hear James yell, just as I hit something flat

and hard. It slams against my ribs. Or maybe my ribs slam against whatever it is. It leaves me breathless, clawing at anything I can. I think I hear my name again. And then nothing.

"Felicity, can you hear me?" James' voice pierces the silence, the darkness. I burst awake, choking as I try to breathe. There's still water trapped in my oesophagus. I throw myself to the side, emptying my guts on the soft ground around me. I clench my fists around damp bracken.

James' hands are on my side, stroking my arms. He helps me lie down again when I'm ready. He touches my face, my chin, my shoulder, casting his eyes all the way down my body. Everything he does is with gentle care. Something about my leg has him touching his face, squeezing his jaw.

"What?" I croak. My throat is burning.

"It's nothing. Just stay down, ok? You passed out. God, I think I should call for help."

I take a deep breath, assessing my body for pain. Despite them being icy cold, I can feel and wiggle my toes. My legs ache and there's a biting pain on my left shin. My ribs burn from where they smacked against something hard, but I can breathe. In fact, my breathing is now relatively shallow with James kneeling beside me, running a hand through his soaked hair.

"You know when I—" I cough as talking becomes difficult. "You know when I said your idea was mad?"

James turns his eyes back to mine, tilting his head in a disbelieving stare. "Don't you dare…" he says. "Don't even go there, Felicity. I've never been so *fucking terrified* in my entire *life*. I thought you were dead!"

I try to laugh, shaking my head. For a moment, I assumed I was too. I think about asking him how the hell he managed to drag me out of the river and onto the bank. I want to talk some more about how this is the stupidest idea he's had yet but his expression is agonised, not his usual arrogant smirk I'm so used to, so I decide it's maybe not the time. And anyway, a more pressing concern is bothering me as I look down and realise how exposed I am.

"Where are my bloody clothes, Gloatman?"

James scratches the back of his neck. I'm shivering on the cold muddy ground, but to see him shudder as the chill racks through *him* is a surprise. Especially as he runs so hot. He looks back down the river enshrouded in thick greenery, the trees on either side linking branches over the water as if to provide it with shelter from the sun.

I gulp, realising how serious this actually is. What if I had actually drowned? Or knocked my head so hard I couldn't be resuscitated? What if I never saw my parents, my friends, ever again?

I could've died!

"Please stop freaking out," James says quietly, softly. I peek across at him through blurry eyes. He's right, I am freaking out. But at least he's not saying it like he usually does. There's no accusatory tone there this time. He puts his hand on my shoulder, rubbing his firm-skinned thumb in circles. "It'll be ok, alright? I'm going to go search for our bags."

"You lost our bags!?" I sob.

"Well, Felicity," he chuckles, exhaustion sitting heavy on his features. "I prioritised saving *your life* over our clothes. I'm sorry if that now presents an inconvenience to you."

A memory flashes back to me. I was flitting in and out of consciousness as he hauled me onto the muddy bank. My brain has retained snippets of hot skin plastered on mine. Strong arms lifting me. Curse words being hissed.

"I'm so co-old," I whimper. "But thank you," I add as he rolls his eyes.

"Good to know you're back to your usual self. I was going to turn your phone on and call for help but then I realised it's fucked off down the river somewhere with our bags."

I gasp. "Oh god! James, what if it's broken?"

"We'll figure it out," he says, shuddering again. He looks back down the river, peering as if he might be able to spot them in the rocky waters ahead. "Stay here. I'll go look for them."

He rises to his feet. As he walks away in his drenched boxer shorts, which are leaving very little to the imagination (he has a really nice arse), he calls over his shoulder, "Don't look at your leg. Just stay like that."

My leg!? Shit, what's wrong with my leg?

I sit up fast. In doing so, I bend my knees and a sharp pain has me hissing. That's when I remember the jagged rock, the blood trickling through the water. It *was* me bleeding. Specifically, my shin, which now has a nasty two-inch gash across it. Luckily I'm not squeamish, as the blood has poured all the way down and over my trainers.

In order to not make the gash worse I restrain myself from touching it, lying back down and crying into the grey skies above me that promise drizzle. Slow, lazy tears wet my cheeks and ears as I wait for James to return. After a while there's the promise of heavy breathing and footsteps crunching through the overgrowth.

He stops a few steps away from me with a strange expression on his face. He places two soaked bags down on the ground in front of him. They land with a squelch. Another sob racks my chest.

"You looked at your leg, didn't you?" he says, coming to sit beside me again.

I suck in air to calm my breathing. "What're we going to do!?"

James sighs, raggedly. His breathing is still choppy from having hunted the bags down. "I don't know. We need to find out if you can walk on it first."

"Where were the bags?" I ask through fresh tears. So much for never letting this man see me cry.

"All the way down there, getting pummelled by the current on the rocky part... I saw an otter," he adds, as if that somehow sweetens the situation. "We need to get somewhere dryer. I need to clean your leg up. Can't believe he didn't think to give us a first aid kit. Maybe he is trying to kill us off..."

"Are all our clothes wet now?"

James squeezes the back of his neck, as a breeze plays with the branches in the trees around us. "I haven't looked at the clothes, but I suspect so. Definitely everything nearer the top of the bags. But I did check just now, and your phone isn't turning on."

I sniff, covering my face with my hands.

"We've been walking for a day now. We're not in a desert,

Fliss. This is Scotland. We'll find somewhere, or someone, to help us very soon. I promise."

I note how he's started calling me Fliss intermittently over the past few hours. I decide not to comment on it yet. Instead, I power up my threshold for pain and try to sit up. James notices what I'm doing and offers me his arm like a gentleman. I let him help me, feeling like a fool and a baby for needing help at all.

Once I'm standing, we're both relieved to find I can put weight on my leg and won't need carrying. The clothes are drenched. My bag was hit worse than his for some reason.

James offers me his top, which although wet, is long, falling down over my buttocks to provide a modicum of dignity. He puts his shirt on, not bothering to button it up. It hangs loosely to the side of his toned abdomen. His wet boxer shorts are officially leaving nothing to the imagination anymore. I bite my lip to remind myself not to look, since he's providing me with the same respect.

After hobbling off the bank, we find miles and miles of bracken-covered undulating Highlands. In the far distance, I can see the blue outline of mountains. The birds are well and truly alive here. We must spot at least three birds of prey in an hour. Ravens hop across our path, eyeing us suspiciously, before flying off again, crying out in their creepy way.

We don't make it far, finding a patch of clear ground, where James pitches the wet tent, with a small lake about ten metres away. I sit and watch, as I'm ordered, sipping water from my steel bottle. He finds some fallen branches from a nearby patch of trees, using rocks to raise them off the ground enough to hang all our drenched clothes over.

Somehow the sleeping bags are only wet on the outside. He shakes off the water droplets, hanging them out to dry too as I shiver on my perch.

"I'm going to attempt to make a fire," he tells me, peeking over with a frown.

"Is it even legal?" I ask, my quivering voice giving my chilliness away.

"We don't really have a choice, do we? I need to help you wash your leg. You're not going to be able to rely on my body heat tonight as I'm also freezing. Plus, there's hardly any sun here." James rubs his face. "We really need to get you to a doctor. Your leg might get infected."

"I'm sure we'll find something tomorrow," I say, slumping at the thought of spending another night in a dripping tent, fighting midges and digging holes for toilets. And now I have an injury to factor in as well. "Do we still have the tampons?"

"No. They were ruined." He pauses, not looking at me. "Why? Do you need them?"

I snigger. "No, not for that! Don't worry."

"I'm not worried… I have three sisters, remember? But I can't nip to the corner shop for you right now, can I?"

"You do that?"

"What?"

"Buy tampons."

He gives me a look. "Of course, I do. I don't care."

"None of my ex-boyfriends would do it, it was always a categoric no."

"They're idiots," he says, ripping something. I turn to see what he's doing. He's taken the nice white shirt he wore on his journey here and is tearing it into strips. "Come on.

Better get you down to the lake as it's easier than using bottled water."

Once I'm seated on the rocky beach, long grasses tickling my arms in the breeze, James takes off his trainers and steps in barefoot, squatting down to my eye height. He cleans my leg diligently, taking care to be gentle when I hiss, clenching my fists and biting the insides of my cheeks. He watches me, his blue eyes warm when they connect with mine. I try to ignore the heat building in my core whenever he's nice to me. It's the last thing I want to be thinking about considering he's both my colleague *and* my nemesis. I'm waiting for him to suddenly lash out with a smart comment or jibe.

"Why're you being so kind to me?" I say. I mean it in a jokey way but it comes out more vulnerable than I was going for.

James is carefully cleaning off the dried blood near my ankle. "Would you prefer for me to pick another fight?"

I can't stop myself from smiling. "At least it will feel somewhere closer to normal."

"Alright, give me a second." He's quiet for a moment then chuckles suddenly. "You know I'm way better at rattling you when I don't have to think about it. I can't come up with anything right now."

"Nothing? Not a single thing to annoy me?"

He presses his lips together and shakes his head. "Nada."

"How disappointing."

Once he's finished, he rises to his full height again offering me both his hands to help me up too. I take them, but hold back, watching, as he returns to our makeshift camp.

If I didn't know better, I'd say he actually cared about me all of a sudden. It was like he purposefully didn't take the bait to nettle me just now. I don't believe he can't think of at least one thing which would set us off.

Maybe I read him all wrong these past six years. Or maybe he read me all wrong.

Then I remember how he tried to discourage me from going for the director role earlier in the day and it stings in a different way. Somehow, that discussion got right to the centre of me. The place that harbours my lack of self-confidence and people-pleasing tendencies. And it hurt. I look over at the man who is now fiddling with the tent. I'm used to snakes. He doesn't look like one right now. But I know who he is really. All this flirty nonsense between us needs to end here.

I will not fall for James Gloatman.

Eleven

James wraps the driest sleeping bag around my shoulders as I perch on the rock back by the campsite. My gash doesn't look quite so bad now without the blood. He's been careful to only clean around it, trying hard not to get any more unsterilised water in, or around, the actual cut itself. Without any phones to use, it all feels a little more serious than it did this morning.

He pulls my leg out in front of me to inspect. It just so happens he is one of the first-aid-trained staff in our company. "I don't think you'll need stitches. I'm still worried it might get infected though. Should we pour some of the vodka on there? I've seen that done in a film before."

"That sounds painful."

James winces. "Probably will be. Let's just keep an eye on it, yeah?"

"So, what? Do we just leave it?"

He leans back to take the strips of his shirt from where they're hanging. Turning back to me with a grimace, he says, "I think we should bandage it to prevent dirt getting in. I found this leaf." He's holding a big waxy leaf he's picked off a bush somewhere. "I'll use this as a gauze. You don't want to risk it getting mucky. And given our current situation that could pose somewhat tricky."

"Have you done this before?"

He laughs nervously. "*No*. I'm massively improvising here. Please don't sue me if it goes wrong."

"Only person I'm suing is Michael."

"Well, well," he says, smiling. "That's my girl."

My eyebrows shoot upwards, realising what he's said. James must realise too, as his smile vanishes. He coughs to clear his throat, rearranging his already arranged strips of shirt. "I'm glad you're finally starting to see him for the raging lunatic he is."

I nod. "Right."

He clears his throat again, his Adam's apple bobbing as he hands me the bottle of vodka. "Painkiller."

I unscrew the lid. The first sip is as awful as it was earlier. I squint, stick out my tongue and shudder as James places the leaf carefully onto my cut, slowly and meticulously wrapping his shirt around it to secure.

James passes me another protein bar, making a joke about fine dining with a view. I look around at our surroundings. We're in somewhat of an angular glade, so you can see right out into the distance. There's no sign of human life. It's all wilderness for as far as the eye can see. Bracken is thick across this part of the world, leaving a layer of soft greenery for the wildlife to hide amongst, but today we've seen all sorts of creatures, from grey rabbits to red deer, their antlers held fiercely above them as their calves pootle around their legs, looking for teats. Unfamiliar with human activity, they're slow to dart away, so we both get a good look.

"I'm sure we could eat something out here," I say. "What about fish in the lake?"

"Do you know how to fish?"

"No," I laugh. "But if I get desperate enough, I'll go all savage and stab them with sticks like they do in the movies."

James snorts. "I'll make traps out of shredded shirt sleeves. We'll be the wild people of Scotland."

As the first midge appears, I suggest we play a game to pass the time. But James is dead set on getting a fire burning before the light completely diminishes. For the next thirty minutes he busies himself looking for stones and firewood. Once he's got a half-decent set up, he gives me a look, and asks, "You know how to make a flame?"

"You're kidding, aren't you? You just did all that, and you don't know how to make a flame?"

"I don't have matches."

"Aren't you supposed to scratch sticks together?"

He has a go, trying several different things. Then, through sheer force and persistence, he manages to spark a flame. He does the same thing again and again until, at last, a small fire is glowing a few metres from our tent. I practically launch forwards, tucking myself fully into my sleeping bag like a slug, with just my face visible. I perch on the ground once again.

The heat is lush. James disappears to find a few more pieces of firewood to keep it alight throughout the evening as I interchange between sipping vodka and taking bites of my protein bar. When I get back to normality. *If* I get back to normality. I will never touch one of these nasty bars again. The taste and texture are already turning my stomach.

I drink more vodka. When James returns, he smiles. "Look at those red cheeks. You feeling a bit better?"

I nod. "I've had quite a bit of this," I say, holding up the bottle. I noticeably sway, even in my seated position. "You should have some now before I drink it all."

He comes over and sits beside me. His sleeping bag is dry too, so he steps into it, making himself cosy. He positions himself so that he's hugging his knees over the material. "What game did you want to play?"

"What about that one where we choose a celeb and the other has to guess who we are?"

"Boring," he says.

"Fine," I say. "Let's play truth. Except instead of me asking the questions, you just have to give me deep, pressing, emotional truths and I will do the same." Hmm. I'm not sure how good of an idea this is now I've said it out loud. Can I trust Gloatman, or am I dangerously tipsy and at risk of being too candid and vulnerable?

James is looking at me with a face that is undoubtedly sincere. "Me first?"

I nod. He shuffles, getting comfy as he takes a bite of his bar. I watch his face run through a mix of emotions as he considers what to tell me first. He's clearly got a lot of truths he could say. I'm not even sure I have enough about me to play this game. Why did I suggest this again? I take another sip of vodka whilst I wait.

"Alright, let's see," he muses. "Well, I've had two serious girlfriends end things with me," he announces. And *wow*, wasn't expecting that. "One was my sixth-form girlfriend, who didn't want a boyfriend before university. And then again before I moved to London. Er, actually, I moved to

London when I was twenty-three because of the breakup. Our town wasn't big enough for the both of us, as the adage goes. Especially as she broke up with me to get with my best friend."

I'm dead still, listening. Did he really just tell me that? Is it even true? Was he in love with them? I can hardly imagine him with a girlfriend, let alone being dumped by one.

"Have I stunned you into silence?" he asks when I don't say anything.

"Yeah," I reply with a laugh. "I didn't have you down as the long-term relationship type."

He laughs too but doesn't share any more details. "Your turn."

"Right, ok. Sorry about that. That's… It's really rubbish. I sort of wish I'd known that about you before now." James gives me a pleasant smile. It's too intimate in the lowering sun, dropping an orange glow behind the landscape. I swallow as heat pools in my core again. "Because I'd have been able to jibe you for it, obviously."

James makes a humoured face, nods. "Fair."

"Ok, my turn. Um, so, my parents told me they only stayed together for fifteen years of their marriage because of me, and I guess I feel like I can never pay them back for that sort of misery."

James nods again to show he's listening but doesn't say anything, so I assume he wants me to say more.

"It's fine. Mum always talks about how she wasted her younger years raising me and looking after Dad. And then my dad's out there making all these terrible decisions all the time and I don't know how to stop either of them. It's maddening.

"Also, they tell everyone I'm this big, successful businesswoman in the city. It's lovely but also, *it's so much pressure*. I see how happy it makes them and I can't stop myself from pushing forwards. And don't get me started about parental responsibilities of only children. I think about this a lot, but what happens when they get old? Where do I put them? They hate each other. I can't have them in the same house. But I want to look after and provide for them both."

I take a deep breath. That felt good to say out loud.

"That sounds hard," James says. "I'm sure they'll be proud of you, whatever you did. And clearly, nothing about their marriage or divorce was about you, no matter what they said. I'm sure they don't blame you at all. Have you asked them?"

"Please don't be so pragmatic," I laugh. "Let me be insane about this."

He chuckles too. "Ok, ok. Do they live near to London?"

"Near-ish," I say. "I grew up in Sussex. Down by the coast. They both still live in the area, but separately, of course."

"I'm sorry... I don't have any advice."

"That's ok. I didn't ask for it." I suddenly feel embarrassed.

James puckers his lips in agreement. "You're right. This is a moan fest. Not a problem-fixing session."

"I'm cool with that."

He shuffles beside me, takes another sip of vodka then hands it back. "Right, second thing... The rumours are true."

"What rumours?"

James frowns. "How many are there?"

"Quite a few."

"I slept with a client."

I open my mouth like a dead fish, staring into the flames growing in height. I can't believe what he's just said. There's no way. No! He wouldn't. "You didn't."

He laughs at my reaction. "I did."

"Who!?"

"Mrs Horley from Copper & Steel International."

"*Sara?* But she's like…"

"Forty-nine. Got an invite to her fiftieth birthday party the other day."

I gasp. "Oh my god… are you still…?"

James snorts and shakes his head. "Nah. It's been over for a while. She doesn't like to keep a toyboy for too long. Apparently, they get clingy. She was really nice though. We had some fun. She took me to Santorini for a long weekend. Felt like a prince."

"Shut. Up. *No.* I refuse to believe this. When did you go to Santorini with a client? And, wait, what if Michael had found out?"

He gives me one of those patronising looks again. I swear he thinks he's dealing with a child. It's like I'm completely innocent and he's this worldly being who's harboured all this incredible knowledge. "Michael knew. He knew the whole time. Sara told him."

Something hard forms in the pit of my stomach. A hot rage washes over me. "No."

James shrugs. "It wasn't a big deal, really. It was just sex."

"It is *never* just sex. Never ever."

"I promise you; it was. It depends how you're doing it.

But let me guess, you'll only have sex with a guy after three dates or something?"

I scoff. "Five."

"Five?! Oh, brilliant." He laughs good-humouredly. "I get it. That's absolutely the right way to do it if you want to avoid getting burnt." Then he adds, "I bet you're something else to date." But he doesn't say it with the sort of burning tone he usually uses. It's more inquisitive.

"Stop trying to change the conversation... Why did you date Sara?"

"Why are you making such a thing about it? She's an attractive, wealthy woman. She made the rules very clear from the start. I knew where I stood. We made each other feel good for a time. It was fun. There isn't much else to it."

"Did your sisters know about her?"

He nearly chokes on the water he's just sipped from his bottle. "Why on earth would I tell them that?"

"I'm guessing you didn't because you knew they wouldn't approve."

"Of course they wouldn't. I wouldn't approve if roles were reversed, but it's none of their business and same goes for me with them. We're adults, Felicity. You've never done anything remotely controversial?"

I look away, forcing the heated feeling inside of me to settle. I can't work myself out. There are butterflies flighting in my stomach at the thought of James sleeping with this woman. And not just any woman, but Sara, an older, highly successful woman at that. There's also an ingrained sadness that James' experience of Michael is so extremely different to mine.

"Your turn," he says again.

I groan, taking another sip.

"And you need to make it better than mine. I want juicy gossip, Felicity."

"Alright," I say, accepting his challenge. "How's this? I haven't been with anyone in over two years. I've totally fallen off the horse. Sometimes I think the longer this goes on, the more impossible it will be to get back on."

I'm looking ahead as I say it. A weird moment of silence occurs where I wonder if I took his challenge of providing juicier gossip too far and actually just stepped right into one of his manipulative traps. Warmth rises slowly up my neck. That's when I feel the bottle move in my hands. James is carefully removing it from my grip. I give him a worried glance. Our eyes collide with fire as a small smirk rises on the side of his lips.

"At least now I know why you don't get drunk at work dos."

Oh, god. I throw my head back, crying out with laughter. He joins in too. It's true. I don't drink at work dos. Or if I do, it's minimal. I don't trust myself not to act like a prat or say something I'll later regret. When I finally glance at him, he's looking at me with a fresh curiosity. It's like I'm a puzzle he's trying to figure out.

"I'm sorry, I shouldn't have said that. Please don't ever repeat it. I'm just in this phase of my life where I'm incredibly fussy. It's strange because I finally like myself and actually only want to sleep with decent people. I feel like I deserve that. Quality over quantity, you know?"

Now I'm all hot again. Who knew I'd go from a shivering wreck to a boiling, sweaty mess so quickly. I'm sure the fire isn't helping. Maybe I have a fever. Does it work that quickly?

Oh balls. It's James. He's making me all clammy and bothered with his messy hair and relaxed boy-next-door look. Like this, out here in the wilderness, he's completely my type. And now he's looking at me like it's for the first time.

We're quiet for a while, sipping our waters and eating another protein bar each. The flames are successfully keeping the midges at bay. And when the light has completely faded, James lets the fire die down a bit before we start to climb into the tent again.

"You know we can zip our sleeping bags together, right?"

I'm glad it's dark when he says this because I can't help the smile blooming on my lips. He wants to sleep with me. Me! If nothing else, that's a compliment. Even if he does mean literal sleeping and nothing more.

"You don't have to," he adds when I don't respond right away.

"Actually," I say, pinching myself. I can't believe I'm agreeing to this. This morning I swore I'd never allow it to happen again. He's just so warm. It's like I have no control over the words that come out of my mouth. "I think that's a good idea."

Twelve

Something makes me stir. Amongst the night creatures going about their business, I manage to ignore much of the twig-snapping sounds of nearby animals inspecting our tent and fire. This time, however, I'm sure there's a thud or a cry. I roll over, reaching for James. His warmth is missing but I'm too sleep-drunk to worry myself with his disappearance, especially as the patter of raindrops on the tent is so soothing. I deflate into another deep sleep.

This one takes me somewhere new. Or maybe somewhere old. I'm in a garden enclosed with high hedgerows. There's a large oak tree in the middle, sucking the moisture out of the lawn, its roots weaving through the ground like snakes turned to stone. I realise where I am. I turn around to see the red-brick exterior of my childhood home.

The sun beats down on my face when I look up at the perfect blue sky. I see how the leaves are turned yellow as the rays of light catch them and turn them opaque. The smell of barbeque wafts over from the patio that wraps around the side of the house. Dad stands with his back to me, handling the food with utensils, looking at peace in being exactly where a dad ought to be. There's a hissing sound as something drips onto the coals. His polo top isn't

WORK TRIP

straight at the collar. He's got a line of sweat running from his neck down to his hips. His hair is darker, like mine. I squint, looking for his silver hairs, but they're not there.

A warm sense of homeliness comes over me as I walk across the lumpy lawn to the blue hammock Dad bought me, and perch there, watching the afternoon unfold. The recently watered grass glitters in the sunlight. Dad doesn't look at me, his full concentration absorbed in the task at hand. That's when Mum appears at the garden doors dressed in summery dungarees over a flowery top. Her hair, blonde but thick like mine, has been tied back with a scrunchie. She's got a salad bowl in one hand, plates in another. The most noticeable difference is her face. She's at ease, content with her surroundings. I've not seen her like this in so very long.

"Help me set up, darling," she asks me in her merry voice.

I nod, hopping down from the hammock and skipping into the kitchen. I spin in a circle. I think I'm dreaming. This is the kitchen we had before we renovated. Something feels strange. There's a crying sound outside. Mum goes to Dad's rescue, a tea towel in hand. He's probably just burnt himself. I decide to stay in the kitchen.

I want to venture further into the house full of happy memories. A place I can't reach anymore in real life. I want to soak it all in and stay for a while. But my feet anchor me to the floor.

Mum calls for me. I can't reach her though. It's like I don't even have feet to move. I've faded into a bodyless being. A sleep-induced blob.

I try to shout back but my voice doesn't work.

When she finally reappears at the door, the sun-bleached

garden casting her into a silhouette, her arm is linked through— I blink. It should be Dad. Dad was outside. When the other person appears alongside Mum, his smile is as terrifyingly jubilant as it always is.

His pale skin and ghostly eyes catch on mine. Despite knowing exactly who he is, it sends my pulse reeling. I'd stumble backwards if I could. Run and scream. Why is Mum holding arms with my boss?

Michael's grin doesn't fade as he yells, "Fliss!"

I judder awake, clenching my fists around anything I can to ground me. My soft sleeping bag fills my palms. This world is in total darkness. I'm inside the tent. I thrust around, looking for James. Where's his heat gone? We fell asleep with our sleeping bags zipped together. I had my back to him – he promised not to physically touch me unless I started shivering.

Where's he gone? I sit up, blinking into the night. Has he abandoned me?

My heart launches into a vicious beat as I clamber out of the bag, unzipping the tent with frantic fingers. I emerge under a drizzly sky, a whisper of moonlight pushing through the clouds. The fire is down to a lightly glowing ember. Smoke billows upwards lazily. Neither offers much in the way of light. It's silent apart from the menacing cry of an owl in the distance, the trickle of water nearby and the constant swaying of the long grasses and bracken branches up here.

"James!?" I call.

"Fliss." I hear my name muttered quietly. It's almost eerie.

I climb up from the ground, patting my knees as I rise to a standing position. The ache from my injured shin makes me wince. I can't see any sign of life around me. "I swear to god, James, if you're messing with me, I will murder you and feed you to the otters."

"Can you hear me?" he croaks. His voice is muffled, as if he's in pain.

"Yeah!"

"I'm behind the tent," he breathes. "But be careful, ok? There's a drop just to the left. The other side of the grass."

"What do you mean?" I ask, walking in exactly that direction.

"Stop!" he shouts, his voice echoing in the dark. "*Listen*."

"I am," I insist, standing absolutely still for a beat.

"You need to *not* step through the grasses or you're going to land on me."

"What the hell are you talking about?"

"Just walk behind the tent to the right. Follow it round the slope and you'll find me."

I do as he tells me, exasperated to be out in the dark with just a (still) slightly damp top and knickers on. It's making me shiver already. With bare feet, I'm cautious to place each foot down carefully to prevent impaling myself on a sharp rock or spiky twig. I should've clambered around in search of my trainers. That would've been smart.

"Stop," James croaks again. I pause, my hands out in front of me as if that'll help me find my way through the darkness somehow. "Down here."

I squat down. Behind what I assume is a sort of rocky edge, we're in total darkness again. A hand grabs mine. I squeal, batting at it.

"It's me, you ninny," James says.

"You made me jump! Why're you on the floor? If this is all some stupid game, it's not funny."

"Don't be daft! I fell."

"Why did you do that?"

James coughs a laugh. "Because I fancied taking flying lessons and I wanted to see if I was any good at it."

"You're an idiot," I say. "Did you know there was a drop *this* close to where we pitched?"

"Clearly not," he says, audibly frustrated. "It was obscured by the grass. I'm in so much pain, Felicity."

I kneel carefully, wincing as the tight-fitting bandage rubs against my wound. There's only a slight pressure there now. I think it's best though not to put my weight on it. I realise I'm possibly still a bit drunk. Must've been why I was in such a deep sleep. I groan. This is not going to help my mood in the morning.

And no caffeine. *Weep!*

"Why are *you* freaking out, right now?" James complains. How the hell can he tell in the dark? "I'm the one who may have broken his back without any way of calling for help."

"There's no way you've broken your back."

"I'm sorry, when did you become a doctor?"

"You'd be screaming in pain, Gloatman, or else you wouldn't be able to move at all. You're probably winded." I offer him my arm to help him up to a sitting position, but he just groans, being a big baby and refusing to move. I place my hands gently on his body to try to work out what position he's in.

He's topless. I think I find his abs, his chest. I walk my hands upwards to find his face. Except, I happen upon…

NOT his face. I get a good handful... *A really good handful.* I yelp, snatching my hands back.

"*Really*, Felicity? Fuck's sake," he says. "First you plaster yourself to me all night. Now you're *groping* me?"

"Why the hell are you naked!?"

"I was taking a piss. My pants are halfway down my legs. I can't sit up to pull them up. I'm sorry. Alright?"

I laugh with disbelief, staring up at the moonlight leaking through another break in the clouds. A force of wind pushes itself through the valley, rocking some nearby trees as the rattle of leaves makes it hard to hear.

"Let me get this straight. You were taking a piss and fell?"

"Yes. Well, I'd finished."

"Then you stepped forwards?"

"No. I turned and stepped backwards."

I laugh again. "Did you fall into your pee?"

"No, luckily... But now I'm in a precarious position. I've been waiting for you to hear me calling, hoping no animals or, god forbid, people, find me first."

I sigh. "If only you did see a person. They might have a phone and then we can finally get the fuck out of here. I'd charter a helicopter at this point," I say. "And claim it back on expenses." I chuckle.

James moves slightly, making a hissing sound as he does.

"Ok, so then what happened? How long have you been down here?"

"Must have been about an hour ago now," he mumbles.

"Why didn't you yell?"

"I did! I've been calling your name for ages. You were really out for the count, huh?"

I scrunch my face. I've been told I do this. It used to be an enjoyable game at sleepovers when I was a teenager. Once I'm asleep, I'm deeply asleep. Usually sounds, smells and even someone touching me are incorporated into my dreams. It's almost a little scary at times. I worry I won't wake up for a fire alarm. Somehow, I've trained myself to know when my actual morning alarm is going off. I would really hate to be late for work.

"I think I had too much vodka. I'm not really much of a drinker," I say. "I was also having a really weird dream."

James sniffs a laugh. "Fine, fine. I just want to get back to the tent. Any bright ideas on how to get me up there?"

"Where's the pain?"

"Everywhere."

"Ok, well that's actually probably a good thing," I say, not really having any clue but trying to motivate him to get up. It's not exactly like I'm going to be able to carry him. He must weigh two stone more than me. I'm not one of those amazing women who can bench my own weight. Quite the opposite. Me and my flatmates went to a bootcamp in the local park a few weeks back and I couldn't even manage a single press-up. It was pretty pathetic. I found myself at an intersection; keep training and better myself, committing to the cause; or never return and hope the embarrassment will one day fade. Obviously, I went with the latter.

James sighs. "Can you help me up now?"

"I did offer a minute ago."

"Well, I'm ready now."

I offer my arm out again. James takes it and applies some of his weight to pull himself into a sitting position but, *shit*, he's heavy, I topple forwards, landing on his bare chest with a thwack.

"Argh!" he cries out as I panic, pushing off him with both hands on his chest. He grabs me, squishing me tight to him. "Stop. Stop moving. Just stay there. Argh, that's so painful."

"I'm sorry…"

His arms bunch around me, squeezing. "Just don't move. No more moving."

"Ok…" My eyes are wide, my cheek flush with his cool bare skin. Well, this is intimate. I try very hard to stay still. The issue is, at my very core, I'm a chronic fidgeter. It's bad enough I haven't had a phone to scroll through over the last few days – that usually allows me to sit still for a while, but the chances of me staying totally still for long are always going to be slim. A phantom fly lands on my forehead and I whip my hand up to get rid of it.

"Stay. Still."

"It's impossible," I complain.

"You're the worst," he groans.

I sigh, trying to go to my happy place whilst I wait for him to release me again. We're going to get cold out here eventually. Then I think of a clever idea. "Whilst I have you," I say.

"Whilst you have me? Are we on a Teams call?"

"Whilst I'm on top of you…"

"Gawd, don't say that!" he moans.

I laugh. "Ok, whilst you hold me captive, whatever, can I ask you something?"

"You're going to anyway."

"True. What's your long-term plan for The Starr Agency?"

"My *long-term plan*?"

"Yeah. Like where do you see it in ten years?"

James scoffs. "Well, if I'm still there in ten years will you do me a favour and shoot me? I really don't think my mental health can handle that."

"Why not? You're not seeing all this hard work now as a long-term investment? Or strategy?"

"Hell no! Or well, yeah, in a way. None of it is for Starr though."

I scowl. "You're planning on leaving then?"

"I'm planning on travelling the world. Having enough money to buy my own house. Some nice cars. Get a decent retirement pot under my belt so I can call it quits at forty and hang out on a Mediterranean island for the rest of my days."

I'm quiet for a moment. I'm not sure why my head goes there but I compare his happy place with mine. They don't fit together too well… Of course they don't! This is James Gloatman. Why on earth is my brain even attempting to match up our long-term plans? It's not as if I want to do what he's doing – far from it. Maybe it's just one of those "last man at the end of the world" things. He's the only option out here, and therefore my horny mind is doing the math and equalling Gloatman.

Disgusting, really.

I mean, he's not necessarily disgusting. He has a nice body. His hair is kind of cute now it isn't gelled into his usual style. When it flops over his forehead, and he has to push it back, it makes me want to reach out and tangle it in my fingers. Just thinking about it makes my hands tingle.

Must be the vodka talking. I'm beer goggling.

"What about you? What's your plan?" he asks, still holding me tight to his chest.

"Well, obviously, part of it was to grow the image and awareness of the brand. Make The Starr Agency the real go-to musical event organiser. Find new revenue streams and more but I guess…" I pause, biting my lip.

"What?"

"My vision sort of planned on you being there. Despite you being the worst person in the office, you're also pretty good at your job. The hospitality sales are nearly always on budget and you're brilliant at finding new revenue streams."

"I know."

I laugh and roll my eyes. James grunts as I accidentally move a leg. "Always so, *so* humble, Gloatman."

"It's one of my strengths," he says. "What about you?"

"What do you mean?"

"Where do you see yourself in ten years?"

"Hmm…" I consider telling him about my happy place since he told me his. And yet, I decide not to. It feels like we've healed some long-weeping wounds between us in the past twenty-four hours, but that doesn't mean I'm ready to get *that* vulnerable. It's bad enough I've divulged as much as I have – this is *precisely* why I'm not a heavy drinker. "That's easy. I'm going to be a director at Starr."

James, once again, says nothing about the promotion, letting the conversation run dry. I suspect he doesn't think I've got it in me to be a director. Either that or he dreads the thought of me becoming his boss. But the silence I've been met with since he told me not to set my hopes on it the other day seems to be getting louder in my head. Is he hiding something from me? Does he know something

I don't? I'm about to ask him. I'm about to push him for his opinion and demand to know what it is he doesn't like about my plan, when he shivers beneath me. The remaining ounce of empathy I have for him and our situation overrides my ability to fight with him. Instead, I lift myself up and put on a brave face.

"Come on," I say. "Let's work out how we're going to get you back to the tent."

Thirteen

It took us a long and gruelling time to get James back into the tent. Initially, he managed to use me as a leaning post to guide his feet back up the slope, wincing and groaning the whole way. I pointed out, helpfully, that he wouldn't be able to stand if it was a broken back, so respectfully, he was probably being a big baby. He slithered to the ground outside the tent, hissing like a snake. Then, wiggling as a half-squished worm might, he somehow managed to get himself inside the tent and in his sleeping bag, where he promptly fell back to sleep.

I wake first, the promise of morning light pushing through the thin material. I yawn, and then I realise James has both hands on me, his fingers twisted into my baggy t-shirt. If I didn't know it was James, I'd find it very endearing. Boyish, even. The need to hold onto something in his sleep, like I'm his teddy bear. I forcefully push away any of the feelings this is trying to stir up in me. I blink across at his sleeping face, relieved he can't see how I'm reacting. He is so relaxed in slumber, his hair sticking out at hundreds of different angles. I stifle a laugh, biting my lip. His eyelashes are offensively long. Always something I've found rude in men – they don't *need* long lashes, it's such a waste. In the morning light, I can't help but admire how beautiful his features are.

God, am I really suggesting James is beautiful? I mean, I have always liked the little bump on his nose. It suits him. He's this perfectly smart, suited man, but he's *clearly* not perfect. Just like his nose.

I sigh. I need some fresh air. My "end of the world" horniness is going to get me in serious trouble if I don't escape the confines of this tent.

Cool down, lady.

I unravel myself from James' grip carefully, trying not to wake him. He grunts, turning himself slowly away from me. I take that as a good sign. His back can't be too injured if he's rolling over in his sleep.

Pulling on my trousers, socks and trainers, which at this point are working up all sorts of aromas, I unzip the tent and emerge under a glorious morning sky. Long strips of fluffy white clouds smear the rich blue landscape as if they've been painted there with a fat brush. I stretch my arms upwards, sensing that familiar post-drinking body ache. It could also be from all the walking and the fact I was dragged down water rapids yesterday, but, in an attempt to start the day positively, I push that from my mind. It's impossible not to notice the foreign feeling in my shin though. I can't bring myself to check on my wound just yet. Hopefully it hasn't got infected overnight.

I take our bottles down to the little lake and fill them, remembering how we washed my bloody knee into the same water the day before. However it is clear to the bottom now, and I noticed the lake is fed by downhill streams, so I assume it's ok since this must be fresh hill water. I think about it for another minute, scrunch my face and decide if we die out here from water poisoning, at least this whole stupid journey is over and my parents can sue the bejesus out of Michael.

When I get back, I take a seat on the floor beside the almost completely burnt-out fire, and start returning the ground to how it was before we arrived. I've seen on adventure shows like *Bear Grylls* that you should leave it all the way you found it. I aspire to be a non-destructive human being to the best of my ability.

James makes a wailing sound from inside the tent. When he finally emerges a few minutes later, he looks adorably awful. His face is scrunched, one eye still struggling to open against the bright morning light. He doesn't sit down, slowly pacing around the spot we've claimed as our own, doing strange stretches with slow movements.

"I'd offer you a coffee if I had one. Except if I had one, I'd drink it myself," I say helpfully.

James grunts in response.

The silence is dragging, it's making me sweat. I need to get a response out of him before I start to squirm. "At least you haven't broken your back?"

More grunting.

"Hopefully the castle isn't much further now?"

He gives me a look, squinting down at my seated position. "Are you trying to fill the silence?"

"All you have to do is reply with actual words and it soothes me."

"You're incredibly high maintenance."

I pout. "I'm not... I just..." Meh. It's too early to argue and he's clearly in a worse than usual grump. I start packing up all our stuff into the bags, taking the tent down and offering him a protein bar. He takes it, still refusing to sit down, walking a little further towards the lake to glare out at the scenery, doing his Austen hero stance.

It's nothing personal, Fliss. Sometimes people get grumpy, and it isn't you who caused it. You aren't responsible for other people's feelings.

James peers over his shoulder and catches me watching him. I blush, warmth pooling through me. Why am I embarrassed? Was I checking him out? Was he checking me out? Am I officially losing my mind? I kneel on the ground to cram the tent into its packaging. Shrugging my own bag onto my shoulders, I pick up James' to meet him down by the lake. I take one last look across the place we camped to check nothing has been left behind.

It's as if we were never there.

"Here," I say. "Do you think you'll be able to carry it?"

"Yeah. Sorry I called you high maintenance just now. I didn't mean it. You're not. And you didn't have to pack everything up on your own."

"Well, it's done now."

James nods, giving me a look. His gaze catches on mine. I take a deep breath as his eyes flit down the length of me then away back to the river so fast I almost can't trust it even happened. He's definitely checking me out. I know he was. He must be suffering from "last two people" syndrome as well. Poor soul. Let's hope our horny arses can make it to the castle without doing anything we'll regret.

"Better get going," I say, striding off in the direction we think we should be heading in. At this point, who even knows. We don't have a compass. Our map skills are so wanting we're essentially having to guess and hope for the best. Our generation have been spoiled with Google Maps and Citymapper. We don't have the same navigation skills as our parents. I remember watching from the back seat of our car as a map the size of the windscreen would be held up, twisted and argued over as they worked out which road to take next. I haven't had to do that in forever.

James stumbles along behind me, dragging his feet. Every now and again, his foot catches on a stone or a lump of grass, and he trips or sends something flying.

"So," James says out of nowhere. "What was your worst date?" I wonder if he's now trying to fill the silence for a reason, or if he is considering my need to fill the silence. Maybe he feels bad for snapping at me this morning.

I don't look back at him as I respond. "Mini golf. Two years ago. Guy got so angry with his lack of skills, he threw his putter through a window."

"Jeez." I'm pleased when I hear James snort a laugh. "You?"

"Few months ago, I went out for a nice dinner with this girl on a dating site. Was all going really smoothly. She was alright. Funny, pretty, had some decent banter. Then she started telling me about her boyfriend."

"What?!" I laugh.

"Yeah. It was like her kink or something."

"What!?"

"I don't know. Clearly, I got caught up in something. She wanted me to go back with them. I'm up for some shit but that's too much even for me."

I'm gawping at the path ahead. His story doesn't surprise me. There were several dates I had myself where it was pretty obvious the guy was fielding calls from other women. Sad part is, they were usually the ones most keen to meet up again. Lowers your opinion of people in general.

"I hate dating. I hardly do it these days. It's far too stressful," I say.

"Stressful?"

"Very. You just never know where you stand, or what the other person's expectations are. Some dates would be going great then I'd suggest splitting the bill and the conversation would nosedive. The whole vibe would change. I really thought our generation was better than that."

"Fragile masculinity."

"It is. But it's more than that, it symbolises, to them, that the date isn't going to be simply transactional. I'm worth more than a meal."

"You are."

A warm swell surrounds my heart, squeezing it. I bite the inside of my cheek. "I know. That's why I've given up. Also, I swear none of these guys know what they want or even what they like. They can barely talk about themselves or their lives. It's all very superficial and boring."

James is laughing. Without turning I can almost hear his head shaking, and his eyes rolling. "I know where you're coming from." He pauses. "What *do* you want then?"

"I'm not telling you."

"Ok, I'll guess. You probably have quite a list for dates to pass before they're even considered. So, must be above a certain height. Must have good teeth. Must have a decent job or working towards a career. Must have similar interests. Am I about right?"

"Yes..." I admit. "Apart from the height thing. So far, I'm

yet to meet a man shorter than me, but if I did, it wouldn't necessarily put me off. As long as they were confident in themselves. I'm not about propping up egos. And I'm not wasting my time on someone who still lives with their mum. Or if they do, doesn't even have a plan to leave."

James snorts. "Ok, once you get on the date... Must want... marriage?"

"No, actually." I shrug as I step across a small ditch in the ground. "Must be willing to commit long term. I want someone to share a mortgage with."

"How romantic."

"And I want a dog. Something like a cavapoo or corgi."

"I can see that."

"They don't even have to want kids. I don't even know if *I* want them yet," I add. "And I do find some guys are really put off by my career. So they need to have their own professional ambitions and be supportive of mine."

"Yeah, I can imagine."

I stop, turning to face James. He steps right up close, his face barely inches from mine. I'm suddenly thankful we've had toothpaste in our bags and been using it twice a day. His minty breath blows down across my nose. I find myself locked in his blue eyes, watching how his dark hair hangs down across his eyebrows.

I clear my throat. What was I going to say? I stare into his eyes and then blurt, "Why do you say that?" My voice doesn't sound like mine. My limbs are buzzing, my fingers tingling. Either that water from the lake is finally getting into my blood and I'm about to die, or I'm having a weird meltdown.

"Some guys are intimidated by successful women."

"Oh. Right. I know," I say. And then for some mad unknown reason, I ask, "Are you?"

James takes a moment to answer. "No. Although *you've* been known to intimidate me from time to time. You're a lot of things I always wanted to be."

I'm very cautious of my breathing right now. It doesn't sound normal. It sounds choppy. Desperate. My eyes drop to James' lips. I've never noticed how pink they are. Slightly parted. Kissable. I bite my bottom lip, imploring my sex-starved brain to silence itself. "Like what?"

"Educated. Positive. Funny."

"You find me funny?" I interrupt.

"And annoying," he adds to keep me grounded.

I laugh in a breathy way, forcing myself to look away, focussing on a patch of pink wildflowers swaying softly in the breeze. James' eyes are on the side of my face, I feel trapped by them. I can't look back now, or I might actually lose my mind. I'm not in control of my own body. This is really quite unacceptable.

Must remember that not only is this a work trip – granted, it's a terrible, dangerous work trip – but James is my colleague – a colleague, until about five hours ago, I absolutely could not stand. I can't *want* him. And I certainly cannot allow these thoughts to get the better of me. He should be firmly set aside in the no-go zone in my head. I hate him, don't I? He ruins everything. He adds to my stress and anxiety all the time in our normal daily lives. So, why does telling myself this make me flush even more?

"I kind of like how you're not always thinking about money," he says. "I wish I could do that. You know, find pleasure in other things. For me, having money has always been this insatiable need. It can be really toxic. It makes you do things you're not proud of."

I can't help myself. I look back to read his face. Connecting with his eyes once again sends a shot of sensation through to the spot between my legs. Instinctively, I cross them. James catches the movement, dropping his eyes.

This is so, so inappropriate.

And then he steps even closer. I panic, putting my hands between us. They land on his torso and because he's simply much bigger than me, it ends up producing the opposite effect of pushing him away and has me stumbling backwards. He grabs my arms to steady me.

Oh hell.

Now he's holding onto me. Too close. We must look like a couple on a romantic hike. At least nobody is going to see it.

Fliss, wake up!

I shake myself out of whatever the hell is happening here, twisting out of his grip and striding off again, way too quickly. I seal my lips shut, willing this persistent buzz in my body away. James jogs gently to catch me up, as if he waited a few moments to gather himself, a slight hitch in his breathing.

The first signs of civilisation we encounter are the occasional grey stone walls. They're scattered about at random, as if they used to have a purpose holding something in or out, but now they've crumbled and only the best parts of the walls remain. We cross a stream, James helping me through again, this time far more successfully than the river. We then follow it until we finally reach a bridge over a brook.

The bridge is another sign of human existence. The only problem is it doesn't look as if anyone has crossed it in hundreds of years. Clearly it was once a track of some sort, there's an underlying sturdiness that suggests a dirt road. Now mother nature has reclaimed it, saplings growing on top of the bridge as well as under. A sign of how long the roots have been able to plant themselves.

"It looks safe enough to cross," James says, leading the way.

It's wide enough that it was probably designed for carriages. I trust it was once able to hold the weight of horses and therefore is capable of carrying two humans. However, my faith in there being a fully functioning castle hotel is diminished. I'm about to vocalise this to James, but he walks steadily on ahead with a sense of purpose.

As the castle finally comes into view, my heart drops like an anchor thrown from a ship. It's a total ruin, complete with toppled turrets and massive gaping holes. It's surrounded by thick forest, eagerly encroaching on the structure, more unruly saplings and weeds claw back the space, claiming what was once theirs. Even if it was hundreds of years ago.

"This would've been a home," James says, peering up at the slanted tops.

"What makes you say that?"

"There's no moat. It's not a hill fort. There are practically zero safety measures. Looks like they have some arrow slits in that tower over there, but this forest is ancient. No way they would've used this for battle. It was someone's home. Or maybe a hunting lodge."

"How do you know that?"

James shrugs. "I read quite a lot of medieval history books as a teenager. Believe it or not, but I may have been a bit of a nerd back then. Now I mostly watch historical documentaries instead."

I nod, listening. It's good to know he's got other interests outside of work. That he's a whole human being. James ventures further into the ruins, touching the walls as he goes. Ivy hangs down from what looks like a collapsed second floor. "Be careful," I say. Who knows when a wall might fall on top of him when he's that close.

"Don't pretend you care about me now, Felicity," he says in jest.

Oh, crap. Yes, caring about James all of a sudden would be a real one-eighty. Most importantly, we can't let Michael think his insane task succeeded. "Just don't fancy being left with a dead body in a rural, creepy-arse, derelict castle," I shout at his disappearing back. "Seriously? You're abandoning me?"

He doesn't reply, fading in between the walls. I hug myself, a dreary dread pouring through me. A gust of wind pushes through the dense, dark trees surrounding us. They're so close together you can see the spider webs intertwined. They creak as they sway, branches colliding in an ominous crackling. I shudder. I have no choice but to follow him in.

I take tentative steps towards the "home" as James called it, listening out for his footsteps whilst also hoping any long-ago residents aren't still occupying the halls. It's not a huge castle. It sort of reminds me of where Drew Barrymore's character in *Ever After* would meet the prince. All hanging ivy, gorgeous shadows and that real rich unknown history charming the walls. So much so, as I walk under an archway, stepping down into what must have been one of the old rooms, I disturb a flutter of small white butterflies. They surround me, lifting up into the rafters. I stop, mesmerised.

"James?" I call out.

My body is tense in here on my own. Has he come this way, or not? My imagination is running away with me, seeing things I'm not really seeing. The shapes of trees swaying through gaps startle me, playing tricks on my mind. The call of an animal nearby has me freezing with fear. Are there predators out here? I'm pretty sure they culled wolves from the Scottish landscape some time ago but now I'm worried I got that snippet of information wrong.

I wait, standing stock still, but I don't hear so much as a twig snap under James' shoe. Has he already fallen down a hole or been crushed by something? My lungs accelerate as I move to search harder, quicker, spinning under more archways, up and down unstable steps, into courtyards and through pitch-black tunnels.

I stop when I see a stained-glass window of greens, blues and purples still enclosed perfectly in its frame, the outer wall completely gone. A man and woman, embracing passionately, stare back at me, as if I'm intruding on their intimate moment.

That's when something touches me from behind and my heart explodes. I spin on the attacker, launching myself backwards with a high-pitched scream.

Instantly, the attacker stops, crunching over with laughter.
Gloatman.

"Arsehole! You nearly gave me a bloody heart attack!"

This only makes him laugh harder. Big, gulping belly laughs.

"You're such a shit. Honestly." I hold a hand over my recovering heart. His laughter, despite being irritating as hell, starts to rub off on me and I find myself smiling like an idiot. "What happened to the flippin' castle hotel thing, hey? Can I say I told—"

"Don't!" James says, straightening up to his full height again and giving me a daring grin. His eyes connect with mine, the fire between us fuelling up for a fight or... I don't know. Just fuelling. "Don't you *dare* say it," he breathes, our faces so close now that I can see the flecks of gold in his irises.

"But I did te—" I start to say as James' lips collide with mine.

Fourteen

His large hand curls around the side of my chin and cheek, fingers lacing through the knotted hair at the top of my neck. Tingles surface on my skin everywhere he touches, sprinting downwards to inappropriate places. He kisses me hard, as if he's been starved all day and I'm the only thing that can replenish him. His lips push against mine as he steps into my body, my back butting up against a cold wall.

I'm in shock.

Gloatman is kissing me. Me. *Oh my god! Gloatman is kissing me!* James Gloatman. And I'm doing absolutely nothing about it.

He places his spare hand on the wall beside me for balance as his other hand curves further behind my head, tipping it up gently. I realise what he's doing. He's trying to progress this kiss. He wants us to use tongues. And hell, I'm up for it. I'm clenching my core as shivers fly up and down my spine like one of those drop towers at an amusement park.

But, no, no, no, no… This cannot be.

This is madness. We must stop. We must.

His tongue traces the crease of my lips, inviting me to

open for him, and that's it. I laugh. I laugh against his lips whilst he's still kissing me.

Oh, shit. This isn't going to land well. I'm fairly certain it's a rule you can't laugh when someone tries to kiss you – same goes for laughing during sex.

James stops what he's doing, slowly extracting himself from me. He takes a few steps back as my laughter grows harder. I cover my face to hide it, but the damage is already done, I see it written all over his face.

"I'm sorry," I squeak.

"Oh, no. No. Go ahead and destroy my ego. I know it's one of your favourite pastimes." James' tone is jokey, softer than usual, as if I have, in fact, destroyed his ego. Oh, well, it has always been a life goal of mine. I never thought it would be this easy to achieve though.

"No, no. It's not you. Well, it is you. It's just… *This*…" I gesture between us. "*What?* Why? How? No… We can't. Can we? Oh god, this is weird. I hate you. But I sort of like you too," I say. "Can't believe I'm even saying this out loud."

"You're making zero sense, Felicity," he says, rubbing his chin.

"Ok, sorry, what I mean is…" I laugh again. Christ my cheeks are hot. So are my thighs. *Get a grip, Fliss*. I sigh, calming myself. After a few deep breaths I say, "Do you think this is just a reaction to this situation?" I'm overusing hand gestures. I link my fingers together behind my back to hide them. "It's so intense, this forced proximity, the last-two-people-in-the-world thing. Have we just succumbed to our baser desires?"

James blinks. He cups his cheeks as he blows out a breath. Then he laughs too. "Oh god, that's it, isn't it?"

"*See.*"

"Argh, this is embarrassing. So, you weren't laughing at the kiss, then?"

Oh, man. I've really bruised his ego. His self-conscious thoughts are manifesting both verbally and as worried facial expressions. Who knew he had them? "Oh, well. No. It's the situation."

"Right," he nods, looking around like he's lost and just found himself in a ruined castle in Scotland. How did he get here? How did *I* get here? Oh, yes. Our crazy boss. "I'm sorry. If you weren't into it, if I overstepped."

A wild buzz spreads through my limbs and cheeks. "No, not at all, that's sort of why I laughed."

"No?" He frowns. "You're still not making any sense."

"No, as in I was dangerously into it… But you're James Boatman. You're the worst person I know. You're a bloody nightmare. I can't kiss you. You can't kiss me. That's not a thing we can do."

He nods. "Dangerously into it?"

I laugh. "Why is that the only thing you heard?"

"Hmm, only bit that mattered, really." He swallows, his face suddenly serious again. He reverts back to his Austen hero stance, as if he walked straight here from a seventeenth-century battle and is surprised to find his hunting lodge has burnt down in flames. With a light feathering of stubble on his chin and his hair falling around his ears, it's almost believable. Unfortunately, his black t-shirt and walking trousers tarnish the image.

"What about you?" I say, my voice low. I suddenly realise

that I'm scared of his answer. I've put myself into the more vulnerable position. He knows exactly what I'm thinking but as usual his thoughts remain enigmatic.

He steps closer to me where I'm leaning against the wall, until his body is once again flush with mine. I have to tip my head back to look at him which means my body arches into his. *Wanton wench!* James' breathing isn't normal. It's choppy, harsh to the ear. His eyes lock with mine, blue fire sending shockwaves to my core.

"I think I'm dangerously into this too," he says, as his knee slides between my legs, his thigh pressing against me. I gasp as he leans in closer.

This time his lips only trace mine. It's so gentle, so subtle, I barely even feel it. His minty breath plays on my senses as his hand finds its way back to my cheek, fingers tickling my skin so gently I squirm as sensations burst then explode outwards like mini fireworks.

He comes back again, gently. Taking his time. His lips press on mine as if I'm made of sugar paper and might rip if he's too hard.

I think I know exactly what he's doing. He's playing with me. He's daring me to kiss him back. And I'm completely up for winning the game he's started. But I'm not sure what the winning response is… Maybe I should pull away. That doesn't feel right. Instead, I grab at his top, the material bunching in my grip. I finally get my hands in his hair, tugging his face closer to mine. Dear lord, it's better than I'd imagined. His hair is long enough, soft enough, that I can properly weave it in between my fingers. I groan into his mouth as we both open to take it further.

His tongue collides with mine in this big hot mess. He

holds me tighter, his spare hand roaming down the side of my body, finding my shoulders, my waist, then curving over my butt and pulling me into him.

We kiss harder, longer, desperately. It's quite literally the sort of kiss you'd expect from two people who are as horny as hell, going at it at the end of the world. That's when I take hold of James' bottom lip with my teeth, nipping and pulling it into my mouth. I feel something hard bridge between us and James grunts in this guttural way before pushing off me. I release him, wondering if I've gone too far.

He turns his back to me. I stand stunned, waiting for the butterflies in my core to settle down, the buzz in my limbs to fade. My breathing too, is frantic. I place a hand over my heart to feel it jumping in my chest.

That's when he starts to laugh.

"Now *you're* laughing?" I say.

He turns to face me with a challenging glow in his eyes. "You bit me."

"Yeah... Sorry, it's sort of a party trick of mine. It doesn't work for everyone."

"It worked, don't worry."

Oh wow, this is mental. I rack my brain for ways to change the conversation. When I do speak, my voice is squeaky. "I think, on that note, we should probably find somewhere to camp. This place is going to turn into midge city in about twenty minutes."

James sighs. Nods. Then follows me out of the ruins and we walk in silence, calming all our senses as we seek a spot to pitch up for the night.

*

We find a piece of land next to a quietly trickling stream. It's covered in little stones and rocks we move in order to provide a semi-comfortable space to lie on. The grey skies have finally broken and although the rain that dampens our clothing again removes the issue of midges, it provides the same result. We need shelter.

Once our tiny tent is pitched and ready, we both climb in, James lying down on his back, groaning as the pain from his fall last night and the long walk today start to take effect. He fidgets, rolling from side to side slowly trying to find a comfortable position. I sit up cross-legged. This is partly because, clearly, there is a chemical reaction occurring between us now and I feel that the more space between us (albeit entirely limited due to the puny tent we were provided with), the less likely it is a reaction will occur.

James finally rolls onto his back in defeat, blinking at the ceiling. "This is our last night out here, right? We can't be that far now... right?"

"I'd get the map out so we could play guess where we probably are again, but I don't see much point."

"Please give me hope."

"I see. You wanted the answer you want to hear, not the likely, most probable one?"

"Exactly."

"Yes. We'll make it back tomorrow. Can't you hear all that city traffic? We're practically in the suburbs," I add as the sound of more raindrops *tap, tap, tap* on the material we're sheltered by.

James grins. It's a calm grin. "Could be worse."

I try not to accept that as a compliment but granted it's difficult. We've been at each other's throats for so long, it seems crazy he might actually be enjoying spending time with me. I lean over to grab a protein bar from the bottom of James' bag because I can feel the early evening hunger coming on. When I hear his stomach rumble too, I laugh, pass him the first one, before getting another for me. We chew in silence, pausing to take gulps of water from our bottles whilst we listen to the world outside our tiny tent.

James clears his throat. "Do you think I'm an uncle yet?"

"Oh, you must be. How many days has it been?"

"This will be our third night out here."

"There's no way labour can last three days. Right? *Right?*"

He laughs, rubbing his face and pushing his hair back, holding his arm above his head. "Nah, I think they get surgical before then." He gulps, his face dropping to a serious expression. "I hope she's ok."

"I'm sure she is."

"I should really be there. If not for her, for my sisters too. And Mum. She'll be losing her mind if anything is wrong."

"I'm sure everything's fine."

James nods. "Yeah, you're right. Sophie is strong."

"Like you," I say. And what? Is he strong? Do I think that or am I just trying to make him feel better? I can feel a blush creep into my cheeks. I look away, my eyes settling on his socked feet at the end of the tent.

He sighs. "I'm not strong out of choice. Mum had a… bad patch… after my dad absconded. She was left completely on her own with four kids on a nurse's salary and a shit heap of a house. I don't know when it happened, but I just started taking charge. Somehow it felt like the natural thing to do.

"I was the one who got all the girls out for school in the morning. I made sure we had dinner on the table. We mostly ate jacket potatoes and beans on toast because it was all we could afford. I'd just turned fourteen when I started working weekends at the shop, and sixteen when I started working full time." He's staring at the ceiling of the tent when I realise my gaze has strayed back to his face. "I'm strong because there wasn't another option for us, my family. I wasn't going to let anything happen to my sisters."

I nod. "You didn't have to do that though. You're strong because you chose to be, despite what you think. Some people never improve their situation, or else use it to enable their own bad behaviour. You've done more than take care of your sisters. You've worked hard to get where you are now."

James grins again as he swallows. I watch his throat working. I have this sudden animalistic urge to bend over and kiss him there. Feel the taste of his skin on my tongue.

Maybe I should go and stand in the rain for a bit. Cool off.

"What about you?" he asks. "Why are you so brave?"

"I'm categorically not brave, James."

"You are. You have no problem standing up to me. You get up and present in front of huge teams and really important client meetings. It's like it doesn't even bother you."

I shrug. "That's *work* brave. Not *life* brave."

"What's the difference?"

"At work I'm Head of Marketing. I know what I'm talking about and I'm confident enough not to feel nervous doing those things. People respect me enough to listen. I'm not necessarily trying to prove anything. Sure, I want to progress. But I know I'm nailing it. In life? I'm fairly certain I'm failing quite spectacularly."

I laugh at the absurdity of it all. "I live with four full-grown adults in a three-bed flat covered in mould we all just pretend isn't there for our own sanity. Surely, by the time you're Head of Marketing you should be able to afford to rent your own place? My parents honestly cause me constant stress and anxiety. Why can't my mum just figure out some of her own life issues without using me as her personal therapist? And why can't Dad make some good decisions for once? I so often feel like I'm the bad guy, coming in to tell them off or call them out on their shit."

I close my eyes tight, breathing slowly, as I realise I've wound up a pang of anxiety. It's sitting heavy across my abdomen. I want to take all those words back, because compared to James' story, they're nothing at all.

"If it makes you feel any better, my mum's the opposite, always breathing down my neck," James says. "She loves to remind me that my sisters have settled down."

"Bet you pay her hardly any notice."

He shrugs, turning his head to look at me. It's very intimate being this close as a cloud must cover what's left of the sun, blocking out the light. His eyes are as dark as midnight. "It's a stark reminder that I've had my heart broken. It's like she either forgets or doesn't think it bothers me anymore."

I can't look away. I really think I should. Because clearly it does bother him. Whatever happened in his past. My heart rate is increasing, as if I'm facing some sort of threat.

Maybe this is what exhilaration feels like. I've never had this with a man before. I don't know why he's opening up to me so much. Allowing me to see something he normally wouldn't.

He grins softly. "We're a pathetic pair, huh?"

I just shrug lightly. I think we both know we're not pathetic really. We're just both at a stage where we're trying to figure out our lives.

I feel a shiver rack through me as the temperature drops. It's getting later. The sun is fading, and with the thick blanketing of cloud it's getting darker earlier than usual. The rain picks up. It's so loud in the tent, thundering down on top of us, I can barely hear myself think. The stream nearby is picking up pace. Wind rattles through the trees. I hug my knees closer to my chest.

James leans across to the zipped-together sleeping bag that's been shoved in the corner. He pulls it upwards, laying it out and climbing in. As he slides his trousers off with much shuffling and removes his t-shirt, he says, "Climb in before you get too cold."

Clearly, he's now in tune with my body.

Warning signals go off in my head.

You'll be back at work with him next week, Fliss. You'll have to face him. You'll have to face everyone knowing what you did. That's if you do something. Probably just don't do something. Don't give in to those urges.

But I am cold. And James, by experience, is very warm. I strip down to my knickers and vest like I did the previous nights. He pretends not to be looking. I climb in beside him, trying and failing to keep my hands safely at my sides. By default, my hand happens to be in the same place as his crotch and I swipe it with my hand before knowing what I've even done.

James sucks in a breath.

"Oh, god, I'm sorry. That was an accident."

He nods, repositioning himself.

"Are you in much pain today?" I ask, trying to change the conversation swiftly.

"It's manageable."

"Good, because we ran out of vodka."

"You drank it all for your leg. How's the cut feeling now, by the way?"

I peek down, which is pointless because now I'm covered by my sleeping bag. "It's a little sore but it's fine. Should probably see a doctor about it once we're out of here."

"You'd probably have a fever by now if it was infected."

"Yikes. Could you imagine?"

James rolls over again, trying to find a comfortable position. His shoulder wedges up against mine. Then his leg is against my leg, the hairs rubbing on my smooth skin. The sensation has me clenching my core. I bite my lip. I stay on my back, closing my eyes in the dimming light, willing the buzz away.

I need to not fancy this man.

He doesn't stop moving, however, shifting this way and that. It's only small movements but it's enough to get me properly riled up. "Oh my god, James. *Please*. Please stop moving."

James laughs awkwardly, breathy. "I'm trying to find a position where I can make you warm but not get turned on by your body being so close."

I laugh too. "How's that going?"

"*So* badly."

"Oh, sod it. Should I just go and sleep in the rain? Should we hike in the dark?"

"If only we had some distress signals."

"What? Get rescued by helicopters because we're too horny to be left alone right now?"

James' head twists so he can scan my face properly. My lips part as our eyes collide. There's so much hunger there. So much need in both of us. I think it would seriously take hurricane winds to pull us apart and prevent this from happening.

I act first this time, turning onto my side so my hand can loop through the gorgeous dark hair at the back of his head. He makes the most throaty sound I've ever heard as he leans down to take my lips with his. His long, heavy leg links between mine as he seems to forget any of the pain and kisses me back with ardour.

Fifteen

James groans into my mouth as the kiss gets hotter and harder and just as wanton as it was back in the castle. It's totally inappropriate for me to want to do this with *this* man. I scold myself royally whilst carrying on regardless. I'm thankful we both cleaned our teeth before eating our protein bars – his breath is still freshly minted as I take hold of his bottom lip with my teeth again, like before, tugging until he's cursing with pleasure.

Whilst one hand plays in his hair, my other roams lower, feeling across his chest and the tangle of hairs there. James takes this as a cue to do the same thing, sweeping his long fingers down along my back, tracing my spine, until he's cupping my bum and sliding his warm palm under my knickers. He leaves it there. A dare. A challenge.

He's asking – *are we really doing this?*

And my answer, as I gasp into his mouth, is clearly, *yes*. Whatever yes means. It feels as if I have a raging fire whipping up through my core that needs to be soothed. There's a level of panic which tells me it's impossible. I can't be soothed. Not here. Not in this tent getting drenched on the outside. The wind is stroking the skin on our faces as it streams through the material, not strong enough to keep it out completely.

And in addition to the setting, there's a pressure, a disappointment, lingering before we've even begun because it's been so long since a man has really given me his time.

James is attentive now, slowing his kisses and venturing down my neck, touching points where my pulse meets my skin, lingering there until I'm squirming. He takes a pinch with his teeth, making me jump. I play his game, using my nails to scrape up his back. He arches and I know I've got him.

"God, *Felicity*, what're we going to do?" he whispers into my neck as he spreads more kisses there, nibbling over my collarbone. "What do you want *me* to do?"

"Anything," I say but there's an undertone of panic in my voice I can't even hide. Do I even know what I'm doing? It's genuinely been that long. I've been too busy, too stressed. But maybe this is what I've needed all along.

What if I do something wrong?

He must hear my hesitation because he freezes for a few seconds, as if he's considering his next move, then lifts his head to look at me. "What is it? You not into this now?" he asks gently, removing his hands from my body.

It's the worst thing he's ever done to me.

I shake my head violently. "No! God, no. I mean, *yes*. I'm into this. It's just..."

James' eyes bore down on me with concern, realisation slowly flitting over his face. He pushes his hair back from his forehead and that act alone makes me melt further into the ground. *God damn him and his sexy, floppy hair.* "Oh.

Right. What you told me yesterday about scaring men away for two years?"

I scrunch my face. "I don't think that's what I said."

"It was implied."

"Was it?"

James quirks his lips. "I refuse to believe it's because there was a lack of interest. Look at you, Fliss. And besides, are we really arguing right now?"

More compliments from James. Or at least I think they are. Maybe he's right about the scaring part though. Between work stress and life stress, I've been frightening men away this whole time. Maybe what I need right now is someone who is definitely not afraid of me to step straight through that invisible armour I've made for myself.

I take a deep breath as James kisses me again. This time slowly, deliberately, tugging at my bottom lip in the way I do but with more care. He cups my cheek and neck delicately as if he's cradling glass.

Slowly but surely, the fire that ebbed, as I started to worry, builds again.

Extracting my hand from his chest, he slides his fingers with mine, leaning up enough to kiss my knuckles, sending shots of fire straight to my core. The core that's now pulsing as if it's got its own heartbeat. I never knew knuckles could be sensitive like this. When he pops one of my fingers in his mouth, I feel it in my brain and my toes. Since when was this a thing? He takes another, his tongue rolling across them.

After releasing my hand, he carefully, slowly drops his hand lower. I close my eyes because, yes, I'm up for this, but, no, I can't have him looking at me with those intense eyes, because holy shit, Gloatman is about to be touching me. *Touching me*, touching me. And I'm totally up for it.

When he's almost there, he changes direction. It's brutal. Completely the sort of underhanded thing he would do. I whimper as he reaches down as far as he can on my left leg, circling the area he knows I want soothed but never actually giving me what I want. Whenever I think he's getting close, he moves away again. He strokes my belly button which makes me hop from my pelvis. His hand skirts the side of my waist, and back down before finally curving over the spot I need him to be touching *so, so* bad.

Then he snatches it away again. I gasp.

"You're teasing me," I moan as James laughs in this devilishly dark way that makes my ears tingle. He leans in close, his tongue and lips and teeth playing with sensitive spots behind my ears and down my neck until I'm squirming again. He finds my hand, purposefully holding it still over my stomach as he does so.

Then, because I'm desperate for something and really don't know what else to do, I twist my face in search of him. His lips find mine, colliding in passion. I find myself rocking my wanton hips into his body, trying with all my strength to move our hands lower.

"You want this now?" he whispers.

"Please."

He releases the lock on his elbow and moves our hands lower until he's tracing my clit with his fingers, under the thin material of my knickers. Then, as I begin to hum, closing my eyes tight again, he places my hand there, his pressed over the top of mine. "Show me," he says.

At first, I'm not sure he's serious. I wait for him to take

control again but he's busy now, kissing my neck, playing with the spots of pleasure I didn't even know existed. Steadily, I begin to circle myself in the way I usually do. The pressure builds gradually, James' fingers are quick to follow the movement. He groans as if me going along with his suggestion is as good as having outright sex.

I moan out loud too, totally uncontrolled, as a wave of pleasure rolls over me.

But we're not there yet. James is nibbling along my collarbone. His breathing is choppy, as if he too is experiencing my building eruption.

Slowly, his hand moves over mine. He lifts it again, taking it away from where I want it. He kisses my knuckles before placing it back on my chest. "I'll take it from here," he says. "You can trust me."

And, oh god, I really shouldn't trust Gloatman but here we are. I let him take over, his fingers roaming lower until he's in the same spot, moving gently over it in exactly the same way I did. But, oh.

He's so, so, *so* much better than me. Or is it just because it's not me? His fingers are warm as they move anti-clockwise. Occasionally, he dips lower, using my own moisture as natural lube. It's so bloody intimate. It's so wrong that it's James. But it feels so very right.

I bite my lip to prevent too many sounds from exiting my lips; my breathing is slower now and yet, louder, as if I'm running a race. "That's it," he says into my ear, sending shivers racking through me.

It's getting closer.

The pressure is rising now. It's building like there's a pool or a dam holding back a tidal wave.

I moan again.

He nibbles on my earlobe.

He's circling a little quicker now, waiting patiently for me to come undone. But I need something more. I need him to get meaner.

"More," I say.

"More what?" he asks. No panic in his voice. No offence taken that I'm asking for something. "I need you to tell me."

"Be meaner with it."

Be meaner with it?!

"Gladly," he says in that devilishly dark tone again, picking up the pace so suddenly and so abruptly I find myself thrusting into his hand. It all starts coming undone.

It's too much. The pressure and the intimacy and the whole damn bloody moment. I twist to escape. But James is prepared for this reaction. Before I know what's happened, he's got a strong thigh between mine. The hairs scratch on my skin exquisitely. He pins me, keeping pace the whole time. Not letting me escape. Not letting me roll away. He's entered this game with only one possible outcome.

And, *oh!*

The feeling washes through me exactly like an eruption. Boiling hot lava invading my veins. My body goes lax as the wild endorphins roll through me. I suck in a long breath as James slows his fingers, moving them further down to find a slick wetness between my legs. I can't help myself at this point. I roll onto my side as James' hand skirts up to my waist, holding onto me. I try to push my hand towards his boxers, but he stops me.

"No, it's ok," he says.

"But I want to."

James laughs now. I feel the sting of it in my chest.

"You don't want me to?" I ask, suddenly ridiculously self-conscious.

"God, it's not *that*," he says. "It's just we're in a tent in Scotland and all we've got are the condoms in the bag which Michael provided for us."

"Oh hell! Why would you remind me of *that*?" I say, a breathy laugh finding its way out of my mouth when I realise he's got a point.

"I tried not to…"

"Well, I can…"

"Fliss… I'm telling you it's fine. I'm too… It's too… If I let you down there, and you want more, I'm not going to be able to stop, which means using the condoms."

I cover my face with my hands, rolling onto my back again. I'm being typical Fliss. Overkeen to get a task done. Always feeling the need to return the favour. I mean, I *want* to. I could feel it against me the whole time, the gorgeous solidness of it through his boxers. I just sort of want to make him as vulnerable as he made me. But he's got a point. If we get too giddy now, surely that's just going to escalate until we're properly fucking, and then we have to use a condom that was supplied to us by our boss. What does that make us? *Seriously. What does that make us?* No, we can't do that.

But gawd, I really want to.

"Hey," James says, trying to remove my hands from my face. I finally submit but I know the colour in my cheeks is embarrassingly red. "You don't owe me *anything*. You did half the work anyway and I don't give to receive. I really enjoy giving. I promise. This sleeping bag massively restricts my abilities. There's a whole world of things I want to do to you right now. But not here."

I smile awkwardly. "Thank you?"

"Take it back," he says calmly. "You're literally not allowed to thank me. That is just a big fat no."

I want to say "then I owe you", but he's already said I don't. So, what now? I decide I may as well use the opportunity to play with his hair, wrapping my hands around his head and bringing his lips down to mine again.

We kiss slowly, dreamlike, until we're exhausted and collapse into a heap within the sleeping bag. Our limbs are entwined. Our hearts seem to be beating in unison. It's overwhelming to feel this close to someone. It's dangerous really. We aren't the people we are right now. I can feel something twinge in my heart, like an old violin string wound too tight at the thought of it ending. But it will end.

Has it really even begun?

Who are we beyond this tent? Who are we beyond this whole crazy adventure? We've never got along before. What's to say we can make this work when (or *if*, at this rate) we ever get back to normality? I've acted on my instincts instead of my head.

We both have. And now we'll have to suffer whatever the consequences are.

"Stop freaking out," James mumbles into my thick, bushy hair.

I laugh breathlessly. "How can you tell?"

"I can hear your brain. It's buzzing."

"Shut up."

"I'm serious. You actually hum a bit when you're overthinking."

"No, I don't."

He nuzzles in closer, tickling me with his fresh stubble. "I promise. You do. Stop thinking about it. Just let what happens, happen."

I don't respond after that. The weather has settled down again and we're bathed in total darkness. James reaches up behind us and fiddles with the zip. I'm unsure why he's doing it until I open my eyes. A bright sky, littered with stars, glows down on us between the thick trees. We stare at it in soft silence, watching its peaceful twinkling as we drift off to sleep.

Sixteen

It's the gentle murmur of voices that wakes me. At first, they're incorporated into part of my dream. I'm ordering a coffee, the sweet smell of delicious caramel lattes wafting into my nostrils. I ask for a millionaire shortbread to go with that too. Oh, how I long for sugar and caffeine. But the lady serving me is asking me questions. I keep blinking at her until I realise it's a man's voice coming out of her lips. I startle awake.

James is talking too. There are *two* voices.

"We're here on a work trip, of sorts. It was kind of unplanned and unexpected."

The other voice mutters, "Christ."

"Our boss is… insane. Thought it would be some kind of fun team-building challenge to drop us Londoners off in the middle of nowhere with two badly packed bags and a fifty-pound note."

"That's fucking wild," the man replies. "This area is hiking on steroids. It's for the pros."

"Mate, I know. We're a bit worse for wear. That was our third night."

"You're kidding? Hope you're going to sue."

James snorts. "We'll see, huh?"

"Well, look. You want to follow this path through the forest about another three miles and you'll find a road. Could hitch a lift from there."

"Yeah? Great. Cheers for that."

I turn around in the sleeping bag, and consider climbing out, but decide to leave James to the talking, partly because I must look like hell right now. Straight up cavewoman. My hair is all over the place. I occasionally touch it and can feel how knotted it has become. It's like in the noughties when we thought it would be a good idea to back brush our ponytails for discos, then spent three days washing and combing it back out.

Oh no. Last night. There's no hiding from it. We'll have to talk about it today. What happens now? What next? This *thing* we have going on between us. How do we work together on Monday?

James is still talking to the other voice. "Any chance you have a phone we could borrow?"

"Sorry, pal. When I go wild camping, I go wild."

"That's pretty mental," James mutters.

"Your boss didn't give you phones? How strange. Was he trying to kill you?"

"We had our own but mine died the first day out here and my... *hers*..." He coughs to clear his throat. This is going to be so awkward. He doesn't even know what to call me. "Got wet in the river."

"Ah, right," the voice replies with limited interest. "Well, like I said. An hour's walk in that direction will lead you to a pretty busy road. I'm sure someone'll help you out."

And with that, footsteps crunching across twig-strewn terrain fade off into the distance. When I don't hear any sound from James, only the rustling of leaves in the morning breeze, the trickle of the stream, I unzip the bottom of the tent and pop my head out. He's nowhere to be seen. But he can't be far. He was literally just talking to some random guy. I didn't make that up. Did I?

"James?" I call out.

"Yeah?" he replies within close proximity.

"Where are you?"

"Here." Helpful as ever.

I sigh, pulling on my clothes, not bothering with a bra just yet, using folded arms for support instead. I try to smooth down my hair a bit and wipe the eye bogeys away with my fingers. Then, climbing out into the morning sunshine, I'm instantly warmed in its generous glow.

Once I'm standing, he's pretty easy to spot. There, sitting comfortably in the middle of the stream, the water circling around him like he's a boulder in the way, is James Boatman. Almost naked, apart from his very damp boxer shorts now practically submerged.

I pull a humoured face. "What are you doing?"

He squints back at me, flicking his head to get his floppy black hair out of his eyes. I hate how it sets the butterflies off in my stomach. "Cooling off."

"Why?"

He gives me a bemused glance, tilting his head. He's leaning back in the water with both arms propped to hold him up. There's something very sexy, alluring, about it. He looks like he's posing for an eighteenth-century portrait by an opium-addicted artist who also writes poetry about treeline backdrops and valleys of hills, mountains and untouched nature for as far as the eye can see.

"Why do you think?" he asks, with a gentle grin.

"You run at an unnaturally high temperature?"

"Fliss."

"Yeah?"

"I woke up with a raging hard on."

Heat rushes up to my face. I raise my hands to cover it. But that's only going to make it more obvious. So, he does like me? Or is this just a standard morning thing? That's pretty normal, isn't it? Probably shouldn't overthink it.

"Wait… Were you sat like that when that guy walked past?"

He nods. "Yeah. He didn't blink an eye."

"Oh god." Now I'm laughing. This is ridiculous. James joins in too. There's this moment where we're both smiling at each other. Then we realise we're both smiling at each other and get really serious, swallowing in unison and busying ourselves with other things. James plays with the water. I fiddle with my hair.

"Did you hear about the road?" he asks, hardly even looking my way.

"Yeah."

"Shall we pack up and go?"

"Sounds like a plan."

Once we're packed up again, James has clothes on and we're both wearing our backpacks, we make off in the direction we were advised to. James had a quick look at my injury before we set off. He changed the leaf as he has every twelve hours or so. It's looking much better now. I wouldn't exactly recommend leaves as suitable gauze unless you have to, but it seems to be working for me.

My shoulders are burning today. James groans as he hoists his rucksack onto his back. All his muscles are aching since his fall. In hindsight, we're lucky it wasn't worse. Especially since we're both without our phones by this point. He's still carrying more than me. I feel sort of guilty about it. I'm a committed feminist, I should be sharing the load. That's why I calculated the ratios based on my weight, and a guessed weight for James, and decided, actually, I'm doing my fair share. But his tight facial features this morning suggest he's possibly in more pain than he's letting on.

The path dips into a new valley as we emerge from the forest. We stop as the vista before us opens up under the glorious sunshine, beams of light stretching lazily over the long patches of lush spring grass. Ahead of us, we can hear a low rumbling of cars. A promise of escape.

James looks back the way we came. "There's something magical about being the only people amongst such vastness, isn't there?"

"The magic is fading now, huh?"

He gives me a look, scrunches his forehead on a frown. "The low hum of exhausts isn't going to kill the magic."

Then, before I can say too much more, he takes my hand, squeezing as if to tell me this is going to be ok, then releases it again as we descend a gravelly, curving path in between ruts and swamps leading towards a car park about a mile in the distance.

*

Once we reach the main road, James confidently strides up to the edge where a black BMW is speeding towards us. The road has been carved through the Scottish Highlands in the most absurd way. Only humans could create something so unappealing to the eye, surrounded by such incredible natural beauty. It's a long, straight Roman road. We can see it goes on for miles, which suddenly hits me in this overwhelming sense of panic. How are we even alive? How did we, two city people surrounded by unlimited food outlets, taxis and trains and concrete, make it across so much of wild Scotland like this and live to tell the tale?

The first car does not stop. In fact, it speeds up, swerving James as if they half-expect him to throw himself in front of them. I wonder how we appear to passersby. I look down at myself: the stained ripped shirt material bandaged around my calf, the sweaty black top and scuffed, dirty shorts. My trainers are already split. Clearly, budget-priced versions. I peek across at James too, stood with his hand out, thumb up. His hair is completely wild, swirling around in the wind. His t-shirt, also black, is sweaty too, trousers ripped in two places. When did that happen?

Luck is not on our side whilst we look like this. Car after car passes by, giving us strange, slightly terrified glances. James, though, is totally unfazed by the rejection. Meanwhile, I'm dissociating from him with every step backwards from the edge of the road. When there's a gap in the cars he peers over his shoulder.

"What are you doing?" he calls.

"Dying from embarrassment."

"What? Why? Because we're trying to hitch a lift?"

"I've never been a hitchhiker before. It's mortifying!"

He laughs. "Oh, bloody hell, it's not that bad."

I cringe at him, decidedly disagreeing with his statement. This is about as awful as it gets. Especially, looking like this.

As more cars come over the hill in our direction, James steps out again, this time blocking more of the road. It's like he's playing a game of chicken. I can't help but wince as cars get closer, then dart around him. One, then another, then another.

"It's no use!" I shout. "Nobody is going to take us looking like this. We look like murderers from the wild."

James' shoulders droop. He looks back to me, squeezing his jaw. "Well, I guess we follow the road then. Have you got that map so we can work out which bloody direction we need to go in?"

I nod, whipping my bag off my shoulders and sliding the map out of one of the front pockets. It got partially ruined during the river incident. Luckily, we can just about make out the main points when we spread it out across a boulder on the side of the road. The gravel slides under my shoes as I lean over it.

"I reckon this is the road," I say, pointing to the long, straight line with only minor curves in it where it allows for rivers and lakes. "But I'm not sure where we are on it or what direction we're facing."

James crouches down beside me, his hair ruffling against my chin. It smells like the outdoors. Tree sap, mud and water. It's pretty sexy actually. I have no idea why. As if he can read my mind, he squints upwards, his blue eyes blinking at me, before looking back towards the road. More cars pass but they pay zero attention to us.

"I reckon that's the forest we camped in. Look, that's

the castle. So, if we keep travelling this way…" He uses his finger to demonstrate. "That should lead us to this town. Glenbonn. No idea what's there but they might be able to get us to this train station."

I peer at where his finger has landed. There is indeed a train station with a line that travels through mountains on its way back to Inverness. Not that that is even where Michael is, but at least there are taxis from there. We could probably use our money to get back to the hotel I assume he's staying in.

The things I have to say to that man… Then I think about the reason we're in this predicament in the first place. I still want to be promoted. I can see the long-term benefits, not to mention the rumoured six-figure salary.

Being a director is what I've longed for. So why do I suddenly have a sick, twisting feeling in my stomach when I think about Michael and returning to Starr. I guess this whole thing has shone a new, unflattering light on him.

"I'm so done with walking," I mumble, wiggling my aching toes. The blisters my boots caused at the start are practically raw open wounds now. "How far do you think it'll be?"

I half-expect James to groan and come back with something sharp and annoyingly witty but instead I get a face of sympathy. "That's why I was trying to get us a lift. You look beat."

Oh, so he has noticed how dreadful I look. My heart sinks. It was all pity last night. That's why he didn't let me return the favour. I bite my lip to force away the threat of tears. James must sense my shift in mood because he stands and pulls me into him. At first, I'm not entirely sure what is happening as his arms wrap around me. My face is squished into his shoulder. I ride his chest as he takes a deep breath. He rests his chin on the top of my head as I slowly relax, melting into him. It's nice. This hug. I feel safe, and warm, and oddly protected.

"What's this for?" I mumble into his chest.

"I needed a hug. And I think you did too."

"Mmm," I agree. I did. I'm not sure how he read that though. The tears start to overflow but I manage to keep the flooding at bay, calmly blinking them away or onto his top. If he notices, he doesn't say anything.

"What's worrying you about hitching a lift?" James asks. "It's just, me and my sisters have done it quite a lot and, well, usually the people willing to give lifts are really good people."

I scrunch my face even though he can't see me as I talk into his t-shirt. "I guess it's just not something I'd ever do on my own."

James frowns. "Ok, would you rather walk then? We can."

"But I'm so tired."

James laughs now. "Ok, then we'll catch a lift?" He holds me away from his chest, squeezing my shoulders. "What would make you feel safer?"

"I don't know," I admit.

"How about we don't use our real names? Or agree to anything you're not happy with?"

I sigh out some of the anxious energy. "Ok, deal. At least I can rest my legs for a bit. I've never walked this far in my entire life."

James nods. "I've always had to walk places without cars

and stuff but never this far in one go." We're quiet for a moment, ignoring the cars passing us, leaving a breath of dust in their wake. "About last night..." he says, just as a loud horn blares. I jump, peering around James' side to see a huge red lorry, with faded sides, pulling over towards us. James shifts as he looks too, squint-cringing at the sight of it.

"What about last night?" I ask. We were about to have an important discussion but have been rudely interrupted.

The window on our side of the lorry comes down and a raspy voice shouts, "You need a lift?!"

James steps up to open the door. A large waft of cigarette smoke washes over us. I force myself to smile, deciding that maybe I should trust James with this sort of thing. He did say he's done this a lot. He must be able to read the situation. I follow him up to the door to get a better look. The man smiling down at us is missing a few teeth. He wears a stained white t-shirt with a picture of Rihanna on the front. His grey hair is missing through the middle of his head which is smoothly bald, the sides thick and long. I can see the promise of a ponytail at the back. But the most stand-out thing is his Saruman-style beard. And yet, his warm brown eyes are bright, kind looking. Maybe I am overreacting to this whole thing.

"Where you headed?" the man asks.

"The nearest town with decent connectivity," James says in his usual confident voice as if he's about to sell this man corporate hospitality. "Or a train station. Whatever is closest."

"Aye. Well, I'm headed towards a few of those. In you hop." The man gives us one of his friendly smiles.

I give James a glance. I hope it says, *I'm trusting you again, please don't let me down this time.*

He returns a warm grin. *You can trust me, Felicity.*

He reaches out, offering me his hand to help me up. Once I'm seated, I tentatively look to my right. The driver is beaming at me. I smile back awkwardly as James throws both our bags in and closes the cabin door.

Seventeen

The lorry lurches forwards, the gravel crunching under the tyres as the man steers it back onto the road. I keep my eyes focussed directly in front of me. Ahead, the road remains fairly straight, dipping and curving over the lumpy landscape, the blue silhouette of Scottish mountains set as the backdrop. I shuffle closer to James. It's not that this driver doesn't seem friendly. He does. But something is pulling me towards my counterpart in this adventure in a way I can't seem to control.

James instinctively looks down as if I'm acting weird. I am, I guess. I sort of have this urge to lean into his energy. To enjoy this time with him, even if we both know none of it can last.

As if I'm actually trying to cause trouble, I place my hand on James' knee. His thigh clenches as I do. The coarse hairs feel nice under my palm. I think he reads me. Or at least he reacts in the way I'd hope he would, placing an arm around my shoulder and pulling me into him.

Oh, thank god. He's on the same wavelength as me.

But, oh hell, *Gloatman is on the same wavelength as me*. What has been going on these past few days? Were we enchanted in that bloody castle? Was there something in the water? Are the protein bars spacing us out?

"So, what you two doing all the ways out 'ere?" the driver asks.

Luckily, James is happy to do the talking as usual. "We're on a hiking work trip. Our boss is expecting us back this evening."

Crafty, I think. This man has found himself in precarious positions before. He's letting this guy know that if he does try to kill us, he's going to get caught. Someone's looking for us. Little does he know, that's bullshit. Our boss is a raving lunatic who probably isn't even worried about our whereabouts at all.

The air conditioning in here is grumbling. There's a vent right in front of me pulsing cool air across my skin. I shiver, stroking my arms.

"You cold, darling?" James says in a sickly sweet way. I'd have smacked him for calling me *darling* even fifteen minutes ago, but as he passes me the sweatshirt he had tied around his waist and I slip it on, doing the zip right up to my chin, I have to fight off a cosy feeling that swamps me. It lingers in my limbs, as he tucks me under his arm again, even brushing his lips across my forehead as if we're a couple.

My heart is beating slower, yet louder and harder, as his long, strong fingers curl over my shoulder, tapping my arm as if that's what he always does to me. I find myself leaning into him, imagining what he'd actually be like as a boyfriend. He said he's been in love with women before. That's definitely not something I can say. I've had boyfriends, briefly, but there was never a truly deep, meaningful connection. I don't think the word "love" was even uttered before any of those inevitable, boring breakups.

But James is different. It'd be just like *this*. He'd be gentle, clever *and* funny.

He'd also be a know-it-all. Always up for an argument over trivial things, like how you load the dishwasher. Or whether or not we should get a cat, or a dog. Hint: we should get a dog. He'd probably complain about how many books I have but never read. Actually, we'd argue until we're both blue in the face. Then we'd get all hot and heavy. I'd trust James with my body because, clearly, he's not opposed to listening to me.

"Darling?" he says.

"Yeah?"

"Were you listening?"

I blush. Oh, if only he knew where my head had gone. "Er, sorry. What did I miss?"

"Bernie here said he can drop us off near another path. It's only a mile from there to a train station. But he's going the other way."

Bernie nods. "Easy to get you back to Inverness from there, if that's where you're headed."

The thought of walking another mile, although shorter than the miles we've already travelled, makes me feel weepy. But if it's our best bet and Bernie can't drive us directly to the hotel then fine – I mean, he isn't a taxi service. Then I guess I have no choice. I'm sure my shins can hear me thinking, they start to ache along the bone in both directions.

As if he can sense my mood, James leans down, taking

a quick nip of my ear. I squirm. And, wow, does he know how to work my body. Shots are fired somewhere inside of me, exploding like fireworks in my hands and feet, making my fingers and toes tingle. I'm instantly worked up thinking about when we'll be alone together again.

Dear lord, am I ever going to recover from this trip?

This can never work, Fliss.

When James asks Bernie what he happens to be doing all the way out in the Highlands, he talks about his job at a furniture brand. He says he collects these fancy pieces from some place up by the coast. Apparently rich people in London pay a fortune for it. I imagine that's exactly the sort of thing Michael would do. Buy a coffee table with a story about being handmade by a small Scottish family, just so he can make himself seem more interesting. He'd never be seen dead in Ikea. At least somebody is profiting from it, I suppose.

As we near a layby, Bernie indicates and pulls over, coming to a stop. He nods at James' window. There's nothing here. Not even a signpost. It's just more green hills and thorny, angry bushes. The sky is once again an ominous grey.

"You'll want to head in that direction about half a mile then you'll join a proper trail. Keep going till you find the village. The station is there – I've forgotten the name."

"You sure?" James asks, looking dubiously out the window.

"Aye. I walked the trail some years ago. You'll be alright."

I share an exasperated glance with James. Without the need for words, he quietly opens his door and climbs down, turning back to gesture for the bags. I hand one down at a time before I try to climb down myself. Before I know what's happening, James has a hand on my waist to support me. Our faces are close, his nose almost grazing mine. My eyes drop to his lips. Memories of last night spring to mind. I clear my throat when he releases me.

We say goodbye to Bernie, who has disappeared out of sight before we even have our bags on our backs. The path to get out of the layby is steep and my body sags at the thought of it.

"Come on, Felicity," James says, taking my hand, his fingers warm and strong. He practically hauls me up the first part before I suddenly find my steam again and stride ahead.

After about fifteen minutes, a sprawling valley opens before us, swamped in bracken and green and purple flowered bushes, with a thin, icy-blue lake at the bottom. We take a moment to check the map again now we have a better assessment of our location. We both agree on a direction and head that way, stepping straight into a fresh gentle breeze that tangles in our hair.

"Thanks for lending me this, by the way," I say, starting to unzip his sweatshirt.

"Ah, keep it if you're comfortable. I'm not cold."

I give him a tight-lipped smile. *He'd let me wear his clothes.* He'd say he liked it when I lounged around in his boxer shorts and baggy t-shirts.

"About last night," he says, purposefully not looking at me this time.

I manage to look away too just as a prickling sensation spreads through my cheeks and neck.

"We don't have to talk about it."

"I think we should."

I tighten my jaw, ball my hands into fists. Why am I preparing to fight? Or is this me preparing to protect myself? I shouldn't have let it happen. I should never have gone there. It's up there with some of the dumbest shit I've ever done. Granted, there hasn't been a whole lot. But this really does trump it.

Wanton wench – falling for a sexy, shaggy-haired Austen hero. Ugh.

"I really enjoyed it," James says.

"Oh."

"And I know we're colleagues and don't usually get along but… and I cannot believe I'm saying this… I think Michael's idea has actually worked. Turns out you're not as much of a dickhead as I thought you were."

"I think his idea was to make us get along. Not for you to have an epiphany."

He laughs, gives me a warm smile. "All I'm saying is… I wouldn't be opposed to catching up with you outside of work sometime. That's if you're open to it? I think you're funny, Felicity."

"As friends?" I ask instinctively, immediately kicking myself for asking such a dumb question. *What else, Fliss? Are you expecting a marriage proposal?*

James steps in front of me, placing his hands on my shoulders to stop me. I suck in a breath. Here it is. This is where he says, *yes, as friends*. And I'm going to be ok with that. I'm going to make myself be ok with that because he's not boyfriend material anyway. He's slept with a client for crying out loud. He drops his hands, placing them on his hips, doing that bloody Austen stance again. I hate how much I dig it.

"If that's what you want?" he asks, his forehead scrunching into a row of deep wrinkles.

I fight the urge to reach up and smooth them out. I sigh. I'm not going to be that girl I hate. I'm not going to say I don't want something that I actually maybe do. I should just be honest. "I don't know, James. I don't know what's going on here. I kind of think…" I sigh, "… friends would be good, I guess." *Coward.* I inwardly kick myself. Is that really what I want? "But friends don't tend to do the things you did to me last night."

James laughs. "Oh, come on. You've never had a friend who would get down and dirty with you?"

"Not since uni," I say with a smirk.

"Alright, well, usually I'd take a girl out for a few drinks as a minimum before doing what we did last night. So, I suppose I owe you some drinks."

I pull a face. "Hang on. I was the only one who got anything out of it, so maybe I owe *you* drinks."

"On *your* salary?"

"Oh, shut up. God, you're annoying." I shove past him as we both laugh, me in an embarrassed way, my cheeks probably glowing, James like he does when he's enjoying a fight.

"And trust me, I got a lot out of it," he says.

I try to stop myself from overthinking all this. It's as if I'm mentally pinching myself. Reminding myself he isn't future-proof. It doesn't matter how much energy is forming between us now, we don't work. We don't get along away from this. And I know from my childhood how important it is to find someone who can make you happy. Yet I sort of want to explore this. I sort of want to accept the inevitable pain and sprint clumsily down this path anyway. What's gotten into me?

"So, how do we handle it at work?" he asks, coming in step with me.

"I love how confident you are we're going to make it back now."

"Confidence is a skill."

"Too much of it is a flaw."

"Are you going to answer my question?" James presses.

I think about it for a moment. The truth is, I can't have my team thinking I'm dating James Boatman, Head of Sales. That's totally inappropriate. Sales are the dark side of Starr. The gutter. The kitchen trolls. What will my team think of me? I'll lose all credibility.

"It has to be a secret," I say. "If we date that is. We might get back and instantly hate each other again. If people don't know about it, then they won't suspect any misdeeds or falling outs either. And besides… I might be your boss soon if I get promoted. Then that'll be breaking policy."

James goes silent. When I peer across to see what his face is doing, he just looks away, rubbing his chin. I don't know what that means or if he hates the thought of me being a director but I'm not going to let that stop me from putting myself forward for it. I get the urge to confront him. What? Why so quiet? But I also don't want to ruin this thing that's happening between us. So, for now, I leave it.

"Do you agree?" I ask. "About it being a secret?"

"Hmm… Oh yeah. Sure. Well, like you say. This is probably just the unsterilised water making us loopy. Back in London you'll hate me again," he says, smiling. "I'm sure of it."

Eighteen

"There's no way that's a station," James says, frowning at the scattered pile of white-clad buildings posing as a village. For once, at least, we find ourselves looking at a real sign. A wooden post is arrowed towards Dalwhinnie station. The landscape around here is sparse of anything but dull-green fields enclosed with sheep wire. We stroll down a treelined road of pines and spruces.

Ahead of us is a small white building with a bright blue door and a red tiled roof. Behind that is what appears to be a railway. There's no fencing or gates, no screens showing departures. There are also no commuters running to catch their trains, their bags bouncing on their backs. There are… no trains. There are no coffee shops or food stalls for me to get my classic breakfast of beans and smashed avocado. It's like something out of medieval times. Ok, not *quite* medieval, they didn't have trains. But this station can't have been changed much at all since it was originally built back in, what, Victorian times?

I've seen two people in this town so far. One herding sheep with a feisty Border collie, the other driving a car. So, when we finally reach the platform, on the other side of the blue door, I'm surprised to find three people sat waiting on the single bench. To our left there's a small shed-looking kiosk with a glass front. A man, who could not look more animated for what must be the most boring job in existence, sits in the booth, smiling.

"Morning," I say, stepping up to the booth. "We want to get to Inverness airport."

"It's gone midday," the man says with charm.

"Sorry?"

"You said good morning. It's afternoon now. By five minutes."

"Ok," I say, blinking. "How much will two tickets be please?"

James is stood beside me, squinting into the sun, glancing down the tiny platform and beyond where there appears to be a train heading our way. It slithers through the valley like a snake with headlights.

The man taps on his noisy keyboard. "You'll have to change at Pitlochry," he says. "It'll take you two hours to get there."

"That's fine," I say, breathless, as the train rolls into the station. We can't be more than a few metres from where it will stop. I almost say, *it's been three days, what harm is two hours going to do?*, but decide to keep that one to myself. "How much will it be?"

There's more clicking. I can feel an impatient buzz roll through me. *Come on, come on.* Finally, he points to a screen on my side of the booth. "Sixty-two pounds for two," he says.

"Piss off!" I say, horrified.

James scoffs, joining outraged forces with me. "Is that a joke? I thought Scotland was cheaper than London."

"Yous from London?" the man asks, laughing as if something about this whole situation is actually quite funny.

Instead of answering him, James huffs, taking my hand and pulling me away out of earshot. "We've only got fifty pounds."

"No shit!?"

He gives me a sardonic glance as if I'm being the stupid one. "We're getting on this train."

"How? We can't afford it!"

"We're just going to get on." He keeps checking where the train is, as if he's planning on bolting towards it right in front of the ticket man.

My jaw goes slack. "What? We can't. That's theft! It's illegal… It's *immoral*."

James rolls his eyes. He takes a few steps forwards. He's really going to do it. He's not even worried about the consequences. But when I don't follow, he turns back to face me, tilting his head and rubbing his chin. "Hey Fliss, guess what? Rules are made for people who can afford to oblige them. They're there to hurt people who can't."

"What are you talking about?" I hiss. The train is slowing now, coming in line with the platform. It's only two carriages. I've never seen a train that short in London. Not once.

James gives me an imploring glance. "Sometimes you can't afford the things you need. *You* can't afford to get on that train. But you *need* to."

"What, so we just get on? Without tickets?"

"There's nothing stopping us…"

"But what if we get caught?"

"Then they'll kick us off at the next stop."

"They won't fine us?"

The train doors hiss open. The carriages make that compressing sound as the brakes are applied as if they're sighing from exhaustion.

"I dare you, Felicity. I dare you to do something you shouldn't," James says, his eyes glowing in a dangerous, exhilarating way. As if I haven't just spent the past few days doing *precisely* that – something I shouldn't. But even still, I can feel the adrenaline pumping through me as the whistle is blown.

"We *can't*," I say, but without much conviction.

"We *have* to," he repeats.

I open my mouth to object again. James is waiting for me to decide. He's not forcing me on. He wants me to make the decision myself. The decision to be just a little reckless. He's set me a challenge and the people-pleasing part of me doesn't want to let him down.

Clearly, I've lost my mind, because I nod, and then we're charging across the concrete, hand in hand, and up through the doors just as they close and the final whistle blows. The man in the booth points at us, shouts something to someone else who throws their hands up.

I'm instantly drenched in guilt. *They know! They saw! What happens now?*

"Oh, god, what've I done?" I mutter, as the train pulls away from the station, curling back into the valleys of the Highlands. I drop my bag and plonk myself down in a window seat, a slow, thick shame weighing heavy on my shoulders.

The carriage is bizarrely busy. Where did all these people even come from? James looks completely at ease with the situation as he stands tall to push both bags into the overheads. His top slides up and I get a glimpse of the dark line of belly hair below his navel before he takes the seat beside me. There's hardly enough room for his long legs, his right leg stretches out slightly into the aisle.

James focusses on steadying his breathing. He checks his watch and peers out the opposite side as the scenery flashes past us. I take a deep breath too, doing the same on my side, my elbow on the window, chin resting in my palm. There are lots of sheep round here. We can't be that far from where we woke up this morning, deserted still, in a tent by a stream. And yet, this part of Scotland seems so drastically different. It reminds me how small it actually is, whilst also seeming so huge when you're in the middle of it.

I swallow as a sharp sensation builds behind my eyes. It's all a bit overwhelming, really. I wonder what Mum is doing. I wonder if she knows where I am. Does she think I'm on a team-building trip with my colleagues? Safe and sound and tucked up in a castle. I wonder if anyone else has even noticed I've gone. I can go days without seeing my housemates, despite hearing their footsteps and the occasional flush of the loo.

I think about work. All the things that needed doing before I left. The list I wrote and handed to the team. I wonder if they've even looked at it. What sort of state will my inbox be in when I return? If only I could've accessed them whilst I was out here. And then there's Michael. The man behind this whole thing. What is he doing? Eating caviar, sipping expensive champagne on a comfy sofa by a gorgeous grand fireplace?

Bastard. Oh *god*, do I really think that? No, of course

not, he isn't a bastard. He can't be. I can't have worked my arse off to unnatural levels for a man who never actually cared about me or my future. Can I?

And what am I going to do when I get back? How can I trust him, or trust that he won't do something like this to one of my team? I blink as a grey cloud in the distance breaks apart slowly, a faded sky below promising rain.

It suddenly occurs to me that work and my parents are all I really have to worry about right now. Maybe I need a bit more going on in my life. Some closer friends. Some responsibilities. Possibly a hobby. Anything that isn't work.

I'm filled with this sense of doom, as if something's about to change? Something has to change, surely; I know that. It feels like I'm held together with this long thin rope that's being pulled in two directions. Soon it might snap. And what happens then?

This week has been eye opening. The world is a much bigger place than The Starr Agency and Michael and my silly feud with James. It goes so far beyond all my problems.

Do I make other people stressed with my stress? Am I as bad in the office as James makes out?

James reaches across to plant a hand on my bare knee, squeezing. "You're freaking out," he mutters quietly so other passengers can't hear.

I lean my head back, fighting the tears away with a shuddery breath. "I'm not sure how we go back to it all. How do we go to work next week?"

James tilts his head, considering. "I'm honestly not sure I want to at the moment. If that helps at all."

I smile sadly. "Who am I, James? Me. Fliss Rainer, not wanting to go to work?"

"It's probably just holiday blues," he says with a smirk.

"Do they call it that because I nearly froze to death?"

He laughs, looking back at the other passengers to see if they're nosing in. They all seem to be wrapped up in their own little worlds too. They've all got their own problems and places to be.

"Oh shit," James hisses, tucking himself behind his chair. He gives me a smile but his eyes are wild in a way that suggests trouble.

I duck down too. "What!?"

"The ticket inspector," he whispers, gesturing with his chin.

I peek up over the seat to see what has startled James. My eyes go round. My chest starts to constrict. My heart thunders in my chest. I duck down again. There is in fact a train conductor, wearing a hat and all, walking this way, slowly checking other passengers' tickets. But, of course, they're relaxed because they weren't peer pressured into jumping on here without paying.

Oh, but that's unfair. I definitely could've said no, walked in a different direction. And yet... here I am.

"What the fuck do we do?" I demand. There's not even a tiny piece of me that finds this funny, so it rankles me slightly when I see James snigger. "How is this funny!?"

"Oh, lighten up, Felicity. What's the worst that can happen?"

"I don't know... *What is the worst that can happen?*"

"We'll get booted off the train."

"Whilst it's moving?!"

James finds this even funnier. "I certainly hope not."

He sneaks a look back down the aisle. The man hasn't

noticed us. And I suppose, unless he spoke to the station, how would he even know? We're not suspects yet.

James stands to take my bag off the overhead, passing it down to me before grabbing his own. For all the train conductor knows, we're just getting snacks. James' eyes shine with mischief as he offers me his hand. "Come on. Let's sneak into the next carriage."

My legs are shaky as I stand to follow. "Another great idea," I mutter.

"Sssssh. It's fine."

We walk slowly to the back of the carriage which, luckily, is only a couple of rows of seats. Our movement has been spotted though. The train conductor shouts something. I peek over my shoulder, despite James tugging on my arm to speed up.

The man calls, "Hey, now wait a second!"

But James is off with me in tow. We fly to the doors, our lungs slamming against our ribcages. The doors open onto a connection between carriages as we fly through to the next one and along the aisle. People look up with suspicious glances. Some appear to be genuinely offended that we're walking so fast.

James is laughing, smiling as if this is an enjoyable pastime for him. Meanwhile, I feel like the short, panicky girl on *Derry Girls*.

"James," I hiss. "Gloatman!"

But he barely even looks over his shoulder as we hop someone's discarded bag in the middle aisle. He squeezes my hand, aiming for the back of the train. We find ourselves out of escape room and I clatter into his body as he stops.

The man is striding towards us now saying something about bloody kids and chancers.

Does he mean *me*? I'm not a chancer!

"What bloody now?!" I demand of my comrade, or, co-offender.

Suddenly the door opens to the toilet on our left. A man leaving with a newspaper folded under his arm blinks in surprise at us waiting outside, then heads back to his seat.

James gives me a look. It says, *We'll hide in the loo.*

"No," I say. "Ew, no, gross. I have a genuine fear of public toilets."

But really, we don't have much choice. When I peek over my shoulder the rather rotund conductor has nearly caught up with us. James pulls me into the loo. There's a long, blurred window. The curved door closes behind us with a click, trapping me in a train toilet with Gloatman.

How did I get here?

I stand in the middle, trying to balance with the movement of the train. James seems to be much sturdier than me. He has his back against the door, watching me with a funny look on his face.

"Yes?" I ask as the man outside starts knocking politely on the door.

"Excuse me, please. You'll need to come out of there. The train toilets only permit one person at a time."

James sniggers, holding a hand over his mouth.

"This is *so* not funny. You're such an imbecile. Am I going to get a criminal record?"

"What for?"

"For not having a ticket!"

"Oh yeah... You're going straight to a high-security prison, Felicity. You bad, bad girl."

"Shut up," I say, pointing at his chest, but then find myself laughing at how ridiculous this all is. My cheeks must be so red. How did I let him talk me into this? "You've done this before, haven't you?"

His eyes are bright when he turns to me. "I rarely pay for train tickets if I can avoid it. I never paid as a teen and did a lot of running and hiding."

"*James.*"

His lips quirk. "Felicity."

"Excuse me. Please come out," the very polite train conductor asks again, albeit with an element of huffiness.

"Flush the loo," James says, since I'm closer to it.

I lean across to grab some loo roll, covering my hand to push the flush. The toilet makes a sharp, loud swooshing sound. We both watch the door, waiting to see if the conductor will leave but instead, he knocks again. "I'll wait here."

James curses under his breath.

"Next idea?" I ask with a sarcastic smile.

His lips twitch as he glances at my face, his eyes dropping to my lips. "I have an idea."

"Your ideas are exclusively my only problems right now."

"This one will be good, I promise."

"I'm not jumping out of a damn window."

There's another knock on the door. "If you don't come out voluntarily I am authorised to manually unlock the door from the outside."

I don't have to say anything more to James, the look on my face speaks volumes. He cringes through a smile. Oh, this all very, very funny to him. I, on the other hand, fully expect to experience trauma after this trip. I will be having nightmares about running away on trains and hiding in icky toilets for weeks.

Another knock. The very polite train conductor is getting impatient. "I'm giving you ten seconds."

James laughs, stepping closer to me. He plants one hand on my waist, pushing me into the wall, my bag acting as a buffer. He shifts his legs so that one of his is in between mine. It's all a stark reminder of our kiss in the castle. Heat fires up in my chest and abdomen as if someone has lit a match and thrown it on the coals. It's a welcome distraction to the situation. And something more, it's really not like me. This isn't Fliss. Fliss *would never*! And yet, I'm doing it, and it's fun and it's naughty and…

Oh, shit. The door clicks open. Almost simultaneously, James takes my water bottle from the side compartment, turns and tips it into the loo, hunching over to make a horrible gurning sound.

I stare at the back of him in disgust. What on earth am I witnessing?

But then my brain clicks and I jump into action, remembering the situation we're currently in. I rub James' back, pretending to nurse him. I briefly give the train conductor an annoyed face to show him he's interrupting a vulnerable, private moment.

"Oh, very sorry," he says. "Sorry. I didn't know your… he… was being sick." The door slides shut again, locking with a click.

James stands back up with a grin.

"That was exceptionally disgusting," I say, unable to rid the grimace from my face.

James tries to smother a laugh with his hand. It instantly riles me. And yet, I too can't fight the humour of the situation. "It's not funny, you idiot."

"I'm sorry," he says, resting his forehead on mine. I swallow when I realise how easy this has become between us in only a matter of days. It feels sort of wonderful which is terrifying. I shouldn't be feeling this about him. Luckily, a few moments later he steps away to open the top part of the window, and glances out. "Station ahead. We'll get off here."

"But we're not in Inverness."

He gives me a look. "They're not going to let us chill out in here for another hour and a bit. As much as I'm enjoying this—" I snort at his sarcastic tone "—once it stops, we'll charge out the doors, ok?"

"But where are we!?"

"I have no idea."

"Oh, bloody hell." I sigh.

"We're a good team, Felicity. Don't you worry."

"There better be food," I say, huffy, as he grabs my hand again towing me towards the door, readying ourselves for escape.

When the train slows to a stop, James tentatively opens the door to find the coast clear. We've clearly frightened Mr Train Conductor off with James' convincing rendition of a sickness bug. We dart out onto the platform, and I'm tempted to leg it, but James slows me down, linking my arm with his and whispers, "Walk quick but casual. Less suspicious."

"Are you a part-time criminal?" I ask.

"I'm in sales, Felicity. Criminality, sales, it's a role cut from the same cloth."

All I can do is laugh as we exit the station and step into the next unknown. Hell, maybe I'm even enjoying it now!

Nineteen

This town has more substance, I'll give it that. The streets appear friendly enough, with their rustic light-grey stone buildings. There's even a high street with shop fronts offering fish 'n' chips, kebabs, Chinese and tea rooms. My mouth waters from the combined smell of frying fat.

It takes us a few moments to realise people are giving us funny looks. Probably due to the fact that my hair resembles something close to a bird's nest. Oh, and I have torn-up shirt strips bandaged around my shin. We may look particularly grubby too… At least we shouldn't smell, thanks to the deodorant we were supplied with.

But surely hikers walk through here all the time on their way to and from the wilderness? We can't stand out that much. We stop as we come to a T-junction. A bed and breakfast across the road offers value-for-money stays. It's an incredibly old building that leans to the right. It could very possibly be about to topple over. We tilt our heads to read the sign as it's come loose on all but one nail and hangs vertically.

"What do you reckon?" James asks.

"It looks…"

"Dodgy as fuck," he says.

"I was going to say cheap."

"Worth a try, I suppose. We could at least ask about getting our phones fixed. Maybe they can help," he suggests, squinting down at me.

I peek back at all the people we've just walked past to get here. We could've asked any of them for help. Well, I suppose we didn't because we're both slightly out of sorts now. Even James seems a bit more reserved than before. We need a decent meal, a solid sleep and a damn good shower. That'll get us back to ourselves. Especially as we're supposed to be returning to the hotel tomorrow or we'll miss our flight.

"Come on, then. Knowing our luck, it'll be too expensive," I say, pouting as we cross the road towards the building.

The tiny front door is so low James has to duck to get in. The hallway has been redesigned into a reception area with a desk and a bell. The red and white flowery wallpaper is stained and peeling in places along the ceiling. James is just about to ring the bell as an elderly, grey-haired lady pops through a door, wearing an old-fashioned apron.

She blinks at us with her kind yellowy eyes. "Hello there."

"Afternoon," James says. "How much are your rooms please?"

"They're sixty for the night, duck."

I sigh, I'm about to turn away when James says, "Any chance you could do us a solid and meet us at forty? We're sort of strapped for cash."

She makes a face. "Hmm. Can you go without breakfast?"

James looks across at me for confirmation. I say, "Is there hot water?"

"Of course there is," she says, giving me a sneer, as if I've offended her by asking.

"Great, we'll take it." I don't even care if there's only one bed at this point. There's a bloody shower, for crying out loud. With hot water! Luxury!

James fishes through his bag looking for the fifty-pound note. Once he's found it, he hands it across to the lady who makes a face as if we've handed her money from a Monopoly game. "We don't take fifties, duck."

James pauses as he's zipping up his backpack. I blink at her across the desk. There's a moment of silence that drags on.

Then James says, "What do you mean you don't take fifties?"

"Don't get shirty with me, young man. This is probably fake."

"It's certainly not fake." James looks to me for assistance. I shrug. "Does anywhere in the town take fifties?"

"Hmm, the fish 'n' chip shop probably does."

"Perfect," I say. "Come on James. We'll be back in a bit."

The chips smell like heaven. They're perfectly greasy, soaking the white paper they've been wrapped in as we return to the bed and breakfast with two twenty-pound notes. What an excellent excuse to buy two large portions of chips. They weren't super happy to give us change for a fifty, but with James' persuasion, and my quietly-panicked face, we succeeded, returning to collect our key for the night.

Once we've been shown to our room and the shared bathroom, we finally plant ourselves down on the bed – me, cross-legged, James, with his back against the headboard. The room isn't so bad. The bed itself is a little creaky. But it smells alright in here, like rosewater and lavender. There's an adequate amount of light streaming through the window and reflecting off the oval mirror placed above a dressing table at the side of the room.

We gorge ourselves silly. James is attempting to resuscitate his phone, having seen an Android charger behind the reception desk and begging the lady to lend it to him. It won't turn on right away so it's possible it's flooded. Mine is a lost cause. There's water behind the main screen – I didn't even know that was possible.

"We could've asked to borrow that lady's phone, you know? Called Michael and demand he picks us up," I say, scoffing another chip down. *God, it's so good!* Chips are life. Especially when they're covered in salt and vinegar. Each bite requires diligent finger licking.

James finishes chewing on a chip, then gives me an inquisitive look. There's something else there too. It looks like a bit of heat has risen into his cheeks. Is he embarrassed?

"Do you want to? We could still do that. I'm sure we can find his hotel's number pretty easily."

I consider it. Do I want that? I'm sure the castle hotel is very nice. Far, far nicer than this quirky little place. But we'd have to face Michael, knowing what he's done to us. I don't think I can do that right now. Not feeling as depleted as I am.

Besides, I've had worse company. We'd have separate rooms if we went back tonight. Although it's only been three nights, I've sort of grown used to James' heat alongside me, the closeness of his face, his presence somehow keeping me grounded whilst I dream. And then I realise, to my horror, that there's something worse lingering. Something I knew might happen, but I ignored. Something I'm going to kick myself for later.

I sort of like James. *Really* like him.

Butterflies take flight in my stomach as I peer up at his dark blue eyes. He's worried about my answer. I can't tell what he wants me to say. Maybe he does want to go back. Maybe he's been waiting for me to ask exactly this. Or maybe he doesn't? Does he feel the same as me?

I shrug, try to play my feelings down. "It's ok. We're alright here for tonight. We can call him in the morning."

James nods, takes another chip, chewing slowly. I'm sure I see the whisper of a grin on his lips. "Alright then. It's a plan."

Just then, his phone vibrates. We both sit upright, staring in wonder as his screen lights up, slowly loading. James practically launches at it, clicking buttons on the side like he might be able to speed it up. Then he's logging in and searching his contacts. Before I have a chance to move, he's dialling a number.

"I can go," I whisper, clambering off the bed.

"No, it's ok. Stay," he says. "If you want to, that is."

Before I can answer, a woman's voice bursts down the line. "Jamesy!"

"You ok?" he asks. He swallows, his face serious as he stares back at the screen. It takes me a moment to realise he's on FaceTime. I climb back onto the bed, quietly picking at my chips whilst he talks to his sister.

"I'm fine. We're all fine," she sings.

James presses his lips together as if he's almost afraid to ask but then he says, "Can I see him?"

"Who?" his sister teases.

"My bloody nephew."

"Sure, but hang on," she says. "Why've you not been answering your phone? We've been worried."

James sighs but he's grinning. "My phone broke. It's a long story. I'm sorry I've been off grid. I'm alright. We're in Scotland."

"Who's we?"

"Me and Fliss."

Soph cackles down the line. "That irritating woman from marketing?"

James laughs giving me an unapologetic shrug. It says, *you knew how I felt about you.*

I stick my tongue out in response.

"Who you looking at? Is she there? *Is she on your bed?* Fuck's sake, James."

Unexpectedly, James turns the phone so his sister can see me. I try to duck out of the screen but it's impossible, so instead I wave awkwardly.

"Hi," I say, with my mouth full. James smirks at my panicked expression, spinning it back to face him. Soph says something about pretty and cute, but James is talking again.

"Show me my damn nephew," he demands in a jokey manner.

There's shuffling down the line, a soft squeak, the unmistakeable sound of a sleepy newborn. James watches, his eyes widening, his lips parting slightly. He tilts his head.

"Soph," he whispers. "*Look.*"

"Isn't he perfect?"

"Absolutely perfect. You sure you made him?"

"Shut up, you prick."

He guffaws. "You'll have to curb that potty mouth."

"Piss off," she says sweetly.

"Can't wait to meet him. What's he called?"

"Bernie," she says, and I nearly choke on a chip while James sniggers. If Sophie hears she doesn't say anything.

James looks at me over his phone. "Want to meet my nephew?"

"Oh, it's ok," I say, not wanting to intrude on his family moment. But James nods at the spot beside him. I crawl across the bed, planting myself so we're shoulder to shoulder. If someone had told me this would happen three days ago, when we were abandoned roadside in our work clothes, I'd never have believed it. Look at us. So comfy in each other's company.

It doesn't mean anything, Fliss. It can't last. It's just a reaction to the situation.

And I know this. I do. But there's a wonderful energy leaking from his pores now he knows his sister is well and his nephew is perfect. I want to stay right here soaking it in, but I can't because this is going to end badly. I can sense it.

I hop up, swinging my legs off the bed.

"He's adorable," I say. And he is. His soft cheeks, those tiny lips, the little fingers curling round his mummy's hand. "But I really need a shower. I'm going to…" I don't finish the sentence, waving to Sophie on the screen and dipping out of the room, clean white towel in hand.

I'm deliriously relieved to discover this quirky B&B, with a pink bathtub, flowery-patterned roller blinds and bubbly linoleum flooring, has a power shower. I close my eyes and let the hot water wash over my hair, face and body. I give in to the way it pummels perfectly against my shoulder blades. In fact, I'm pretty sure I'm moaning.

I wash my hair using the shampoo and conditioner that's been left for me. Then condition a second time, praying that'll be enough to get some of the knots out. Especially as I'll need to use my fingers to comb it in lieu of my hairbrush. I scrub all over, trying to get the smell of damp, muddy countryside, and my own aromas off my skin. I crave the feeling of cleanliness.

Once I've climbed out, I grab my towel hanging on the back of the door, wrap it around me, and sigh contentedly, as my wet hair drips down my left shoulder. That might be the best shower I've ever had. I pat down my body, slowly realising the towel she's given me is actually very short, barely covering my butt cheeks. I stare at the pile of clothes on the floor for a moment. I could put them back on. That would be the smart thing to do. No need to stoke the fire between me and James further by returning to the room practically naked. And yet the thought of putting those sweaty, mucky things back onto my clean body makes me want to cry.

No. The towel will have to do. I sneak through the door, stepping quietly down the hall to our room, listening for voices. When it's quiet, I peek in to check I'm not intruding on James' family conversations.

He's scrolling on his social media accounts. As he notices me, he glances up, smiling. "How was the shower?"

"Good. *So good*," I say, coming into the room a bit more to reveal my incredibly short towel arrangement.

James gulps as he sees, blinking at my legs. He presses his lips together, then opens them to say something, then closes them again.

"I couldn't bear to put my hiking stuff back on. Sorry," I say.

"It's ok," he says, voice strained. "Tell you what, I'm going to hop in the shower now too. Leave you to get dressed."

He's gone, closing the door behind him before I can say I need clean clothes and probably should've thought that through before getting in the shower in the first place. I groan, peeking round the room, hoping something will give me inspiration. There's an old, flowery bed throw I could fashion into a dress.

A dress! I stride across to my bag, whipping out my black skater dress from the flight to Scotland. It's still a little damp, having not been left out to dry at any point, but once it's on, it covers enough of me to go downstairs and ask the landlady if she has a lost property box I can pillage.

In luck, I find myself a slightly baggy black vest top, beige cardigan and a pair of leggings. There are even pink sneakers in my size. Then, in a rush to get dressed, I whip some items out for James. He's tall so there's far less choice for him. He'll have to make do.

Once he's out of the shower he stands there, towel folded in at his waist, bare chest glistening, his hair even darker now that it's been washed and cleaned, frowning at my choices for him. "I'm not sure I believe this was all they had."

"It's all there was, I promise."

"Hmm," he says, unconvincingly. He pulls the top on over his head, shaking his hair loose as he glances down at me. "Go on, laugh."

I cover my face as a snigger bursts from my lips. "You look…"

"Like a hippie from the seventies on a peace protest march?"

The tie-dye top I found him is blue, yellow and pink, practically glowing with joyous fun. It's probably a few sizes too short, riding up at his belly button, tight around his shoulders. "You look like you're about to shackle yourself to a tree."

He shakes his head, looking across the bed. "I can't believe you even found me some lost boxers."

"Marie promised me it was all clean."

"Wow, and what are these?" he asks, holding up a pair of beige chino shorts that happen to have approximately fifty pockets.

"I believe these are what are called dad pants."

"Dad pants?" he chuckles.

"The pockets are for snacks, bottles of milk, first aid kits, dummies… It's the modern-day alternative to bum bags."

He smirks at me before shaking his head with a sigh. "Turn around then."

I do as I'm told, twisting away to look at the wall whilst James pulls the second-hand boxers and shorts on, when my eyes catch on the mirror on top of the dresser. There he's stood, naked from the waist down, in all his glory. My jaw drops open. He hasn't noticed me gawping. I quickly look away, pinching my leg.

"All done," he says.

I take a second to compose my face before turning back with a guilty smile.

"What?"

"Nothing," I squeak. "It'll do, right?"

"Yeah sure. Hey, fancy some more chips?"

"We have no money left," I remind James with a confused frown.

He waves his phone in front of me. "I have contactless set up on my phone."

I can't fight the smile on my face. "Then, yes. Let's get wine and all."

Twenty

We return to the room with a carrier bag full of delights. Amongst the two cheap bottles of white wine, James grabbed Jaffa Cakes, cheesy Doritos and went rogue with some Space Raiders. I grabbed a pot of Ben & Jerry's ice cream, cookie dough flavoured, a pack of strawberries and a jumbo-sized bag of Skittles. On the walk back I realised I didn't have a spoon to eat with, so James snuck into the fish 'n' chips shop again to steal me a wooden one. Clambering back onto the bed, we settle under the covers as James switches on the ancient box TV across from us.

It hums to life, doing that thing where the screen fuzzes grey. James presses some more buttons until we get Channel 4 on, just in time to watch a dating show about country and city people taking turns to live each other's lives. One of the contestants is talking about how she finds her partner on the show adorable. It's all a bit soppy for my liking.

"They won't last," James says.

I just laugh, half-agreeing. "He is sort of adorable though."

He gives me a look. "Like me?"

"Ha. You're not adorable."

"What!? This is news to me."

"Your hair leans into adorable when it's super floppy, but your attitude is mostly mean and arrogant. Sorry, I mean *confident*."

James snorts, completely unfazed by my comments. "You actually are quite cute though."

"I'm not cute!"

"If you were a character in *Winnie the Pooh*, you'd be Piglet."

"Piglet!?"

"You're small, brave, colourful and you like jam sandwiches. And sometimes you get angry but you're never scary."

"I'm not convinced those are Piglet's characteristics. Does he like jam sandwiches?" I say, then ponder. "How do *you* know I like jam sandwiches?"

James takes a sip of wine from the bottle, munching on a crisp before pressing his lips together guiltily. He doesn't need to say anything more. I fold my arms across my chest with a jokey scowl. "YOU!"

"What?"

"You're the kitchen bandit who steals my sandwiches?"

James munches slowly on another crisp.

"Oh my god! You cretin!"

"They're just so cute," he laughs. "You wrap them up in brown paper and they're never the same jam. You mix it up. My favourite is the sweet chilli one."

I sit there gawking at him. "It is not ok to steal people's lunches, James."

"I don't. I steal yours. Specifically, I might add, when you insist on asking questions at the end of long meetings that mean my lunch break for the day vanishes."

I blink. Actually, that sort of does add up. I remember how it was always when I was going to have a rushed lunch, because meetings overran, that I found my sandwiches had disappeared. "You never bring your own lunch?"

"No way. I'm not that organised. I spend at least fifty quid a week on Pret."

"That's so bad."

He grins across at me, a small dimple forming in his cheek. I bite my bottom lip to prevent myself from smiling too. It's annoying really. His smile is quite infectious. And although I've just found out he's been stealing my sandwiches for the past few years on our busiest days, I can't hate him for it. It's too small. We just survived walking across the Highlands without our phones and limited supplies.

James shuffles slightly, his shoulder pressing alongside mine. Come to think of it, should we be more concerned about the bed-sharing arrangement? I know we've shared a tent the last three nights. And things happened. But that doesn't mean to say this isn't an inappropriate situation considering we're colleagues.

"I meant it though," James says out of nowhere.

"Meant what?"

"That I think you're cute. You've always been sort of cute. Annoying. Frustrating. Argumentative. But cute."

I swallow down his compliment before I know what to say. He sounds sincere. I'm not sure whether cute is really the vibe I'm going for. Blood rushes through my veins and my brain starts to hum, because, oh god, Gloatman is giving me compliments, and after last night's shenanigans I should probably divert this fast. I don't know if I trust myself anymore.

Butterflies take flight in my stomach. Nope. I definitely do not trust myself.

"Ilikeyournose," I say so fast it comes out as one word.

"My nose?" James says, reaching up to touch it.

"Yeah."

He frowns inquisitively. "Why? It's my worst feature."

"It's perfectly imperfect. Like you. In the office you always look like you're about to walk down a runway for Moss Bros. Always so done up. But your nose breaks through the image. The little bump. It's perfect."

James drops his hand, our gazes locked, unsmiling. Our breathing is heavy. I look away first, pretending to watch the TV but I can still feel him watching me, a slight groove forming in his forehead as if he's considering what I've said.

"You know I said the other day I didn't have long-term plans at Starr?" James asks softly.

I look back, feeling the heat of his gaze soak through me like an old whisky. "Yeah?"

"It's not entirely true. I don't want you to think I'm just going to pack up and leave. Partly, I do enjoy some of it. But mostly, I'm too afraid of finding myself skint again. I have nightmares about it. Being broke really weighs on me. Having strange people knocking on your door, calling your home line at weird hours until you have to unplug it for sanity, the emails and letters, it breaks you." James takes a calming breath. "I just want you to understand me. Understand why I do the things I do and say the things I say. Where my ideas come from."

"I get it," I say.

"And I know you haven't had it easy either, Fliss. You had to deal with your parents and the fallout of their separation on your own. You didn't have siblings who understood, to some extent at least, what you were going through."

I feel the threat of tears building behind my eyes. Somehow, between James opening up about work and his family, and the way he's acknowledged *my* baggage, his words have wrapped around my heart and squeezed.

"I didn't have it anywhere near as bad as you. It can just be lonely sometimes, that's all. I thought I'd outgrow that feeling. As a teenager it was hard to manage the emotions but I'm thirty now and sometimes I still wish I had a sibling to call up and moan about my parents with. To share the responsibilities as they get older."

"We have a WhatsApp chat specifically for bitching about Mum's antics," James says with a snort. "It's called 'Lads Chat' so she doesn't pry."

I wish I had that. I wish I could trade some of that emotional workload I have to juggle for Mum to someone who fully gets it. Someone who feels the same way. It would be like taking a load off my shoulders.

As if he can read my mind, James reaches across slowly, tucks a damp strand of hair behind my ear before gently running his fingers across my cheek.

"What about you? Any confessions?" he says.

I laugh just as a tear escapes. James catches it with his thumb.

"I honestly do want someone to share a mortgage with."

A huge smile splits across his face. "And I thought women were supposed to be the romantic ones."

"It's just really impossible to get a mortgage on one salary these days."

"You're right. It's the modern-day marriage."

"They should celebrate it more."

James drops his hand, sighing as he returns to staring at the screen. At some point he must've muted it. I feel the need to be honest with him in this silence, the dragging anxiety surfacing from the lack of noise between us for even a second. And besides, he was brave enough to tell me.

"There's something else too. I *do* want my own house. A place to build a life. But, also, I want recognition. I know it's sometimes a bit over the top and maybe I need to look inwards and work on that. But I want to feel like I've achieved something worthy. I want people to look up to me. Is that wrong?"

James considers this. I gulp at the intensity of his dark blue eyes. The sun has started to fade outside the window, casting the room into darkness, the light from the TV forming colours on his cheeks.

"No," he says. "It's not wrong." He frowns as if he's pondering over it. "I think people already do feel like that with you, Fliss. Your team are very protective over you. And I know this because Connor is dating Amy."

"What!"

"Oh, yeah. And what's the guy with the bright blond hair called again? I think he does graphic design."

"Benji?"

"He's with Mohammed."

"No... The sneaky..."

"They don't tell you because they look up to you. Not because they're afraid. They genuinely want to be like you. But clearly, they've got great taste, hence their reasons for secretly dating salespeople."

I scoff. "I wouldn't call that great taste."

James just grins. It says, *you practically threw a strop last night when I stopped you from taking it further*. I'm glad when he doesn't actually say the words. Blood rushes into my cheeks.

"I'm sad they don't feel like they can tell me though. I'm jealous your crew tell you."

"Sales and marketing people are different. My crew overshares on a dangerous level. Your people are more reserved."

"I guess," I say, though I think he's just trying to make me feel better. Maybe it is something I should work on.

"But look, don't let your need for recognition take away the things you deserve. Just because Michael says you're amazing, doesn't mean he's providing the goods. First thing Monday, I want to see you in that office negotiating your salary."

I sigh. "But what if he says no? What if he fires me?"

"Honestly, Fliss? Is that the sort of place you want to work?"

I press my lips together. "After this week shouldn't we both quit?"

"I have no idea what's going to happen on Monday."

"What do you mean?"

"Exactly that. I don't know what I'm going to do. How I'm going to feel. How I'm going to manage this."

The way his gaze intensifies as he says this, I understand what he's telling me. He's not just talking about work. He's talking about this. Us. Whatever it is that's going on here. I swallow again, a lump forming hard in my throat.

"I don't really want to think about Monday."

James takes a deep breath. "Me neither but it's going to come around and... I don't... I don't want to hurt you. If..."

"It's fine. I get it. I feel the same way." And I do. I don't know what this week has done to me, but I've never felt so disconnected from the world. It's been like an out of body experience, picking me up and placing me in a universe I can't escape from through a black mirror. I've felt connected to this man whom I usually hate. We've had something. Sparked a flame.

"I'm not an idiot. I'm not as breakable as you think I am," I practically whisper.

"I never thought that."

"Then stop trying to be gentle about this."

"Ok... Fine. I'm not worried about you. I'm worried about me."

I frown. "What?"

"You're going to hate me again on Monday when we go back to being who we really are. I'll make your blood boil with an email and then you won't speak to me."

"Then let's make a deal."

"A deal?"

There's two parts of me now. One side is terrified. It wants me to run downstairs and beg Marie to let me have another room. A safe place where I can't hurt my heart. The other side is a flame, flickering dangerously close to a match. It's daring me to take a leap. To push myself out of my comfort zone.

"Let's promise that tomorrow we go back to normal. Not our fighting normal. But we take a step back, reassess. If what's happened this week is just a case of us being in an insanely intense situation, then neither of us get hurt. Our hearts shouldn't be on the line along with our careers."

"Fliss..."

"You don't think that's the best thing here?"

"I don't know."

"Just let us have tonight. We can see this out. And tomorrow we'll go back to colleagues. No mess. No pain. No drama."

James sighs, squeezing his chin. "That's what you want?"

I think about what it would be like for us to extend this thing we're doing beyond Scotland and all I can see is a trail of pain. I see us fighting. I see hearts getting broken. So, I nod.

James nods too.

"Alright, deal," he says. "Then what now?"

I feel my heart quicken in my chest. It's almost completely dark in our room now except for the light flickering on the TV. The sound of our breathing fills the room. James doesn't move as I slide closer towards him. His face drops into a serious expression as I turn, placing one leg across his, sitting astride him. His fingers move slowly, carefully to my hips, sliding between my leggings and vest as he takes hold of me, shuffling to be more central.

"Then this," I say, leaning down to kiss him.

Twenty-One

Without another word, James' hands cup my face as he kisses me like I'm the answer to all his problems. Sensations form where his fingers meet my skin so very gently, bursting like thousands of tiny fireworks behind my ears. I gasp as I relax into him, straddled across his hips until I can feel him growing beneath me. He groans into my mouth, tasting of wine and sugar.

He rolls his hips upwards as I press into him, forming a rhythm of movement between us. I've kissed like this before. Hot and heavy. I've let kissing consume me until I was naked and panting. But it's never been like this before. This time I have so much confidence in my partner it's driving me a little crazy; biting, nipping, scratching at him and we haven't even taken a single item of clothing off yet.

His hands travel over my body, gently pushing my cardigan down from my shoulders. The soft material glides down my back as it falls, sending a quiver back up my spine. James teases me with his lips, leaving my mouth and playing with the places he knows make me squirm. I give in, dropping my head back, closing my eyes. His fingers leave my face, gently caressing my shoulders, my collarbone, dipping lower. He groans as he skirts over my breasts, feeling the bud of tension there.

He takes my breasts in his hands and lifts, feeling the weight of them. His breathing hastens as he bucks into me again from below. Meticulously, he hooks his fingers under my vest and bra, tossing them aside. Once he has full access, I feel the thrill of it in my core, like there's a coil there, twisting.

I drop my head again just in time to glimpse his agonised expression. He catches me watching him and smirks. "You're absolutely gorgeous, Fliss…"

"Call me Felicity," I say breathlessly.

He looks at me half-surprised. "Felicity," he breathes.

And there, *yes*.

That's the sound I'm so reactive to. For so long it would make me tense, furious even. But now it's more. Now it's his name for me and I want him to use it because he knows me in a way nobody who knows Fliss does.

I lean down to pull his bottom lip between my teeth. I feel him harden further and know I've got him right where I want him.

His arms wrap tightly around my back, holding me so close it feels crushing in an exquisite way I can't even explain. We start to rock again, James in control. He takes hold of me, rolling my hips back and forwards as he raises his knees. We're so close it's like we're one entity. Once he's finished positioning me, he refocusses his attention on my breasts, teasing my nipples into firm buds. All the time I'm aware of the movement, the kissing, the sensation in my nipples, all colliding together in a perfect pressure between my legs. My breathing hastens. So does James'. He senses my growing tension.

Am I really going to come apart still clothed from the waist down?

It's like he knew this would happen as I break away from his lips to gasp.

Confident cretin.

But I suppose it's all starting to make sense as to why he is the way he is now. His infuriating confidence. It's deserved. In bed, at least.

His fingers come back to my waist as I feel his smiling lips press against my jaw, his stubble divine against my soft skin. He pulls me into him further, pressing harder into my sides in an almost painful way. But that pain too finds its way to my core, raising the heat until I'm making sounds I have no control over.

"That's it," he whispers in his devilish tone. "Give it to me, Felicity."

The undoing whips up my spine so fast I grapple with James' shoulders, clawing into his skin as he holds me tight. My thighs clench around his hips. I press my chest into him. At first, I throw my head back, but then when he doesn't stop the movement it all becomes too much. I buckle over him, sighing into his neck.

"You're perfect," he says. "You deserve to come undone multiple times, every time. Promise me you'll never settle for less?"

All I can do is nod, my lips and teeth gently pressing into his shoulder as the energy inside of me subsides into a relaxed stupor. The fire hasn't been put out, it's back to an ember and I'm not ready to fully extinguish it.

"I want you," I whisper against James' skin. "We should…"

"We only have those bloody condoms. I could run back to the shop…"

"Oh, I don't care anymore," I say, sitting up as if I'm about to climb off him. James grabs my wrists, laughing at my eagerness.

"Are you sure this is what you want?"

"I'm sure," I huff, wriggling to escape. James relents, releasing me as he leans back, one hand behind his head, the other rearranging himself down below.

Once I've retrieved a condom, I spin to find him watching me.

James' eyes sweep down my body. I'm only conscious enough to hold a hand over my stomach and the pesky roll I have there. When he sees me do this, he leans forwards to pull me closer, removing my hand and bringing it to his lips to kiss. "I don't stand a chance in fighting you on this one," he says with a smile. "I just want to know you're absolutely sure. There's no undoing this. No going back."

But there's also every chance this is our last opportunity. I know why I feel like that. I'm not ready to admit it to myself just yet. Not here. Not now. I need time to work it through in my head. My next steps. My new plan.

"I want this," I tell him, placing my hands on his cheeks this time, so he has to look right back at me. His eyes smoulder like midnight in the dark of the room.

As if this movement has rendered him speechless, he parts his lips and nods. With this I reach down to tug his tie-dye top over his head. Then, before he tries to talk me out of it again, I unbutton his shorts. He raises himself enough so that I can pull them off with his boxers. And there he is.

I've gotten James Boatman naked. He's right here in front of me. Not a stitch of clothing. Despite how serious I was just a moment ago, a flurry of amusement washes over me.

James smirks as he watches my face. "If you laugh right now, Felicity…"

I can't help it. A whisper of a laugh escapes my lips as I smile across at him.

"It's not *that*. I'm not laughing at *that*," I say, nodding downwards. "It's just *this*. This whole thing. I'm in a bed with Gloatman and we're both naked."

James acts swiftly, placing a finger in the crook of my armpit making me squeal.

"I warned you," he says, laughing too. "Trust you to get me naked and be the first girl to ever laugh at me."

"I'm not laughing at *you*. I'd never. It's lovely. It's perfect."

Before he can tickle me again, I lean forwards, placing my lips on his. This time I take control, pushing his back against the headboard as I take him in my other hand, hot, smooth perfection. His body tenses as I deftly roll the condom on and position him where I want him.

As I slide onto him, he wraps his arms around me again, his tongue exploring my mouth, holding me still, as if he's adjusting to the sensation. We move in the same way, breathing into each other, feeling our way across each other's bodies. He keeps me steady, rocking me when I try to pick up the pace. He takes back control, his thumb circling my clit, raising the pressure again until I'm on the verge of climaxing for a second time. I collapse into him as the final waves of pleasure roll through me. I want to make him come too.

Luckily, he senses this, lifting me and spinning our

bodies so that my back falls into the bed, the soft mattress absorbing me as James drives into me again, kissing me, my collarbone, my earlobes. He finds a new, harder rhythm.

He whispers my name, endearments, into my ears as his lips press into my neck, my shoulder. I wrap my legs around his waist, bite his bottom lip again. In my mind there's nothing but him, this moment.

And when he comes, we kiss, slow and heavy until we're both sleepy, him rolling onto his side, my legs entwined with his. He holds me like nobody has ever held me before. And then a creeping, negative thought forms in my mind, pulse slowed, breathing steady: he's probably like this with other women too – intimate. But I allow myself to pretend it's more than that. Just for tonight.

I make a promise to myself that tomorrow I won't bother him, I won't push for more, I won't even bring this whole thing up.

A clean break. A fling. A work trip.

Twenty-Two

As the sun reaches through the thin blinds and fills the room with morning light, I instantly feel an uncomfortable sensation rush through me. Like the way you feel on the last day of your holiday when you have a flight to catch. This has hardly been a holiday; it's been a nightmare really. What with being abandoned in Scotland with a man I hated. And yet, there's an unmistakeable heaviness in my core as if I'm saying goodbye to something.

Today I return to my reality.

I roll onto my front and turn my head to find the space beside me empty. I can hear the low hum of the power shower down the hall. Seizing the moment, I roll out of bed, pulling my clothes on before he comes back. I make the bed and sit there anxiously, scrolling through the TV channels.

I'm restless. I'm ashamed of the feeling but I'm dying to get my phone back. To be reconnected to the world. I want to talk to my parents, check my emails. James offered me his phone to use, but I don't know either Mum's or Dad's numbers by heart. Why would I? They're in my phone.

There's also a familiar dull ache between my legs, reminding me of last night. I take a deep breath as footsteps approach the door. James comes in fully dressed. Thank god for that. No more nudity between us. Colleagues again now. That's for the best.

He grins shyly when he sees me. His damp hair has been combed back with his fingers, almost like normal.

"The water is still hot if you wanted a shower," he offers.

"Yeah," I say, hopping off the bed and walking round to the door to grab my towel hanging on the hook.

As I open the door James says, "Felicity?"

I pause. "Hmm?"

"We ok?" His face is one of concern as he squeezes the back of his neck.

"Of course. That's the plan, right?"

He frowns, nods. "Yeah."

And with that I shoot out of the room and down the corridor, banishing the heaviness forming across my abdomen. A pressure that's warning something bad is happening, or that something bad might happen yet.

I let the water wash over me, scrubbing all my emotions away to the smell of the lavender shower gel.

We check out of the B&B and get a taxi to take us back to the hotel. Turns out, we aren't all that far away. The forty-minute drive takes us on a picturesque journey through Scotland. I make sure to look out the window and maintain space from James. This was the agreement. I get these sudden bursts of memory, scenes from last night, and feel myself blush, hoping James doesn't notice.

I sort of want to reach over and squeeze his hand or stroke his hair, now dry and floppy again. But then I remind myself of what things will be like on Monday. Only forty-eight hours away. I picture the morning meeting, how Michael will make a decision regarding our next event and James' idea. My stomach tightens from the fear of it all. Will we be able to keep this professional? Will we be able to act as if nothing ever happened between us? What if he tells Michael?

"You're freaking out," I hear his low voice beside me. I don't look around though. There's no way he can tell without even seeing my face. And so, what if I am? It's none of his business now.

The taxi rolls down the driveway to the looming castle, stopping just outside reception. We stand side by side, both unsure how to confront this situation.

"We can't let him think he's won," James says.

I exhale slowly. "So what? We hate each other again?"

"I don't know, *do* we?"

I blink, finally turning to look at him. He's watching me with an unreadable, blank expression. I want to ask him what he's thinking, why he's being distant, but I know that's dangerous territory. It's easier to be practical about this. We both agreed.

"I'll go first," I say, striding off, composing my face into one of pure annoyance. By surprise it isn't hard to achieve. I think that's because I *am* annoyed. Furious, in fact. I want to find Michael and scream at him.

But Michael isn't even here.

I ask the receptionist to point us in his direction. She says she was expecting us and passes me a note. Strangely, this time, it's specifically addressed to James, and when I turn to find him a few steps behind, I pass it to him with a glare.

Why would it be for him and not for us both?

James casts his eyes over it. He glances my way once he's finished. He looks tired or resigned. He sighs. "Michael left yesterday. Wanted to spend his weekend in London."

"Wow," I say, shaking my head in disbelief.

"He booked us return flights. And he's put money behind the desk for a taxi."

"What else does it say?" I ask. There's more than that on the note.

James scrunches it up, tucking it in his pocket before I can snatch it off him. Well now I'm fucking suspicious. He shakes his head. "Nothing else."

"Show it to me," I demand, my hand out, palm flat.

James takes it back out with a huff, passing it across to me. It reads, *If you have arrived at the hotel together, I assume you have achieved the objectives I set you.* Why isn't this addressed to both of us? I glare at the paper but the rest of it is just about flights and taxis as James already told me.

"What does that mean?" I say.

James stares at me for a second like I might figure something out, then simply shrugs. "I don't know."

I open my mouth to start an argument because something in my stomach tells me that isn't true. That he's hiding something from me. But I don't say anything. Instead, I leave him right there, brewing, as I spin on my heels and storm back out of the hotel lobby and into the surrounding countryside.

I half-expect James to follow but he doesn't. That's ok, though. That's a good thing. And when he finally does join me again, a good thirty minutes later, he has our suitcases.

He passes me mine. I mutter a thanks then we climb into the taxi.

We don't talk again until we arrive at Heathrow. James is taking a different train to me, which comes as no surprise – I vaguely know where he lives. He's closer to the office than me. He gets a direct train into London Liverpool Street. I've heard he even has his own flat. Not unexpected now I know how much more he earns than me.

James squeezes his chin as I stroll out of the arrivals gate, walking towards my platform. I have my wallet back now but still no phone. At the ticket machine I tap in the location then pay, turning to find him still hovering.

"What are you doing? You'll miss your train," I say.

"I can come with you if you want. Get you to your flat at least."

I take a deep breath, uncertain why he's offering this. Does he think I'm incapable of getting back, or is he worried about me? "Don't pretend you care now, Gloatman," I say, remembering the words he said to me as he faded in between the ruined castle walls.

He frowns. "You haven't got a phone. I don't... I just... When you get in will you let me know?"

"How?" I laugh. "I don't have a phone." James sighs, pulling something from his pocket. He passes a business card across to me. I blink. "Seriously? You're giving me your *business* card?"

"Use a flatmate's phone. Just to let me know you get home safe." Then after a moment, he adds, "As a friend."

"As a colleague."

He laughs, blinking away from me. He's doing that Austen stance again, his jaw flexing. "Can you not be a dick about this? Did I… Have I done something wrong?"

"No." I bite on my bottom lip for a moment wondering what to say. "We agreed, didn't we? That being colleagues is better?"

"We can't be friends?"

"Is that what you want?"

"No," he says, sharp and blunt. "I don't think so, no."

I can't ignore the way that hurts. It's not a surprise really. He never did like me before. Didn't he admit he considered abandoning me by the roadside only two days ago? "Right then. Colleagues."

James makes a frustrated sound. "Yeah, Fliss. Colleagues." He shakes his head. "As my *colleague*, please can you text me whichever way possible when you get home? Please."

"Fine. Yes. Goodbye, James."

"Bye, Felicity," he says, turning and striding in the direction of his platform. I'm sure I see him shrug as if I've personally offended him.

The flat is quiet when I arrive, I imagine my flatmates are all out working, or home with their families. They all tend to get away from the flat more than I do. It's annoying because I was hoping at least one of them might have a phone I could borrow. Instead, I drop my bag in my room then nip out to the nearest store.

I return an hour later with a new phone and groceries to get me through to Monday. Thankfully the technician was able to get all my data across, including contacts, photos and apps. I make myself a blessed cup of tea with three sugars, sighing as the caffeine soaks into my arteries, and cross my legs. I finally text James.

Home, I write. No kisses, no emotion.

Thank you, he replies.

I frown at the screen. I don't know where I stand with him. How would colleagues text? I write a few things then delete them, finally giving up and closing the app. Instead, I call the one person I'm eager to speak to.

It only rings twice.

"Flissity!?"

"Mum," I say, but it comes out weepy.

"What's wrong, darling? How was your work trip?"

"It was good." I always say this, don't I? Isn't that the problem? I never want to offload my problems to Mum. "Well, actually, it was strange. And, well honestly, I'm really confused," I say with a gasp as my eyes start to blur. "I'm sorry I didn't call sooner. I lost my phone."

"Oh, it's ok. I've been busy sorting the garden out. Such lovely weather this week. What's your plan tonight then? Resting up?"

I sniff, wipe a tear from my cheek. I don't know why hearing her voice has made me emotional. All I can think about is how much I've missed her. How much I want to tell her everything that happened, and yet I don't. Because I carry her emotional baggage, not the other way around. She rarely wants to hear my difficult things. I think she likes to believe I'm living this huge exciting, happy life that I'm totally in control of.

"Mum I..." A sob racks my chest.

"Flissity? What is it?"

"I've just had such a *weird* week."

I give Mum a rundown. I miss out a few key details but mostly she gets a play by play of my week with James. She hears how I nearly drowned in a river and how I slept in a tent for three nights. I remember my cut, reaching down to touch it. It's healing fine – doesn't require a doctor after all. I tell her about the lorry and not buying a train ticket. She asks if anything happened between me and James and I say, "Yes, yes it did," because it's true and I need someone to vent to. And for once she listens. She doesn't try to give me advice, but empathises.

I tell her I want to quit my job. It flies out of my mouth so fast I almost can't believe I said it.

"Give it another week," Mum suggests.

"I don't know if I can."

"Is it because of what Michael's done or because you don't want to face James?"

"Both," I say. "I can't do either."

"You can, darling. If anyone can, it's you. You've had a wild week by the sounds of it. If you make a rash decision now, you might regret it. Yes, another week is what you need."

I tell Mum about the salary discrepancy between me and James. She sighs. "Hmm, I don't know an awful lot about that."

"I need to negotiate. I deserve to be paid the same as him."

"Absolutely!"

I groan, throwing myself back into my bed. "I can't do it, Mum."

"You can, Fliss, darling."

"What if he hates me again?"

"Michael?"

"No, James."

"Well," she sighs. "Then you know it was... What did you call it? Last people disease?"

"Last-two-people-at-the-end-of-the-world disease."

"An awfully long slogan for someone in marketing. You should work on that."

"It's not really a slogan, Mum," I laugh. "What've I missed with you then?"

Mum goes into her week without me. It's all the usual stuff: shopping, gardening, tea with a neighbour. She works part time at the GP surgery in town and there's always a ton of gossip there. I pop her on loudspeaker as I unpack my bag, whimpering when I see the state of my red ankle boots. They're damaged beyond repair. I take them out to the kitchen and pop them in the big bin, stuffing my hiking gear in the washing machine.

As I'm emptying the final pockets of the bag that I've lugged around with me all week, a note falls out. The note from the start. I hold it in my hands for a moment as Mum natters on in the background. I read it over once more, then, instead of binning it, I'm about to place it in my top drawer for safekeeping, when I notice black ink on the other side.

This note was also addressed to James.

I grab my phone, turned face up on my bed. "Sorry Mum, my flatmate is calling me," I lie, trying to keep my voice steady. "I'll call you in the morning, ok?" I barely register her response as I frown, that tight-chested feeling returning.

I hold it in my shaking hands. *What does this mean?* I read the letter over again.

In order to proceed to the next step in your career you must overcome the need to compete and find a way to cooperate. I would like to hear how you worked together as a team. See if this week will shine a light on your management skillset. Don't let me down!

Was this addressed to James? Was the whole challenge set for him?

Then it dawns on me. *He knew!* He must've known the whole time.

I sniff as a rogue hot tear runs down my cheek. My brain starts to spin with all the possibilities. All the how's and why's and if's.

Because, if this note was written for him, and only him, then was the challenge even hiking across Scotland? Was the challenge about survival and teamwork? Or was the challenge, in fact, horrifically... *me?*

Oh my god. He tried to stop it a few times. Whenever I said I planned on being a director he acted offish and awkward. I get a sick, twisted feeling in my stomach with the thought of seeing him at work on Monday. How the fuck am I supposed to manage this now?

I fall asleep that night with shame and a stomach full of betrayal and deep, wretched embarrassment.

I hate you, James Gloatman!

Twenty-Three

The office looks and smells exactly the way I remember it. It's clean. Bright. The waft of coffee is heavy in the air. How can it be only a week since I was here last? And why does it feel like this place is so foreign to me now? I blinker myself as I stroll through the central area where the customer service reps usually sit. They won't be here for a few more hours. The glass walls between us are too revealing. It feels dangerous. I want to hovel away somewhere. Out of sight. In a small, dark den. I don't feel like being approachable and available today.

Admittedly, I came in later than I usually would. If I arrived too early, then I might find myself alone with James again. And I hated the way my body responded to that. It felt good. And horrible. I can't handle this chaotic pile of emotions today.

But obviously, I couldn't be late. Mum was right. I can't give up just yet. I can't let it all go after one bad week. What if I've got the wrong end of the stick about the notes?

All the hard work. Six years of slaving away out of hours. All those weekends I'll never see again. And for what? To throw it away because I had a fling with a colleague. Oh god, is that what I'm calling it now? Was it a fling?

Me, Felicity Rainer, having a fling. It's preposterous.

So, here I am, at quarter to eight, in my bright blue dress and fun shoes, staring at my screen as it comes to life. None of my team have arrived yet. They don't need to be here until nine. And even then, I try to be relaxed about when they arrive and leave, as long as they do their hours.

I don't need to look to know when James arrives. His team are all in early, keen to get on the phone to make sales as soon as they can. They chant and joke as he comes in. He replies with good-natured quips. My heart rate increases, my palms feel clammy when I hear his voice. I can't move. I'm sat statue still in my chair as I watch over one hundred emails pour in as it loads. I sigh, tapping my fingers restlessly. The sales team settle down and I pray this means James has too.

Gemma arrives with a Starbucks coffee for me. "Thank you," I say with surprise as she sits at her desk. The gesture relaxes me a bit. So, they don't hate me then like James alluded to early on in the trip?

"What do I owe you?" I ask.

"No, nothing. We missed you." She smiles, looking across at the few who have poured in after her, setting their water bottles, notepads and bags down by their desks. Then she gives me a conspiratorial grin. "Did you *really* have to camp with Gloatman?"

I feel his name in my gut. I panic. Look around. I catch the back of his head in the sales den. His hair is perfectly gelled again, the sight of it almost breaks my heart. What did I expect? Of course, he's back to his usual self. He was hardly going to come into the office in his hiking gear stinking of pine and mud.

"Who told you?" I say.

She shrugs. "There were whisperings about what Michael had planned for you both. I think it was Millie who spilt the beans."

I nod. "Well, that makes sense, I suppose."

I don't like being the topic of gossip. I picture the whole team huddled together, placing bets on who was more likely to succeed. Little did I know it wasn't even a competition. Nothing about last week was mine for the taking. It was all for James'.

I feel fleeced, cheated and robbed of something I've worked exhaustively for over the past six years. I'm angry. Though I've adopted a calm composure... for now.

Once my team have all arrived, I call a meeting to see how they're getting on. My emails are utter chaos. So, instead of wading through them, I sit and listen. I'm taken through all that was achieved in my absence.

"We finished your list," Gemma says proudly. "Dylan and Mo sorted the campaign for the August event. We've got the ticket sales set up on the website. The radio advert has been recorded and it's just going through their internal approvals system," she rattles on.

Gemma even attended some of the meetings I should've gone to, taking notes and providing me with a full rundown of decisions made. I can feel my heart beating slowly. It's adjusting to the truth James already knew. The one he told me about always being replaceable. It's true. They don't need me. In my absence everything was fine, it all ran smoothly.

It takes all my effort not to burst into tears right in front of everyone. I subtly take a deep breath of air, biting the inside of my cheek. They carry on sharing details about the week and the challenges they faced but ultimately overcame. Problems I'd usually take the brunt of. The ones they'd knock on my door and ask for help with, or for me to intervene. Not this time. They didn't need me. They forged on bravely.

They're so proud of themselves. I can't help but smile despite the sadness swelling inside of me. All the effort. All the pain and long hours. All the times I arrived before everyone else. None of it was really necessary. I've burnt myself out, like a charred, exhausted piece of kindling. And now, maybe, I'm no use to anyone. I need to find somewhere to be alone for a moment. I need to reset. I need to strengthen my façade.

But it's not possible.

When I check the clock, I see it's nearly nine thirty. Time for the Monday morning heads-of-department meeting. With five minutes to go, I'd usually be in there already, clicking my pen impatiently.

This time, however, I go back to my desk first. I select all unread emails and click delete. "Gemma, if anyone asks, I've deleted any emails I've received in the past week. I'm not reading all one hundred and fifty of them. If they're important, they'll send them again."

She seems to find this hilarious, cackling away. "Go you! I might do that from now on if someone emails me at the weekend."

I lift my eyebrows, realising she means me. Her cheeks colour slightly, and I think she notices her mistake, but we both laugh at the same time because life is too short. And the world outside of these walls is so very big.

I'm three minutes late to the meeting. Rajesh is just opening the door. Mel has taken my seat near the head of the table opposite James, who is watching me seriously, a notch formed deeply between his brows. Thankfully, Fiona is between us, and as my seat is on the same side as his, I don't have to stare at him the whole time.

Everything hurts being this close to him, my limbs, my heart, my chest. Part of it is still recovering from sleeping on the ground for three nights and nearly getting drowned in a river, but I'm certain some of it's also from being in close proximity to him. I'm sure at some point it will return to normal. I'll hardly feel a thing. Maybe he'll do something to really piss me off in this meeting and we can go back to the way it was before.

Michael comes in, his usual jubilant smile on his face. I've never wanted to punch someone harder. I notice James move in the corner of my eye. He clenches his hand into a fist, leaving it to rest on top of the table.

"Good morning, team," Michael says.

I can't even look at him. Instead, I doodle on my notepad.

"I want to start by congratulating James and Fliss for their brilliant efforts team building last week."

I'm speechless. I should be kicking off. I want to, but my mum's advice thrums on loop in my head: *you'll regret making a rash decision.*

Will I, though? Right now it feels like I should scream and storm straight out of here, smashing a few glass dividers as I go. Michael seems unfazed by the collective silence as he runs through current stats. He talks about the upcoming event and how he's decided not to make any last-minute changes. I should be celebrating. I won! I won the argument with Gloatman.

But there's a problem: a strangely exhilarating feeling lingering in my bones. I don't care anymore. I'm not interested in the outcome of this event or anything after it.

I thought long and hard last night about what I was going to say to Michael. How I was going to make him pay for last week. How I was going to demand a pay rise. How I was going to assert myself over the director position. Yet, I have no desire to do any of that anymore.

I laugh. Everyone turns to look at me. I've interrupted Michael.

He smiles at me as I finally face him. "Did you want to add anything, Fliss?"

"Sorry," I say. "No. Carry on."

Michael makes a strange face as if he wants to frown but can't. He carries on anyway, eyeing me suspiciously.

I watch the way he talks and wonder if anything he says is even real, if he's ever actually meant any of the compliments he's given me. Does he really think he can pay me in recognition?

"And finally," Michael says, clapping his hands. "I'm pleased to say that the board has come to a decision about who our next director should be." Michael pauses for effect. The room spins. He can't possibly have made a decision already, can he? I didn't even get an interview. But, of course, his ideal candidate already passed their final test with flying colours. Fuck, I'm stupid.

"James," he says. "Congratulations!"

There's a lump in my throat that drops to my stomach.

The notes *were* for him then. I *was* the challenge. It slices through the core of me. I knew it; deep down I already knew this. It shouldn't come as a surprise.

My mind races. I could leave. I should just get up and storm out. He doesn't even want it, I remember. They've let *me* win a battle because inevitably, I'd already lost the war.

I feel so *gullible*.

But I clap along with the rest of the room. And I smile.

I say, "Congratulations. Well earnt." And I mean it. He deserves to stay here forever.

James hasn't said anything. He simply frowns and blinks at Michael, then shakes his head ever so subtly at me. Whatever. He can pretend he doesn't want this right now, whilst I'm sat beside him, but he'll be lapping up the extra income. Isn't that what he said? That's all he cares about, isn't it? Money, money, money.

Well, I hope it makes him happy.

"Felicity," James says, hot on my heels as I stride back to my desk. I don't stop to hear what he has to say. The heart-wrenching pain I'm in is most probably because I'm confident he knew that was going to happen but chose not to say. I'm trying to work out what game I lost. When, over the last week, did I miss it? Or was it before all of this? Either way, he was hanging onto something. Hiding it.

"Fliss," he says, when I don't stop or turn, his voice low but urgent.

"What!?" I spin on him. He comes to a halt in front of me. Some of the people at nearby desks turn in our direction.

I can feel their wide-eyed expressions on us before they go back to their work, pretending not to listen.

James exhales slowly. His face is contorted as if he's in pain. But how can he be? He's just been made a flipping director of Starr.

"I'm sorry, I didn't think he'd announce it then."

"Ok," I say with a shrug. I want to say, *so you knew, so you didn't tell me, so you're precisely the arsehole I always thought you were.* But my lips are firmly sealed for two reasons: not fighting him right now is probably the more painful way to defeat him, and because, miraculously, I'm already over it. Over here. Over this. Over it all.

The ache in my core, however, suggests I'm not quite over him. But confronting him about it all would make me splinter in front of the whole office and that certainly isn't an option. Better to let him stew over it.

He watches me, a mix of emotions flitting across his face. I miss his floppy hair. I miss the way it falls over his eyes and has to be pushed back. I miss funny, kind, compassionate James. The one who pulled me from the river and bandaged my leg with his ripped-up shirt and told me stories about his sisters. Not this version. The corporate, slimy, scheming James.

Was any of it even real? Was all of it just a way to complete Michael's stupid challenge?

"Why aren't you saying anything?" he whispers.

"What would you like me to say?"

"I just…"

"What happened to you suing, Michael?" I ask in hushed tones. "What happened to you hating it here? You seem to have settled right back in."

He scoffs, his eyes alight. "And you haven't?"

I open my mouth to say, "No." But instead I say nothing, turning away, leaving James running his fingers through his hair.

I log in to my laptop, typing as fast as my fingers will go. I read through it once and then hit print.

My heart races as I walk to Michael's office. I don't bother to knock, what civilities or courtesies does he deserve at this point? No, I let myself straight in, marching right up to his desk, allowing the door to slam shut behind me. Michael looks up in surprise. I slap the letter down in front of him. He blinks.

"I quit."

"Pardon?" he asks, confused. I cross my arms and stand my ground. "Fliss, surely you're not quitting because I promoted James. You're better than that, and we both know it."

I smile, relief flowing through my veins.

"Actually. I can. Effective immediately, in fact. I'll just collect my things and be on my way now. I'll expect to be paid three months' severance."

"Well, hang on now. I don't think so…"

"For six years you've not given me the respect I deserve. I've worked my arse off for you. And you've been knowingly paying me almost half what you pay James."

"Fliss," Michael says my name with care, surprise, hurt crossing his features. I hate him. The patronising bastard. I can see the confident glow in his eyes. He thinks he can walk me down off this ledge. "The reason James got the role was because he proved himself. He makes The Starr

Agency an incredibly profitable business." Michael rises from his chair, splaying his fingers on his desk. "You don't need to leave. I'll increase your salary in line with his. How does that sound?"

Like he should have thought about that years ago.

I laugh at the absurdity of it. "Goodbye, Michael," I say as I walk back to his door.

He steps around his desk as if he might chase me out of here. "Your contract says you have to give three months' notice. You can't really think I'll just let you leave?"

"Oh, I think you will." I grab the door handle but don't open it just yet, half-twisting to say the next part. "You'll pay me three months, or else I'll sue you for being a fucking lunatic, endangering my life and breaking several employment laws!"

"Now come on, it was an adventure," he says, disappointment rife in his tone. "You can still do big things here. If another position comes up on the board, you'll be the—"

"Stop right there, Michael," I interrupt. "There's nothing you can say that would change my mind. I'd rather shovel shit than spend another second working for you."

And with that I turn on my heel. He doesn't call after me, and I think I even detect a newly found hop in my step – a weight lifted from my shoulders. James' eyes are on me now, following me as I practically glide across the office. I ignore him.

I stride over to Gemma and give her a big hug.

"What's that for?" she laughs.

"I'm going," I whisper, not wanting to cause a fuss.

"You taking an early lunch?"

"Something like that," I say. "Only I won't be back."

"Ever?"

"Ever."

"Good on you," she says quietly, a sad smile on her lips. "Stay in touch."

This time she hugs me, and once she releases me again, I take no time in grabbing my bag. Mel is talking to Michael over by the water cooler. They watch me, whispering to each other.

I take the steps towards the exit slowly. I don't expect anyone to chase me out of here. Partly because nobody except Michael, Gemma and maybe Mel knows I've quit. The rest probably think I've got a dentist appointment or am going to a meeting.

I think about all the times I've climbed these steps. All the times I've arrived early and finished late. I think about the days when I felt on top of the world, like the work I'd done had made everything possible. There's a beauty in working in events. You get to see all your hard work unfold before your eyes. People having the time of their lives because of you.

Then I remember the days when I left the office on the verge of tears, slowly descending these very steps, a quiver in my breath. Nearly every time, it had something to do with James. Somehow knowing that both softens and hardens the memory.

And now the good days, the ones where Michael made a big song and dance about how important I was to the company, cloud over. I know now they were never real, that he's completely disingenuous. I'm grateful James helped me to see the truth. How long would I have carried on if he hadn't?

There's something incredibly toxic about this industry. It's addictive. It's exhausting. But worst of all it exploits your passion. I'm sure there are many others like it.

I close my eyes for a minute, holding the banister, my fingers gripping onto the cool metal. It's time to let go. It's time to adapt and change. My heart beats a little quicker.

Then I let go. And I'm free.

Once I'm out the main doors, I take a deep breath. London smells like cigarette smoke, exhaust fumes and dirty drains. It's not quite the same as it was in Scotland. I miss fresh air.

And luckily, I know exactly where I need to go to find it.

Twenty-Four

As I step off the train, I breathe in the current of sea air that washes over me. It's salty, sharp and damp – just the way I like it. It's been raining here too. Although the sky is clear above me, there are dark patches of cloud far off in the distance, the wind is thick with humidity. It coats my face, my hair, my forearms.

The walk to Mum's is only a short distance up a gradual hill. Seaford is mostly comprised of apartment blocks overlooking the sea, or else Edwardian semi-detached houses. Mum lives in a red-brick, three bed with a charming bay window downstairs. There's a willow tree on her driveway, the roots fighting an unrelenting battle with the concrete. Her front door is bright blue, and although it isn't the house I grew up in, they sold that shortly after their divorce, it's still the place I've been coming back to every birthday, Christmas and long weekend. It certainly feels more like home than my horrible room in London.

I exhale slowly as it comes into view. Some of the stress dissipates, as my shoulders instinctively relax.

I don't have to knock on the door, I have a key. I let myself in and call for Mum. She knew I was coming. It's

Doris who finds me first, Mum's rescue collie, bursting down the wooden stairs, her claws clacking loudly as her wriggly body wiggles around me. I bend down to pat her as she licks my legs and hands.

"Oh, Flissity," Mum says fondly, following closely behind, pulling me in for a hug. She's so like me in physicality. Now that she's gone back to dyeing her hair the same colour as mine it's merely a few more wrinkles she has to contend with. I'm only about an inch taller than her, despite my dad being somewhat of a giant.

"So, you did it," she says, walking through the house to the kitchen at the back and putting the kettle on.

"I did. It was the right thing to do," I say, as I follow her, feeling a little defensive.

She has her back to me, her long grey cardigan falling to her knees. Using her spoon to squeeze the teabag against the side of the mug, she makes a sniffy sound before turning to face me with a frown.

"I'm sure you're right."

"What makes you say it like that?"

"Well, it's hard to know with you sometimes. You always manage to avoid talking about yourself. I don't want to intrude. It's just that I thought you liked the job."

I almost laugh. She can't be serious. The reason I rarely talk about me is because she's so busy talking about herself and her own problems. She can complain for hours on end about the men in the town, or lack thereof. I've heard her ramble on about slugs eating her tomato plants for a whole hour before. I don't get a chance.

"I think you have enough of your own problems without mine to worry about on top."

Mum sighs. "You think I don't know you have stuff going on?"

"I'm honestly not sure."

"I know how it must be for you. I just assumed you had someone else to talk to about it all."

"Like who?"

"Your housemates?"

"They're all busy with their own lives. To be honest, Mum, I've been pretty lonely in London. And if I'm being honest," I say, "it hasn't turned out like I thought it would."

"You've been there six years. You've been lonely the *whole* time?"

"I'm not sure, really. It's not all bad memories. Actually, it's something I've been trying to figure out. I'm starting to wonder if I've sleepwalked through it all. Worked myself so hard, pushing through long hours and full weekends with no rest in between because I was actually just lonely. It was a distraction, I guess. And all the time I thought I was doing this amazing job. Like I was somehow irreplaceable. But that's just not true, is it? Some sorry sod will probably step into my shoes next week and be suckered into doing the same tricks as me."

"You're not a sorry sod. You enjoyed your job, even if only a little. And you'll be able to use that experience to get another, won't you? Do you have a plan, darling?"

I massage my eyebrows slowly. "Yeah, yeah, I'll look at new jobs later. I have some savings."

"I think the fresh air will do you good. Give you a chance to think."

I nod, staring at the milky tea. "I've been set on one path, one plan, for so long, not expecting to deviate from that plan, that this all feels a bit... disorientating."

"Then take a few weeks," she says, with a warm smile. "Have a think about what comes next. Where you see yourself in a few years. Reassess. And whilst you're here, Susie's son is back from America. You should pop in and see him."

I frown. Is she really trying to set me up right now?

"No, thanks. What I need right now is space."

"Well, fine, but no one's getting any younger." She winks.

I give Mum a look that says, *don't you dare try that line on me*. She presses her lips together in surrender. "Anyway, did you tell the boy at work you were leaving?"

"He's hardly a boy, Mum. He's thirty-two."

She shrugs. "That's still sort of a boy to me."

"No, I didn't. I just packed my bag and left. I didn't want to make a scene."

"That's very like you," she says. "Won't he be a bit upset you didn't say goodbye?"

"I doubt it. He's trouble, Mum. Honestly, I should never have gone there. It was as if I was under some sort of spell."

"That's a good sign though."

"How can that be a *good* sign?"

"Well, if he was a dullard, you'd have been very aware of it. Clearly, if you were enchanted, you were happy and relaxed with him. Isn't that right?"

I pull a face wondering if I want to get into the intimate details about this with my mother. It's not very like us. In fact, it's strange to have her asking me questions at all. Maybe she's right. Maybe I do hold back or come across as closed off.

"Well… It felt… right, I guess. At the time at least."

Mum hums, nodding, as if she is proving a point.

"What?" I demand.

"And you decided not to pursue it with him? Why is that?"

"Because…" We never got on before, so why would one intense week change that? We would both end up hurting each other. And I was right. He was made director this morning. And he knew the whole time. He let things get heated knowing he would inevitably hurt me, and that I would be working *for* him. We would have been at each other's throats constantly.

I shake my head. No, it was right to leave it the way I did. To give him the space to do what he wants to do with Starr. If that place turns into a giant money-making machine, then it's what Michael has recruited him to do.

Then there's the anger and hurt still lingering right below the surface of my skin. How could he let things happen whilst hiding something the whole time? Where is his conscience? Such a prick! Honestly. How could I be so stupid to fall for him?

I look at Mum. "Turns out he was a lying prick."

She rolls her eyes. "Aren't they all."

And just like that we're back to Mum's world of dating men in their fifties. It's a horror show, and quite frankly not something I want to listen to. I finish my tea and excuse myself to get settled in the guest room.

"What do you fancy for dinner?" Mum calls as I walk up the stairs, Doris on my heels, *click-clack-clicking* against the varnished wood.

"I'm not sure yet."

"I'll pop to Morrisons. You'll eat me out of the house if I don't."

"I'll chip in for groceries!" I call.

"Yeah, yeah," she says as she walks to the front door, reusable bags in hand.

My bedroom, or I should say the guest bedroom I regularly assume as my own, is light and airy with a window that twinkles thanks to the damp leaves shimmering outside. I place my bags down as Doris makes herself comfortable on the end of the bed. She tends to hang out with the guests whenever there's a visitor. Drives Mum potty.

I take a deep shuddering breath as my body wilts into the bee-embroidered pillows, my head resting against the headboard. The pastel-pink walls have a surprisingly calming effect. One by one, I feel my muscles softening, my heart and lungs slowing. I'm finally alone. Except for Doris that is, but she won't judge me. I'm safe where I can feel all the feelings that have been trying to swamp me these past few hours. For some reason my cheeks are getting damp, as if I'm uncontrollably crying.

And when I reach up to touch them, I realise I am. A sob escapes too. My chest feels tight, the pressure expanding across my abdomen, my arms and up to my throat.

It's a familiar feeling, the feeling you get when you've done something wrong. The only issue is I can't pinpoint what, exactly. It's not the job, I'm happy with my decision. I can do all the things I loved there somewhere else, somewhere willing to pay me what I'm owed, somewhere I have a sense of work-life balance.

Maybe I'm just overwhelmed? This time last week I was packing for a team-building trip to Scotland. It's all been so much. So very much. And in such a short space of time. It's the image of James that's welling me up. I keep picturing him sitting in the stream the morning after the tent incident. The way his hair had gone all flat and messy. How his smile was warm, yet tired. How he'd gone out of his way on so many occasions to keep me cosy, safe and even patched up when needed.

Was any of it real? Because a lot of it felt real. Am I really so incapable of reading people, I somehow got it all wrong? The truth is that I'm angry with James. There's no way he didn't know about the director role. It was probably discussed on their way over. I suck in a breath. He was looking for the note after I read it out loud right at the start and he didn't say anything. He could've told me then. But he chose not to.

And yet, the unmistakeable heat between us. It spurs on the urge for me to call him and fight it out.

I push the heels of my hands into my eyes. Even if he hadn't withheld that information, it was never going to work. We were suffering severely from last-two-people-at-the-end-of-the-world disease. Even he admitted it, too. He agreed. He's probably going to go back to his serial dating again.

What if he already has?

Doris's wet nose nudges into my chin where she's crept up alongside my body. I roll over to cuddle her as more tears wet my pillow.

I can't actually be missing him, can I?

This is a trauma response, surely. Why would I be crying

over *missing* Gloatman? Is that really what I'm doing? Something painful rips through the core of me. I feel myself coming undone. I'm no longer Fliss Rainer, Head of Marketing, and I'm no longer James' Felicity. It's all vanished in a matter of days.

I gasp air like I'm going to run out of the stuff.

It will fade, I tell myself. It has to fade.

I'm about to close my eyes, let myself fall into a tearful slumber for a while when my phone vibrates. I take it out my pocket and squint as I unlock the screen. A text has come through.

Where did you go? Can we talk? James has written.

Biting my lip, I ponder on how to respond or whether to respond at all. He's gotten everything I always wanted. He knew he was going to get it but didn't tell me. I'm so mad with him I don't even know what to say back. I'm hurt. Deceived. And yet, not entirely surprised.

Would I have told him if the tables were turned? I decide to reply but only to get him to leave me alone.

I left.

When you back? he types back instantly.

My pulse quickens, I can feel it hard in my throat when I swallow. I write *never* but then delete it. I put my phone on silent, close my eyes and wallow into my pillow. No good will come of speaking to him right now. He'll ask too many questions, questions I don't have the answers to.

Twenty-Five

That evening Mum and I take a sofa each, beaching out in front of the TV, alternating between episodes of *Friends* and *New Girl*, eating pizza and crisps with dips, and drinking tiny tinned cocktails. The one I sip on now is Malibu and tropical juice. A collective dose of sugar and alcohol, slowly seeping into my bloodstream. It's comforting. But I get a little spike of adrenaline as I check my phone to see if he's messaged again.

I can see he's been online almost consistently since the last one. Probably speaking to other women. *Oh gawd*. I'm not doing that. It doesn't matter what he's doing. I groan as I realise this is when he'd tell me he can hear my brain rattling away. Or he'd ask me kindly to *please stop freaking out*.

Such an irritating man. Honestly, why am I grieving the loss of his company? He's my least favourite person, isn't he?

I refuse to check my phone again. Several hours later I go to bed, tipsy enough that my body sends me right off to sleep.

*

The next morning I'm up early.

"Mum," I call out after taking a very indulgent hot shower. "I'm going to take Doris out down the beach."

I can hear her rattling around downstairs with the dishwasher. It's her day off, so I'm sort of hoping she doesn't offer to join me. Being alone with the sea air and this wonderful, furry bed warmer is my plan. When Mum says she needs to do some more de-weeding out the back, I seize the opportunity, whizzing out the front door in one of her raincoats. I clip Doris onto her lead and stride down the street towards the beach.

Seaford's beach isn't exactly California, with its choppy, murky waves biting at the sand, cold wind whipping off the water and slicing across my cheeks. In fact, it couldn't feel any further from it. Despite this, I find myself standing at the edge of the water, my trainers getting damp where the tips of the waves reach them before bubbling then drifting back out to sea.

If I stand facing this way, I could almost imagine I'm back in Scotland. Back in the town where we found the phone in the church and called for the rescue truck. Thankfully though, there isn't the heavy whiff of rotting seaweed down here. And although it's gusty, the winds in Sussex are no match for the Scottish coast. The gulls cry overhead as Doris trots around me, sniffing and dipping her paws into the retreating waves.

My life plan is warped. I haven't felt so motionless in years. I can't remember when I last found myself without a clear, set five-year plan. It's both disorientating and freeing.

If I'm not travelling in a direction, what am I even doing?

It won't last long. I know that. Within days I'll be bored senseless and will have found myself on a new path, whether that's a somewhat travelled one or something entirely new, I'm not sure.

I could do anything within reason. I could totally change careers. I could go into something where I might free up my weekends.

Maybe I could retrain. But the sharp pang of anxiety says, *no, you're a marketer*. And I am. I love talking all things image, social media, digital designs. I love having control over what colour palette a company uses. Or where and how they get their name out there. It's an art as well as a job.

My feet take me down the beach towards the rock pools. I find a bench up on the main walk and perch, Doris clipped back on her lead, sat sensibly at my feet. She's such a good girl. My cheeks are damp again, but I'm pretty sure it's because of the sea air and the wind making my eyes water. I dry them with my sweater tucked under my raincoat sleeves.

I take my phone out to snap a picture of the view. It's grey everywhere, the sea, the sky, even the sand seems to have gone a miserable colour but it's still beautiful. The way nature moves without human involvement. Totally at its own whim.

When I open the screen, however, I gawp. I've missed fifteen phone calls from James, or Gloatman (that's how he's saved in my phone). And there are messages too. I open them, intrigued, and then I'm instantly annoyed with myself because he'll know I've read them.

YOU QUIT!?

Where are you? We NEED to talk!
Felicity
Call me
Fine. Ignore me.
Michael told me why you quit. He asked me if I really thought you'd sue him. Brilliant.
Damn it, where are you?
Felicity?
Will you please *answer?*

I almost jump when the screen alerts me to another incoming call. I drop it into my lap. Doris gives me a look as if to say, *what is wrong with you?* With care, I reject the call, turn my phone off and stuff it into my pocket.

"Let's go on a really long walk," I say to my black and white sibling with a tail. "I need lots and lots of air."

Two hours later and I finally decide I'm hungry. Doris and I make our way back to Mum's, my stomach a ball of knots. I haven't dared to turn my phone back on yet. My nerves haven't settled since I saw his name flash up on my screen, although I have been walking at quite a pace. I made it pretty far down the coast. I just had to keep walking. It was like the further I went, the more I asserted myself, the more likely I was to answer the massive question mark in my head.

I'm not even sure what the question is, but the knowledge that he's trying to reach me to either have a go at me or... I don't really know... has butterflies lapping circles in my stomach. It doesn't matter anyway. He doesn't deserve my time, the lying— I need to relax. Why am I so hyped up about this? I would have never reacted this way to Gloatman calling me a few weeks ago.

Or would I?

Maybe I would've in a different way. Instantly on the defence, prepared for a fight. Have I always been chemically reactive towards him? There I was taking the mickey out of him back in Scotland for maybe being in love with me the whole time, when it might've been me instead.

Oh god. *No*. That can't be right, *can it*?

I put the key in the door. As I hang the coat on the hooks and unclip Doris, a deep voice has my entire body going rigid. Mum is talking to someone in the kitchen. *How odd.*

Then it hits me. I recognise that voice. I know it so well that it reverberates in my brain. I put my hand on the wall to steady myself.

No, it can't be.

I'm imagining things.

I take my shoes off quietly, creeping through the hall with a frown on my face. As I reach the kitchen door I slowly peer around the frame. His black hair is flat again, flopping down over his forehead as if he's been running. He's drinking tea out of one of Mum's mugs. I blink at the scene before me.

"Oh, there you are! You've been gone ages. I nearly sent a search party out for you. I called your dad and everything, just to check you hadn't gone there," Mum says, clearly annoyed. She folds her arms like I'm being rude. Maybe I am. I'm so confused. "Anyway, you didn't tell me your friend was coming over, Flissity, I would've made some lunch had you said."

"I didn't know," I say, perplexed.

James looks at me now. His eyes connect with mine, blue fire sending a shot of energy straight to my core. It's as if he's both sorry and completely not sorry all in one breath.

"Hi," he says.

Twenty-Six

I laugh but it sounds bitter.

"What are you doing here?"

Mum pauses rummaging through the freezer, probably looking for something to feed us. She gives me a wide-eyed look. "Fliss, don't be so rude."

"Mum." I give her a stern glance, hoping she'll get the hint.

Thankfully, she does. "Right. I'll leave you two to it…" she says, practically skipping towards the kitchen door, then pauses in her step to click the kettle on. "There, you'll probably want a tea after that walk."

And with that, she closes the door behind her, trapping me with James. Oh hell. My heart is somehow leaping up to my throat.

"How do you know where my mum lives?"

James gives me a look. "We work, *worked*, for The Starr Agency. They save all our personal details in the shared file."

"Do they?"

He nods. "Yeah. We could sue them for that too."

"So, you are suing, are you?" I say sarcastically, then shake my head. I don't actually care about that. Before he can answer, I ask, "Why are you here?"

"We need to talk. Please."

"You can't just come round uninvited."

"I tried to call you. I texted. You weren't responding." He shrugs. "You didn't give me another option."

I sigh. "Clearly I didn't want to talk to you."

"Man, ok..." he says, blowing out a breath. He gets up from his chair. Why does he seem so much bigger in my mum's tiny kitchen? I have this forbidden urge to rush over to him in his shirt and work trousers, clearly having come here straight from the office, and hold him again. I miss his heat. I miss the feel of his rigid stomach and chest against my body. I miss his scent. "If that's really how you feel then I'll just leave. But you should know that I quit this morning, too. I'll be filing a case against Michael as well."

"Wait," I say as he's shrugging into his jacket. Then I close my eyes, biting my lip. "No. Yeah, you should go."

James takes a deep breath. When I look at his face again it's torn as if he's in physical pain being this close to me. "Felicity," he says softly, his eyes flitting from my eyes to the floor as if he can't decide where to look. Is he nervous? "Did I do something to hurt you?"

I can't help it; the truth of the last few days has been sitting heavy on a branch in my mind and now it snaps.

"You knew the whole time, didn't you? You knew you were getting the director position. And I was your final hurdle, right?"

James' eyes widen. He presses his lips into a firm line as he dips his chin in a nod. "Yeah, I knew. And yeah, I chose not to tell you."

"Why?!"

"We were abandoned in Scotland. I didn't think it would

help either of us by telling you. I knew you had your heart set on the director role. Hell, you've always worn your heart on your sleeve. And I honestly wasn't even sure if I was that interested. I told Michael I was on the fence about it, but he forged on regardless. But that was before Scotland. Before everything that happened, I swear. I don't know what he was playing at yesterday, but he ambushed me. I didn't know what to do in the moment. You weren't exactly talking to me. We didn't have a plan."

I close my eyes, praying the prickling sensation behind my eyes will fade. Why am I crying again? I swore I wouldn't do this in front of this man. He moves closer, his footsteps clicking on the tiled floor. He's wearing work shoes; I can tell by the sound. His breathing is calm. I wish mine was. I sense it getting more rapid by the second.

Gloatman is here. In my mum's kitchen.

"Please, believe me," he says, his voice closer now, desperate. "Felicity. I quit. As soon as I found out you had, I realised there was nothing keeping me there."

"You... We... *Things* happened between us. You can't just skip past that. You kept things from me and still let it happen."

He sighs, rubbing his face in his hands.

"I promise it wasn't like that. I didn't do that to play into Michael's game. I would never betray you like that."

"What about the money? Don't you want the director's pay?" I ask, and I inhale sharply when I realise how shuddery my voice sounds.

I feel a finger push some of my windswept hair back behind my ear. It's hot and soft and gentle.

"Last week you helped me see that money is something

toxic I've been chasing. It's a vice. I used to snap someone's hand off for a shift, a paper round or any opportunity to bring in some cash. It's as if it's become a part of me. I can't guarantee I won't still do that, but I need to find value in other things.

"I shouldn't've even gone to Scotland. I missed meeting my nephew the day he was born. I missed a really crucial thing that had so much more value than money. I sort of knew that then, but now when I think about it, it physically pains me."

I open my eyes; a treacherous tear runs down my cheek. I swipe it away. James is watching me closely, and staring back at him, I realise we maybe know each other better than we thought we did. I believe he never set out to hurt me. I believe that as things between us shifted rapidly he probably didn't know how to tell me but that doesn't make it right.

There's still a part of me who doubts us.

"But it won't work," I say quietly.

He nods. "I know you think that."

"You don't?"

He laughs gently. "Well, I don't think about things as practically as you do. I just do the things I fancy and let the consequences unfold. I think that's why you find me so infuriating, isn't it? All my unplanned, random ideas?"

"Like coming here?" I practically squeak at this point.

James shakes his head. "No. I planned this, at least since this morning, so it doesn't count. I asked Michael if he knew where you'd gone. You said you left in your message, but I thought you were being facetious. As in you'd just left the building and it was none of my business. But then he said you'd quit, and I laughed. And I couldn't stop smiling. *My god, she's left*, I kept thinking. *She's free of this bullshit.* Then I had a problem. I realised in that moment that annoying you was the only thing I got out of that job – except the money, that is."

I laugh as more lazy tears betray me. "You're such a dick."

"You still want me to go?" He pauses for a moment. "I'm so sorry I hurt you. Please know I never intended to. I'd never consciously do anything to hurt you."

I can't look at him. I find myself staring at his shoes. "I don't think it's worth getting into a legal battle with Michael. I just want to put it behind me."

"All of it?" James asks, his voice husky.

Is he asking if I want to put the moments of *us* behind me too? I push my thumb and forefinger onto my closed eyelids to hide my face from him. Is that what I want?

"I'm not going back to London," I say out of nowhere. It's even a surprise to me. I'd been wondering if going back was the right thing. The discussion with Mum yesterday about being lonely there was true. It didn't suit my personality. I wasn't the type to go out to bars all the time and it was slowly feeling like that was the only way to have friends in the city. And my damp room was not the place to be spending my only free time.

No, my London life might just be over.

"Ok…" James says. "So, what are you saying?"

"I'm saying we are never going to work, are we? Not really? If that's what you mean? And so, yeah, you should probably leave."

James' breath hitches. It's as if I've hurt him somehow

which is madness. He's James Boatman. He'll find someone better than me in seconds. There's no way he's grieving me. I can't even allow myself to accept it.

"I'll just go then," he says, hurt lacing his words. I still can't look at him. "Mostly I came to say that my friend is an employment solicitor, and when I told him what happened, he said we could take Michael for his worth. So, if you fancied coming on board, we've got a better fight together than separately." He exhales slowly. Without touching me again, he moves towards the door. "If you happen to have that note he left us... er, me... with the bags that would be helpful."

I know where it is. It's in my room in London, tucked into my underwear drawer. I don't say that though. Instead, I open my mouth, spilling the words before they can be screened by my brain. "Are you just doing it for the money?"

I turn to catch his face at the door. He squints at me as if he's seeing a different person. Then he laughs, sharply, as if someone has tickled him with a knife. "Yeah. I've got a problem, clearly. It wasn't because for once I wanted to be on the same team with you against Michael."

And then he's gone, slamming the front door as he goes. I breathe out in one long stream, feeling the tension escape my body.

Mum rushes down the stairs, with a face that says she heard every word.

"What are you doing!? Go after him!"

"I can't. We're not right for each other. We'll just fight, Mum. Even in Scotland, it was just bickering the whole time."

"Bickering that turned to kissing?" she says like I'm stupid. "More than kissing?"

I look away, my cheeks on fire.

"Go after him. He likes you, Flissity. He's admitted he wants to be on your team. Honestly! What does he have to do to get your interest?"

"He doesn't even know what his life plan is! He doesn't know what he wants or what he's doing. All he cares about is money. I can't be with someone like that."

Mum puts her hands on her hips. "I don't think that's true. Do you like him?"

"Yes," I say frantically as if that's the stupidest thing she could say. "But I can't see myself *with* him." Mum doesn't say anything, waiting for my words to sink into my brain. The realisation is slow, burning. I blink at the ceiling, letting the tears soak my ears. "He's James flipping Gloatman. He's the worst person I know."

Still, she says nothing, just tilting her head.

"I can't sue Michael. I can't burn bridges like that. What if…" The realisation hits me like a brick. "Oh god. I've got to sue Michael." My breathing hastens, my heart rate quickening. "I've got to sue Michael."

"You both do," she says quietly.

I square my shoulders, pat my cheeks dry again with my sleeves.

"And I have to give things with James a go, don't I?"

"No," Mum says. "You don't *have to* at all."

I laugh. "I know," I say. "But I think I want to."

She laughs too, stepping closer to wrap her arms around me.

"Don't let your silly parents be the reason you don't settle down with someone who isn't quite your image of perfect."

"What do you mean?"

"I know you think we screwed up and did it all wrong. But, Fliss, I don't regret any of it. I'd do it all again exactly the same way to have you. And your dad wasn't the worst thing to ever happen to me. It was as the years went on, we realised we were never truly meant for each other. There was never a spark. Nothing like you and this James boy. If you keep pushing people away who don't meet your list of requirements because… What did you say was wrong with this one?"

"He's too confident. He's only motivated by money… although, he has a good reason for that. But he's really annoying. Never sticks to plans. He comes up with these mad ideas without thinking them through and it makes my blood boil."

Mum sniffs a laugh. "But you enjoy being with him?"

I think about how much I laughed in Scotland, despite the way we almost died. How he kept me safe and warm. How even in the worst moments he would find something funny to turn my mood around. How I felt safe enough, even when I wasn't sure, to share serious discussions with him. It's early days. Despite having worked with him for six years, we're only just getting to know one another.

"Shit, I have to go after him," I say, letting go of Mum and sprinting towards the door.

Twenty-Seven

My heart is beating frantically as I storm down the slabbed pavement towards the station. He won't answer his phone. I've tried three times. But I guess that's fair. I've basically ignored him for two days. I assume he'll be taking the train. Obviously, I don't actually know this. Or does he have a car? He lives in London. Why would he need a car? I shake my head. The train station is my best bet.

A woman in a pushchair gives me a funny look as I hop into the road to get around her. A horn blares as a car swerves past me. *Idiot*. He was nowhere near hitting me. Can't he see I'm in emergency mode? Nobody goes running in jeans and a sweatshirt in early summer!

There are several thoughts swirling around my head. What if James isn't at the station? Or, what if in my moment of stubborn hesitation, I've missed his train and he's already on his way back to the city? My lungs slam against my chest. I can't get enough air into them. I don't ever run. It's quite literally the worst thing I could do to myself. But I deserve it. What an idiot I've been! How could I not hear what he was trying to tell me? And oh god. His stories about heartbreaks and being left and abandoned by people. I'm no better than any of them. He at least deserves a chance. We both do.

The station comes into view up ahead. I can just catch the operator talking over the loudspeaker, something about "London" and "leaving", and I can't run fast enough. I don't see James anywhere, and the staff behind the ticket kiosk give me a funny look as I sprint, red faced and sweaty, to the glass.

"Hi, hi. I just need to speak to a friend. They're in the station. Can you let me through?"

"You need to buy a ticket," a nasally voice responds.

"I'm not getting on a train," I retort. "This isn't the airport."

"You need a ticket to go through the stiles."

I laugh with frustration, then double over trying to recover from the run. *Good lord, Fliss. It was only a minute run.*

"*Please*," I say once more, looking across the stiles at a train waiting, doors open.

When the man repeats himself for the third time, I remember what James said to me in Scotland. It's not necessarily correct but his words play out in my head. *Sometimes you can't afford the things you need. You can't afford to get on that train. But you need to.*

I stand up, give the man behind the kiosk a scowl, then bolt towards the stiles. I try to clear them entirely by placing my hands on the top middle part and jumping, but I'm far too short. I end up with my legs tangled, crying out in pain. The metal is hard as my shins smack across them. Finally, with a shuffle, I end up on my arse on the other side. Someone shouts at me.

I climb to my feet, looking around wildly for James. There's still no sign of him, not on any of the benches or stood on the platform. Maybe he's already boarded the train. A conductor is running towards me now, waving their hands and blowing a whistle. Oh, bloody hell. Who have I become? The train is about to leave, the doors sounding that high-pitched beeping. I only have a second to make up my mind, and because it says it's going to London via Lewes, I leap forwards. Suddenly the doors close behind me, and an angry man is frowning at me from the platform behind the glass. I make a *sorry* face, shrugging as the train moves away from the station.

"Fliss?"

I turn around to see James leaning around his chair to look at me. His face is a mix of shock and confusion.

"I don't have a ticket," I say.

He laughs. "Ok."

"I just had to... I'm so sorry. I think I've projected some of my own issues on you and that's incredibly unfair."

"Alright."

"I mean, you did hurt me. You should've told me from the start that the note from Michael was only meant for you."

He nods, watching me.

Other people are sat on the carriage, some pretending to read their phones, others just outright watching our conversation as if it's free entertainment. "Can we, um?" I nod behind me to the train loo. I frown because it's not somewhere I want to go, but also, I don't particularly want an audience for this discussion.

James climbs up from his seat, grabbing his bag and

walking tentatively towards me. He points behind me, where there are some free seats that look relatively private. I nod, better than the loo. *See, not all his ideas are terrible.* We sit opposite each other as the South Downs whip by.

When I finally meet his eyes, I feel his gaze in my gut again. "I'm sorry."

"Why're you sorry?" he says.

"You came all the way here, but I've been determined to push you away."

He smiles sadly. "I get it. I'm not really your type."

"No. No, you're not."

He laughs, offended.

"But I think that's a good thing because, well my type has always ended up being a bit shit, really. And well, as it happens, I already know all the worst things about you. I know you irritate the shit out of me. And sometimes your random ideas completely derail my well-laid plans." I stop to catch my breath. "But you challenge me – in a good way. Working with you has made me a better person, and truthfully, conflict aside, I wouldn't've had it any other way," I say. "And actually, when I think about it properly, all my plans for Starr included you, you were a central piece of everything. So, sure, I hated your guts. You're an overconfident bastard at times." I exhale slowly. Where was I going with this again?

I look up to see James watching me with an amused expression. "What are you even on about?" he laughs.

"I... Oh, shit. Were you not here to ask me out?"

James seems genuinely surprised by my question.

"No, actually. I just wanted us to double up on the lawsuit against Michael," he says. "See, I had this whole elaborate plan, where we worked together to get our own back against him, and during the course of the trial or whatever, you'd fall in love with me. If I was very lucky. Or something along those lines." He gives me a look that says, *me and my silly ideas*.

"Ok, now *I'm* confused."

"I know you're too good for me, Felicity. I'm not an idiot. I was just hoping if we spent more time together, you'd end up seeing that I'm not a bad guy, and that really, we make a great team. I hadn't planned some sweeping romantic gesture, but you kicking me out certainly wasn't very encouraging."

I sigh happily. "James Boatman, will you go out for drinks with me?"

A huge perfect smile splits across his face. "You mean to say, I don't need to form some huge elaborate plan to win you over?"

"No," I say. "I've known you six years, James. I already know I'm probably going to want to strangle you from time to time, but I also know you're pretty great in other ways."

He suppresses a laugh, folding his arms across his chest. "And you broke onto this train to tell me that."

"Well, you ignored my call."

"Payback, my friend."

"Fair enough," I smile.

"And so, what's your plan from here?"

"Well, that depends, doesn't it?"

He raises an eyebrow in question.

"Are you going to come back to my mum's for a cup of tea?"

"Felicity, Felicity," he sighs. "Is that your idea of going out for drinks?"

"No!" I laugh. "But equally, I might very well get kicked off."

"They'll just fine you. I think it's a hundred quid."

I scoff. "Why didn't you tell me that in Scotland?"

He shrugs. "It was good to see you breaking the rules for once. I didn't know you had it in you. And now twice in the span of a week!" He clucks his tongue at me.

I make a half-laughing, half-infuriated sound. "You're the worst person I know!"

The smile is still on his lips. He leans forwards, crossing the space to sit beside me. "I drink Guinness."

I can't fight the smile worming its way onto my lips. "I might change my mind now."

"What's wrong with Guinness?"

"Nothing, you just seem too confident again."

He chuckles. "Well, in fairness, you did just jump a stile and throw yourself onto a moving train for me, so I think it's safe to assume you're into me."

"The train wasn't moving."

"That's not what I'll tell my sisters."

And with that, I lean in to kiss him, pressing my lips against his. Anything to shut the man up. His large hand cups my cheek, just the way I like it, his fingertips softly grazing the sensitive area behind my ears, sending sparks spiralling through my body.

"You know what I really, really want?" James asks into my mouth.

I stop kissing him, smiling instead. "What, are you a Spice Girl now? A long-awaited sixth member?"

"Very funny. No."

"Hmm, ok, tell me what you want, Gloatman."

He smirks, that annoying, perfect smirk I just want to kiss off his face. "The last word."

Acknowledgements

IT BLOWS my mind that I am sitting here writing acknowledgements for a book **I WROTE!** How crazy is that? I wish thirteen-year-old me could see me now. She'd probably shrug and tell me to calm down, but I know she'd be quietly proud. I've always enjoyed reading acknowledgements at the end of my favourite novels wondering if I would ever do the same. AND I AM!

Thank you Safae El-Ouahabi, my super-agent, who took this early draft on and helped me sculpt it, ready for submission. You held my hand through the process and responded to my (sorry, so many!) emails with total poise and calmness. And to Claire Wilson, thank you for finding me amongst the slush and believing in me. The whole team at RCW has been incredibly professional and personable since day one.

Thank you Aubrie Artiano, my editor, for showing this manuscript so much love. I'm very glad you share my sense of humour and saw these characters for who they are. Thank you for keeping me looped into the process. I've really enjoyed it! And in extension, thanks to Holly, Sophie, Shannon & Yas and the whole Head of Zeus team for reading my work many, many times and being available for support when needed.

Thank you to the early readers on this manuscript – you are warriors! You were all so kind and supportive. Thanks to Amanda Haycock (aka Mum), Janeifer Lawrence and Anna Britton. Thank you to the support networks I have been involved with over the years; Write Mentor, Debut 2025 Discord, Querying Chat and UK Submission Chat (on the site that shall not be named). And then the people who are always available for book nattering and support: Anna Britton again (thanks chum!), Carlie Sorosiak, Lauren Ford and so many more who I won't attempt to list, but please know I am so very grateful.

Thank you to Barbara Henderson who was very kind and shared a lot of details about the Highlands during the specific months I wanted to base this story. Your local expertise definitely helped me to capture the environment these characters were in.

And finally, thank you Dan – I know you prefer bikes to books but thank you for understanding when I needed space to finish that pesky chapter I couldn't figure out in my head. Thanks for all you do to help me write. And my son – please don't read mummy's book, ok? But thank you for not spilling anything on my laptop when I can see your impulses wondering what would happen if you did. I love you both very much!

Thanks again to my mum. You're nearly always my first reader and you never comment on the smut which is honestly the only way we make this work, so thank you. You've been my main cheerleader since I sent you that awful YA fantasy draft. You loved it even though it didn't make sense. The plot holes were craters. But thank you for supporting me anyway.

Thanks to Mr King, the coolest secondary school teacher <u>ever</u>, who would surf on desks, climb scaffolding outside the window during class and make the annoying kids read the embarrassing parts of classics out loud. You taught me if I'm going to lie, make it imaginative. Please know, giving me that A on my assignment, about the two perspectives of the same event, made my year and was the catalyst to this whole venture. You inspired me and you should know that. I hope this reaches you.

Finally, as a book girl at heart, here's to all the authors who have inspired me since I was a young girl. From *Sheltie the Shetland Pony* to my *Twilight* era to the Mills 'n' Boon books I would steal from under my mum's bed (sorry not sorry) – thank you! Here is to all those keeping this incredible community thriving, from Booktokers to Bookstagram, to professionals in the industry, to authors, readers, and everyone in between.

About the Author

CHLOE FORD grew up in rural Sussex but is now based in South Gloucestershire. She has an affinity with all things country, from riding horses to muddy walks. Her love for writing began at secondary school when her English teacher would set a writing task for the whole hour. An avid reader, she started sneaking Mills & Boon books out from under her mum's bed as a teenager and hasn't stopped devouring romance books ever since.

Discover the new swoon-worthy rom-com from Chloe Ford

A KISS FIFTEEN YEARS IN THE MAKING

HOUSE PARTY

CHLOE FORD

A slow-burn romance fifteen years in the making...

Hattie has spent half her life secretly crushing on Freddie—her best friend Sam's irresistibly gorgeous older brother. But Freddie? He's barely spared a glance for Hattie, the girl Sam befriended one fateful New Years' Eve when they discovered they were birthday twins.

Fast-forward to now: Hattie finds herself single for the first time in years—just before the holidays. Enter Sam, who, in classic best-friend fashion, whisks her away to a remote cabin in the Forest of Dean to cheer her up. Snowy woodland views? *Check.* A crackling fire and a steamy hot tub? *Check.* Zero cell service, ravenous wild boars, and an incoming snowstorm of apocalyptic proportions? *Also check.*

And to make matters even more intense, Freddie joins them, unexpectedly. Still *infuriatingly* gorgeous, and still *ridiculously* off-limits. Except this time, he's actually noticing Hattie. But then again, maybe he's been noticing her all along.

Fifteen years of longing.
One night to change everything.

Turn to read an extract...

Chapter One

In hindsight, spending Christmas day alone in my flat might've been the smarter choice.

Instead, I'm sat on an uneven wooden footstall that Mum foraged out of the garage this morning. She changed her mind at the last minute and decided to invite Granny after all, and Granny *cannot* sit on the uneven wooden footstall. And of course, nobody ever has enough dining chairs for Christmas lunch. I mean, unless you're rich – which the Tycers are not. It's especially unfair since I'm one of the tallest people in this room and my knees are almost up to my chest. But according to Mum, I don't count as a guest in this house, even though I don't live here anymore. So, by proxy of being their child, I pulled the short straw.

Worse still: I've been bullied into wearing a ridiculous sweaterdress Mum bought with a giant Rudolf on it (ala red bobble for the nose), along with a fragile paper hat from one of those corny stockings. I'm sweating my tits off – also known as Rudolf's ears – due to the combined heat of the oven in the open plan kitchen and the heating cranked right up to make it extra festive. And now I'm having to watch my socially inept cousin, Dylan, stuff his face with yet another

Yorkshire pudding, whilst my auntie harasses me *yet again* regarding the whereabouts of my ex-boyfriend.

"I liked Adam," she says. The brass on this woman is astonishing. I've long thought it should be studied.

"That's nice," I retort, forking another carrot into my mouth.

"And he couldn't make it this year? Why was that again?"

Dylan gives me a pitying glance from under his light curly fringe. His family come for Christmas every year, but Mum can only stomach her sister's company for so long. They've never been invited to stay beyond lunch before. Why must we suffer this meal every year? None of us enjoy it. And yet we do it anyway. I take my rage out on the turkey, cutting it with force.

"Mum, leave it with the Adam stuff," Dylan warns, giving her an imploring glance.

I catch his eye across the table and offer him an appreciative smile. Maybe he isn't so inept after all. He's well versed in my aunt's linguistic assault tactics. He's only a year younger than me, but we couldn't have less in common. Apart from the fact he's never been in a relationship for more than a few weeks, he also bounces around from job to job and makes wild, unpredictable decisions, like that time when he was in crippling debt, mid-twenties, and he somehow managed to get *another* credit card and took off to work in the Bahamas for a year.

"All right, Dylan?" I say, hoping to divert the conversation to his latest cock-up.

But Auntie Maeve isn't done yet.

"Well, we just want to know what went so wrong, don't we, Martin?"

Uncle Martin is far too many sherries down to care about Adam, but he nods anyway. He's quite resolved to the 'happy wife, happy life' mantra. "Yes, dear," he quips.

"I did warn her you wouldn't talk about it," Mum finally chirps. But I recognise the expression on her face right away. She has never gotten to the bottom of it all either, and she wouldn't mind *finally* knowing the whole story. As *if* I'm suddenly going to give them the entire rundown over Christmas dinner about how my shitty ex broke my stupid heart.

How fucking festive.

I sigh, dropping my fork. "Well, if you insist. But you know it's incredibly difficult to talk about it. Honestly, I…" I pretend to choke up. If they want drama, I'll give it to them. Anything to get them off my back. I fiddle with a section of my curly hair, which has fallen over my shoulder, for extra effect.

Auntie Maeve reaches across the table and places her hand over mine. "Go on," she says softly.

"Well, you see, we were on this boat, travelling to the US for a long holiday and…" Dylan has finally stopped chewing and is highly invested in my story; the corner of his mouth forms a lopsided smirk. I continue, "The boat hit an iceberg and, well, Adam fucking drowned." I finish in my usual dry style, dipping a roastie into the gravy and stuffing my face so I literally can't talk for at least two minutes.

Dylan hangs his head, but I can see he's highly amused. Maybe this is a thing we can bond over. The year Dylan and I become best friends, two peas in a pod. Nah, I just haven't been single at Christmas in a very long time.

"Did Adam really drown?" Auntie Maeve asks, using the

same hand she touched mine with to cover her heart. She's aghast, the colour drained from her cheeks.

Mum scoffs. "Don't be daft, Maeve. That's the plot of the *Titanic*."

"Oh, *well*." She tuts. "That's *very* bad taste, Hattie, very bad," Maeve says, her breaths choppy as if she's about to burst into tears. It's all a show. She loves to play the victim, especially after one of her notorious interrogations. Basically, she's a more vicious version of Mum.

I shrug, my mouth still full of potato.

"It's no laughing matter really," she says. "There's a reason there aren't many children in this house. Me and your mum left it too late."

"Good god, Mum!" Dylan retorts. "You can't say those things these days."

"Why not? She should know. I'm doing her a favour!"

It's official. All Christmas joy has been lynched from my body. I could've been watching *Elf* or *Love, Actually* in peace, tucking into a fruit bowl sized serving of those pig in blanket flavoured crisps.

I sigh. The baby chat isn't new to me. We've all heard Mum's sob story about wishing she'd had more than just one child, how time really gets away from you. Sometimes I feel bad for her, but it isn't something I really want to worry about at Christmas, especially the first Christmas in which I've been single in over *nine* years. That makes it more than slightly grating.

"Excuse me," I say, rising from my arse-chewing stool. "Think I'm going to grab some fresh air."

"Oh, don't make a scene, Hattie," Mum berates.

Me? I'm the one making the scene?

I give her a look to this effect to which she relents, shrugging glumly as if this wasn't her plan for the day and we're all ruining it for her.

I lock myself in the loo to discourage anyone from following me. I stare at my reflection and pull the paper crown from my head, balling it into my fist. The worst part about all of this is that while I'd love for everyone, myself included, to forget about Adam, that won't happen. Adam was a part of my life whether I like it or not. I run my fingers through my hair, careful not to frizz it up. It plonks back exactly the way it was, frothy. Mum used to say if I had dyed my hair black when I was a kid, I'd have been the spit of Tracy Beaker. Not exactly the vibe I was going for. Although I could probably tell a few people to 'BOG OFF' right now.

I take a few deep breaths then stride out towards the back garden, grabbing my coat from the hall on my way.

Once I'm outside, sitting on the frozen garden furniture, I breathe in that fresh, sharp winter air for all of five minutes before I hear the door open and close.

"Brr, it's sharp out here," Dylan says, rubbing his hands together. He draws a long puff from his vape. It's a festive one – apple and cinnamon spiced or something similar. I give him a look, but fortunately I don't mind second hand steam so much when it smells divine.

"Thanks for sticking up for me in there," I say.

He shrugs. "Mum's a right nosy bitch. She's been wondering about your breakup for weeks, making up her own stories." He shakes his head. "She's desperate to know the truth. Which is why I'm so bloody happy you didn't give it to her." He turns and gives me a conspiratorial grin. "Welcome to the black sheep parade. We march at dawn."

I snort. The thing about connecting with other *tragic* people when you feel particularly tragic yourself is you find yourself oversharing. It's like I want him to know I qualify to be in his tragic club. So, I tell him, "He thought he could do better."

Dylan makes a face. "Adam said that? What a prick."

"He didn't say that *exactly*. He said something along the lines of, 'You don't fit in with my finance bro crowd.'"

"Well, what a relief."

I laugh. "*Right?* Anyway, how's your recent venture going?"

"Which one? The dog walking business or the clothing brand?"

"Both of those are new to me. You started a clothing brand?"

"Well, technically, it was just briefs."

I nod to show him I'm listening.

He shakes his head. "That's all there is to it really. I got bored and am now thinking of becoming a travel blogger."

I can't help the teasing smile that works its way onto my lips. "Thanks, Dylan."

He frowns. "For what?"

For helping me realise I have at least a little bit of my life together, even if it isn't quite all of it. "Just for cheering me up," I say.

We sit in silence for a bit, and I work over all the stuff I need to do before the gallery opens again after the Christmas break, which isn't all that much, truthfully. It's part of the reason I love the job, the simplicity of it. It's right on the sea front, owned by a lovely local couple who pay me to manage it. Adam always thought it was too 'provincial', and I could do more with my art degree.

I mean, he hated that I did an art degree full stop. What sort of business was I going to get into with that?

Hopefully none, was always my first thought. Business sounded boring.

But I've found myself in the art business and so far, I'm enjoying it. Adam always belittled me for it, as if having wealth, or aspiring to wealth, was the only route to happiness, so clearly I didn't want to be happy since I was content to 'rot away in that little shop', as he so eloquently put it.

But I love art—I especially love art that's associated with the sea or the seaside. Ever since moving down to the South Coast from the city, aged fourteen, I've always loved the freedom of the beach, the seagulls, the sound of the waves crashing against the pebbles at high tide. The way you can taste it, hear it, breathe it. And anyone who can capture that beauty is an artist to me.

But now I do occasionally wonder if Adam was onto something, because he isn't at his parent's place for Christmas, moping outside and wishing the time away. Well, at least I don't think he is... *Pfft*. Who am I kidding? I checked his Instagram this morning like an idiot. He's skiing in the French Alps. It's as if I'm chasing that gutless feeling it gives me whenever I go looking for updates.

He doesn't want me anymore. He doesn't love me anymore. And I have moved on.

Sort of.

"What's on your mind?" Dylan asks. "You're grinding your teeth. It's giving me shivers."

"I keep panicking that I've wasted my twenties," I blurt out. *Maybe I really do belong in this tragic club, eh? See, look how pathetic I am.* "But so what if Adam doesn't want to be with me anymore? It's been a few months now and it's less sore. I'm ok. I'm enjoying having my own flat near the beach and being able to watch the TV I like and not have to worry if it will be too girly for him. I like cooking Thai and seafood in my own kitchen without having to think about all his undiagnosed allergies. And you know what? I like sleeping alone. He used to take up too much of the bed. You know?"

Dylan scrunches his face up. "Not really… but go on."

"What if he *stole* my twenties?" I say, my voice raising a pitch. "What if he never actually intended for us to be long-term and I was just convenient? Hmm? And now I've gone and given him my entire youth? I'm going to be old soon, Dylan."

"You're twenty-eight."

"Yeah. *Right now.* But what about in two years? Next week will be the last birthday in my twenties."

My pulse is raising. Am I sweating? I can feel a lump forming in my throat. Dylan looks restless, like he's regretting his decision to join me outside.

"I can't take back all those years. All of the good men are all gone!"

Dylan watches me, wide eyed. "I'm not a therapist, Hattie. *Jeez.* You know I'm probably the worst person to be giving advice, right? I haven't got my shit together either. Hell, I don't even know where my shit is. How am I supposed to get it together? You've always been the golden child round here. And now you're coming to *me* for advice?"

"I didn't ask for advice…"

"You need to let your hair down. Stop being perfect for ten minutes. Go and do something, or *someone*, recklessly. Screw rules. Screw that lot," he says, tilting his head towards the house. "Screw giving this final year in your twenties to someone else. Make it your own!"

I nod quickly. "Yes! This sounds right."

Dylan shakes his head. "Meh, it's probably terrible advice."

"No! It's good. You're right. I need to take this year. I need to *own* it."

"What's something you've always wanted to do?"

"I want to see the seaside."

Dylan purses his lips. "Babe, you *live* in Seaford."

"I know, I mean *better* seasides! Croatia, the Greek Islands, California and…" My eyes widen. "Shit! There are so many places I should go. Why haven't I been?"

"Didn't Adam hate travelling?"

"Yes! He only ever wanted to go skiing, and I wasn't invited."

Suddenly, I feel feral. He only ever wanted to go away with his mates, and his excuse was that I wasn't very good at learning new things (which I'm now convinced isn't true) and he didn't have time to train me whilst also getting out on the best slopes.

Dylan cups hands around his mouth and blows. "Are you coming to the family New Year's Eve party then?"

Panic sets in. "Oh hell. I forgot they'd roped me into that too. I take it back. No! I'm taking back the final year of my twenties. It's *my* birthday! I'm making plans!' I proclaim, a little overexcited. 'And you know what? I should do another house party."

"Isn't your flat more of studio…"

I clap my hands at him. "You're becoming less helpful now, Dyl."

"I'm just saying. You being irrational is making me squirmish."

"*Squirmish?*"

"I don't know what it means, I just know that's how I feel."

"Ugh, maybe you're right." I lean back in the garden chair, the icy armrests sticking to my coat sleeves. "I should ask someone sensible first. I'll call Fliss, she'll know what to do."

"Good idea. Check in with someone sensible. Would you be open to signing a waiver that resolves me of all liability from giving advice?" he asks. He's being funny, but there's a nervous glint in his eye.

"No, sorry. You should've thought about that before you gave it to me."

"Crap. I better lawyer up."

I snort as I take my phone out to message my sensible person.

Fliss used to work for a high-end marketing firm in the city. Her mum is friends with mine, so we've always known each other by proxy, but recently she's moved back to Seaford and has been doing freelance work for the gallery's events. We've bonded over our shared love of fish 'n' chips whilst staring out at the grey abyss that is Seaford seafront during winter.

Dylan squints as if he's about to say something else, but then blows out a long stream of apple-scented steam. "Come on, let's get wasted before they ask us any more questions about our life plans."

Thanks for reading!

Want to receive exclusive author content, news on the latest Aria books and updates on offers and giveaways?

Follow us on X @AriaFiction and on Facebook and Instagram @HeadofZeus, and join our mailing list.